SHOCKED
SILENT

For more information, address: judithdriscoll77@gmail.com

First paperback edition August 2018
E-book edition August 2018

Cover and interior design by David Ter-Avanesyan/Ter33Design

ISBN 978-1-7325007-0-9 (paperback)
ISBN 978-1-7325007-1-6 (ebook)
ISBN 978-1-7325007-2-3 (audiobook)

SHOCKED SILENT

A PSYCHOLOGICAL THRILLER

BOOK ONE

JUDITH DRISCOLL

CHAPTER ONE

DRUGS & THE BREAK UP

Florida, January, 1968

Two brown skinned men edged their boat up to the dock. They silently worked securing lines to the mooring cleats. Juan stopped to wipe the sweat away from his eyes; and as he glanced up, he saw a customs agent boarding a boat docked a short distance away. Juan turned and motioned to Luis who looked up with an air of authority. He turned in the direction of the gaze, his face tensing as he recognized the customs boat. Luis growled at Juan, "Hurry up, let's get the fuck out of here!"

The two men finished tying up the boat. Luis knelt on the deck, lifted a loose board, and took out duffel bags from the storage space. They grabbed the bags, jumped onto the dock, and were soon swallowed up by the crowd of tourists and vendors milling around the marina. As the two men quickly walked through the parking lot adjacent to the marina, the older man gazed across the rows of cars. After a few minutes, he pointed to a car. "There it is! Over there, the blue Ford with the gringo." He turned to Juan. "Get in the back seat and watch him." Luis smiled, flashing his gold-capped tooth. "If he gives you any crap, slit his throat."

The white man was seated behind the wheel in dark glasses and dressed in a suit from a different world than the seedy looking men approaching him. The men were a short distance from the car when suddenly the driver pulled out. "What the fuck's going on?" He turned around and saw four men running toward them with drawn guns shouting, "Federal agents, drop to the ground!"

They dropped the duffel bags and started to run. Just then a shot was fired from the open window of a blue Ford that had pulled next to them. The car roared toward the exit of the parking lot as Luis fell to the ground, his face grotesque, a gaping bleeding hole where the top of his head had been. His mouth hung open, and the gold tooth gleamed in the afternoon sun. Juan immediately dropped to the ground and spread-eagled.

The agent stopped running. One of them shouted, "Jesus Christ! He's getting away. Max, get back to the car and call this in. Did anyone get the license number?" No one answered.

The agent, a tall, slim man in his early thirties with dark hair curling around his ears, knelt on the blacktopped lot and opened one of the duffel bags, crammed with plastic bags filled with white powder. He cut one open, stuck his finger in and dropped a bit of the white powder onto his tongue. "Tastes like pure coke. It looks like we got a profitable bust." He motioned to where Juan was lying on the ground, afraid to raise his head. "Read him his rights, and then call for the coroner's guys to pick up this mess. The flies are already circling."

The agent zipped the bag closed, stood up, and gazed around the parking lot as another agent walked over." I called it in, Randy; maybe we'll get lucky."

"A late model blue Ford on the expressway? Sure, it will stick out like a sore thumb." Randy motioned to the man now hand-cuffed to a car. "Make sure he gets a look at his buddy over there, then throw something over what's left of his head. There are kids around here."

The blue Ford disappeared into a sea of cars on the expressway. After weaving in and out of traffic for fifteen minutes, the Ford exited and pulled into the alley behind the bar in a run-down neighborhood. The driver parked and after a quick look around, opened the trunk, took out a brief-case and headed for a gas station he remembered seeing a few blocks back. The phone booth was out in the open, and no one was around; so the man closed the door and took off his sunglasses. He was about six feet tall with an athletic build, thick, brown hair, and penetrating icy blue eyes. After dialing, he silently counted the rings until someone answered. "Frank, it's Elliott. Something went wrong! Those ass holes got busted in the parking lot."

"Do you still have the money?" an anxious voice demanded.

"Yes, I've got it."

"Good! Did anyone see you?"

"No, and Luis was the only one who knew about our operation. I took care of him before I left. I think I'm clean; the Feds were too far away to see my plates. I left the car in an alley. Some kids will have it stripped down by midnight."

"Elliott, get a cab and meet me at Caruso's. We need to talk."

A woman with blonde hair, greying at the roots, kept knocking on the window of the phone booth. Elliott turned his back on her and cupped the phone. "Right, Frank, I'll get there as soon as possible." He hung up the phone and turned his face away as he quickly pushed past the woman.

"Hey, Sonny! No need to push! Where do you think you are, New York?"

The lounge at Caruso's was dim, but Elliott knew the layout by heart. He walked to the rear of the room and slipped into the last booth. A well-dressed man in his late sixty's sat with a drink of seltzer. Elliott waited politely until the older man spoke.

"Life is strange. As soon as you have the money to buy anything your heart desires, your heart can't take any of your desires. But then again, a man in my line of business doesn't often have complaints of old age. Elliott, you have a fine mind. So, I did the right thing and sent you to law school. And you did me proud, always at the top of the class. Now I have a good legal mind working on my special business deals, and you've made more money than you ever dreamed of." Frank waved his finger in front of Elliott's face. "Let's both of us stay happy. No more guns; just legal work. Young guys, you always want the quick solution. In the old days, we had loyalty; and violence was the last resort. It's not just the Colombians; it's the young punks that want to start at the top."

Elliott responded calmly. "Frank, I'll always be loyal to you. You know that, don't you?"

There was a long pause before Frank responded. "I hope so, I certainly hope so. I'm sending you to Chicago, and I want you to stay clean for this operation. You need some messy work done; you pay someone to do it. I've arranged for you to join a top-notch law firm. And you find a nice wife, not the kind of whores you've been fucking around with lately. You know, a classy broad, someone with education and breeding,"

The old man affectionately slapped Elliott on the cheek. "I have plans for you; so I want respectability, and I want it now! I want you to run for a political office in a couple of years, and you should have a wife at your side. Do you understand?"

Elliott smiled, "Actually, I was thinking of settling down."

"Good, so we agree," Frank raised his hand and seconds later a man was standing next to the booth. "Get Elliott a drink, Joe, we have to talk about a few more things.

Two weeks later

The office at the Florida branch of the drug enforcement agency was bustling with activity. Phones were ringing, and everyone was busy except for the slim man with the dark hair curling down his neck, who was bent over his desk. Bored, he threw down his pencil, wadded a piece of paper into a ball, and volleyed it across the room just as the Chief stepped out of his office. The projectile bounced off his crotch.

"Get in here, Sloan."

The caster squeaked as Randy Sloan pushed the chair back and sheepishly followed the Chief back into his office.

"Sit down, Randy. I've some information on that Florida bust you handled two weeks ago, the one where Luis Diego got the top of his head blown off. Guess what? Luis came up as one of Frank DiMato's boys."

Randy's brown eyes brightened with interest. "You think there's some connection between that bust and Elliott Mason leaving town so quickly?"

The Chief shrugged his shoulders. "Who knows, maybe he didn't have anything to do with it. Either way, I want you to go undercover again, this time in Chicago. Mason's move has been anticipated. He got his Illinois law license last fall, and he's started working in a law firm that has handled some of Frank DiMato's troubles." The Chief smiled. "Congratulations, Randy. You went to Marshall Law in Chicago, took the bar, but moved to Florida because of the climate. Your favorite auntie is ill in a nursing home, and you think she'll get better care if you're closer."

Randy nodded. "But what if Mason or DiMato does some checking? I hope I don't run into any alumni from the law school I attended."

"One of our agents, Tom Hartley, went to Marshall and has contacts there. They developed a temporary file for you. He'll also make contact with a couple of trusted alumni. Just don't go to any meetings or functions from your old law school. We found an aunt for you, a Jane Doe, that lapsed into a coma last month. We've given her an identity. She's your Aunt Victoria. Hartley will brief you for the rest of this week. When you arrive in Chicago, you'll be following orders from that area chief. It's the agency's top priority to put Frank DiMato away, and Elliott's the link to getting to Frank. I don't have to tell you that both of our futures are tied up in this case. Take your time, don't rush it, and don't do anything that will blow your cover. We want to corner this bastard with his hands so dirty that the only way out for him is to turn states' evidence against DiMato."

The Chief stood up, "Randy, one more thing. Remember Elliott Mason is known for three traits: brilliance, charm, and ruthlessness. Be careful!"

Chicago, January 1968

The room had glossy oak floors, beige walls, and heavy maroon drapes. It was a man's room, its masculine appearance temporarily altered by the trail of lace and silk leading to the bed. Susan Carey lay on the king-size bed, wrapped in the arms of Dr. Mark Denning. It was an icy, subzero day outside, but Susan and Mark were sweating from their passion. As Susan tightened her legs around Mark's waist, he lifted her hips to pull her closer. He kissed her and gave a loud sigh as he feigned collapse. His sandy colored hair and olive complexion contrasted with Susan's black hair and white, translucent skin.

"This is it; you finally drained every bit of strength from my body. My mother warned me about nymphos. You'll kill me before I reach forty."

"Stop complaining. At least you haven't had a pimple since I've come into your life." Susan laughed as she pulled a hair from his chest.

"Ouch!" Mark rubbed his chest and then touched his cheek. "You're right! I haven't had a zit in the last two years."

"Two years! Has it been that long?"

Mark's face clouded. "Susan, you know damn well how long it's been. We've had a great afternoon. Please, let's not get started on that again."

"I can't help it, Mark. I tell myself to just let things go on the way they are. But my emotions won't listen to my head. I'm twenty-eight, Mark!"

"You're young, Susan! Women are having babies into their late thirties." He slowly stroked her breast and gently rubbed her nipples between his fingers. "Someday I'll be happy to share these."

Susan tried to keep her voice from shaking. "Mark, I can't continue this way. It's been months of talk of the future, but no indication of when that future will come. It's not just that I want to start a family; it's belonging to someone and having a person who wants to belong to me. Maybe I'm old-fashioned, but I want to be married. I love you, but I've got to have more."

Mark lay back on the pillow, silent for a moment. Finally, he found the words. "Susan, I've told you many times, I'm just not ready. I love you, but I can't make that kind of a commitment right now." He took a deep breath. "You know, it seems that lately all I ever do is make you unhappy."

Susan's voice was little more than a whisper. "You're right; I'm more unhappy every day. Maybe we need some breathing space."

"In other words, if I won't marry you, you're going to break it off." Mark's face hardened. "Doesn't that sound like emotional blackmail?"

Susan rolled over and sat on the edge of the bed. "Oh, my God; Dr. Denning, the psychiatrist, has spoken." She stood up, grabbed her clothes from the floor, and dressed in silence. Mark swung his legs over the side of the bed and pulled on his pants.

Susan left the bedroom, and Mark followed behind her. She stood close to Mark. She was close enough to put her arms around him, but this time she didn't. "I'm sorry that I put so much pressure on you. But, Mark, if you can't commit after all this time, perhaps you'll never be able. As it stands, we still have affection for each other; but if we continue to go on like this, we'll end up hating each other."

Mark stiffened away. "Well, if that's the way you feel, I guess there's nothing else for us to do. I think you're right though; since we have to work together, we'd better end it before things get bitter."

Susan put her coat on and picked up her purse. As she reached for the door, Mark put his hand out to stop her. Then he slowly let it drop.

"I'm sorry, Susan."

Susan made no response and rushed out, not wanting Mark to see her tears.

* * *

Susan stayed in bed most of Sunday morning, alternating between tears and anger. She fought back the desire to call Mark. Even if he wanted to stay together, it would only delay the inevitable. After a shower and some coffee, Susan walked a few blocks to the Oak Park train station. Twenty minutes later she was strolling downtown. Somehow being alone in a crowd didn't seem to feel as bad as being alone at home. The wind on Michigan Avenue was whipping up as she pushed the revolving door and entered Marshall Fields'. Susan took the escalator up to the seventh floor for lunch in the Walnut room. She deserved pampering and ordered their famous chicken pot pie followed by a decadent dessert.

* * *

That night Susan sat with a glass of wine and reflected on the last two years. Most of her social life was spent either with Mark or other couples. Why was it that so many women gave up their single girlfriends as soon as they got involved with a man? She sighed. Hopefully, they would let her reconnect.

CHAPTER 2
LINTON STATE HOSPITAL

Chicago, June, 1968

The night shift was leaving, and Susan was easily able to find a parking spot. She turned off the engine and sat in the car looking over the compound. There were four, three-story buildings that housed the acute hospital, administration building, and two adult psychiatric buildings. The complex was built in the early fifties when every government building resembled a prison, and this one even included iron mesh on the windows. Underneath all these buildings was a tunnel system designed to facilitate taking patients to appointments in the acute hospital. Without proper funding for maintenance, the tunnels became a scary place with broken lights and water dripping from the soaked asbestos covered pipes in the ceiling. One building mainly housed adult patients of color from the less affluent side of Cook County. The other building housed wealthier white adult patients.

Susan glanced at her watch, quickly exited her car, and entered the adult building; it was the one that housed the poor and people of color. She walked to the lobby, took the elevator to the second floor, and went straight to her office to avoid any staff who might ask about her boring weekend. The office had previously been a patient's room, and it housed only a desk and two chairs. When seated, the visitors' knees were pressed against her desk. The walls were pale green cinderblocks, a carryover from the institutional look of the state hospital. The floor was concrete, covered with tiles that had yellowed along the baseboards from years of casual mopping. To avoid feeling claustrophobic, she saw patients on the ward as much as possible.

Susan settled back in her chair, picked up a chart, and started to write. She had closed the door to her office for privacy, but now someone was pounding on it.

"Miss Carey!"

Susan frowned, as the pounding got louder.

"I need to talk to you, Miss Carey. They're treating me bad here."

Susan immediately recognized Mary's voice. She had heard it every fifteen minutes for the past two days. "Come on in, Mary." She smiled back at Mary's grotesque, but friendly smile. Mary had smeared on poppy red lipstick that extended over her lips into a large Cupid's bow. She had put on a bright, peacock blue shadow on her eyelids. Today Mary was wearing an orange wool sweater with a cotton flowered skirt and a pair of worn tennis shoes. The hospital's air-conditioning was not working, and the orange sweater had dark moisture circles under the arms.

Mary was on her fifteenth hospitalization. She responded well to Lithium, a drug for the treatment of manic-depressive illness. However, unfortunately, she did not like how the medication made her feel. Soon after discharge, Mary discontinued her meds and was quickly on another emotional roller coaster.

"Mary, in a few days you will be feeling better, and then we can talk about going home. But right now, you and I have a group meeting to attend."

"Okay, Miss Carey," Mary called back as she ran from the room. "I'll go get everyone into the day room."

The U-shaped ward had a lingering odor of disinfectant mixed with urine and body odor. The women's wing was on one side and the men's on the other, with the large day room and nurses' station at the base. Each wing had twenty double rooms, which meant that there were usually eighty emotionally unstable people on the ward. Sometimes the ward was pleasant, with joking and banter between staff and patients. At other times, however, Susan found it a frightening place, an explosive tinderbox waiting for a spark.

Susan looked around her waiting group; a tall Black man had been admitted last night. She recognized John since this was the fourth time he was assigned to her group. His arms and face were covered with scars from numerous self-inflicted cuts, and now there were fresh scabs from a new set of wounds. Several years ago, he had accidentally cut himself after his wife's funeral and immediately experienced a tremendous feeling of relief. Consequently, whenever he felt depressed or guilty, he would cut himself. As time went on, it took deeper cuts to achieve an emotional release. Susan knew that she would have a difficult time finding John a placement since he had run out of sympathetic relatives and friends a long time ago. Their concern had changed into fear and disgust.

Two middle-aged White women sat in the circle of chairs, their faces reflecting a private hell, an agony of constant guilt and despair. They were alive only because society prevented them from choosing death.

A young White man was standing outside the group. For weeks Jeff had been in a catatonic state, spending his days standing next to the nurses' station like a motionless soldier at a guard post. As Susan approached the group, Mary was already starting the meeting. She rapidly pitched one question after another indiscriminately, never waiting for an answer. "Who has any problems? Who wants to talk first? Who wants to have a party?"

Susan stepped in and took control of the group. "Mary, you've got some good ideas, but let's take them one at a time. How about first having the new people introduce themselves?"

Her attention was abruptly pulled from the group as she noticed Jeff starting to move. He turned toward the glass-walled nurses' station, unzipped his pants, and proceeded to urinate on the glass, aiming at the faces of the startled people on the other side. The occupants yelled and jumped back from the window. Susan forgot about the group as she stared at the scene.

Helen, the charge nurse, ran out of the office. "Jeff, stop that! Stop that right now!"

He just stood there, never changing his expression, calmly shaking off the last drop.

Mary, craving attention, jumped up from the chair and pulled her orange sweater over her head. Susan shouted, "Mary, if you take that off, you're grounded on the ward for the weekend!"

Mary plopped back down on the plastic chair, slowly pulled her sweater back over her head, and glared at Susan, her Cupid's bow now a pout.

After the session ended and the group scattered, Susan went into the nurses' station. A housekeeper grumbled as she mopped under the stinking window as Jeff stood guard. Helen looked up, "You've got a real sicko there, Susan."

"Oh, I don't know about that." She smiled. "I think saying 'piss on you' is better than nothing. At least he's communicating."

Helen shook her head. "Yeah. Well, now that we know he can handle charades, how about teaching him some verbal skills?"

Susan sat down with the other two social workers. Maggie was in her early sixties, and Karen was about fifty. Between them, they had over sixty years of service in the state mental health system. Maggie was slightly overweight, but still pretty, despite the lines and wrinkles in her face. She had a ruddy complexion and gray wavy hair that softly framed her face. Maggie was known throughout the hospital for wit and kindness, but also for her sharp mouth which at times could be crude. She knew every patient and never passed one without taking the time to show interest and concern. She had been a nurses' aide and worked her way up to social worker assistant at a time when there was a shortage of college graduates interested in working at a public psychiatric hospital.

Karen had a pleasant smile, even when she was angry or disgusted. Her expression, her mannerisms, her clothes, and a short, severe hairstyle were a uniform that she placed on her trim body every morning. She came with a master's degree in social work and prided herself on professionalism. She was continually embarrassed by Maggie's unorthodox views and earthy behavior. Karen went by the book; and when it came to choosing between institutional rules or the personal interest of patients, she strictly followed the rules.

When Susan had started her job four years ago, she did her internship with Karen and acquired interviewing skills and learned how to write proper reports and social histories. Susan also learned that one shouldn't take risks unless it's for your benefit; and above all, one must demand respect for your position. If a patient doesn't give that respect, then let him or her wait for you to find the time to contact families for home visits or discharge.

After her mandatory internship with Karen, Dr. Denning, the Administrator, called Susan to his office. "I'm going to have you work with Maggie starting this Monday. You've spent time learning the tools of your trade from Karen; now I want you to experience the heart."

Under Maggie's tutelage, Susan learned to pull strings, tell white lies, overlook rules, and to respect and care about patients. Karen never approved of Susan's training with Maggie. Karen felt that Maggie weakened her authority and contaminated Susan. As a result, Karen and Maggie were always at loggerheads.

* * *

Susan returned to her office and started writing progress notes when the phone rang. It was Helen, the charge nurse. "Susan, I hate to spring this on you, but you have to go to commitment court with John today. His seventy-two hours are up, and he refuses to sign voluntary papers. Security will drive, and Ken will be the aide assigned to him. You can either ride with them or drive your car. It will probably be after four o'clock before you're out of court, so you may not want to drive back to the hospital."

"Thanks, I'll take my car." Susan wondered if Randy would be assigned to represent John Tierney. She smiled as she thought about their first meeting last February.

Susan had to appear in court regularly to testify in commitment cases; and on several occasions, Randy had been the court-appointed attorney for Susan's patient. Randy had used his legal weapons on one particular case to gain freedom for a nineteen-year-old with the maturity of an eight-year-old. Susan and the doctor knew that he would not be safe on the streets. But, for a short time during the hearing, with Randy's help, the kid managed to pull himself together. He was judged competent and free to leave the courtroom without having to return to the hospital for treatment. Susan was furious at the decision and waited in the corridor for Randy.

"What the hell do you think you did in there? That kid doesn't know what time to eat, let alone where to get food." Susan's eyes flashed with anger. "I hope it makes you happy to know that you helped put him back on the street where he'll probably sell himself tonight just to get a place to sleep!"

Randy's face flushed with anger, but he waited until Susan finished with her tirade. "Hey lady, don't give me that holier than thou crap. That guy demanded his day in court, and I represented him. You are the people that are emptying the state hospitals. Tell me how many unfit patients have you helped discharge from the hospital?"

Susan was taken back and stood silent for a moment. "I guess I deserved that. I'm sorry. I get angry when reality interferes with my ideals. Can I buy you a cup of coffee as a peace offering?"

The anger drained from Randy's face, and he cracked a smile. "I can certainly relate to that; it's a problem with both our fields. Neither of us works in a perfect system. I accept your truce. I have time for a quick coffee in the canteen." And that was the beginning of their friendship.

* * *

Commitment court took place at the Chicago Civic Center. Susan got there first and was waiting in the hall when Randy walked up and sat next to her. "Hi. Are you here for John Tierney?" Susan smiled. "Yes, he'll be here in a little while. By the way, ask him to take off his jacket so you can get a look at all his self-inflicted wounds."

Randy looked uncomfortable, "I already read his file, but remember I'm his public defender. If we're still talking when this is over, how about stopping for a drink?"

"That sounds good to me. I'll see you here after the judge gives his ruling." Susan looked up and saw John walking down the hall with security on one side; and the aide, Ken, on the other side.

First, the judge asked Susan why John should be committed to a psychiatric hospital. She responded, "John has a history of self-mutilation. He has had multiple hospitalizations because after discharge he immediately discontinues his medications. Currently, he is on antibiotics for his recent cutting and has been refused by all our placements."

The judge looked at Randy and motioned for him to speak. "John has refused my legal assistance and wants to speak for himself." The judge turned toward John. "Okay, John, what do you have to say for yourself?"

"I called my sister from the nurses' station, and she said I could come live with her if I promise to take my medication and stop cutting myself." The judge tapped his fingers for a moment and then looked up. "John, is that what you are going to do? Are you going to take your medicine and stop cutting yourself?"

John responded, "Yes, sir, I am."

"Well, okay then, I am going to give you another chance." Susan interrupted. "But Your Honor. . . ." The judge banged his gavel. "Don't interrupt the court; I've already ruled. Next case."

John, Susan, Ken, and security stood in the hall while Randy looked on. "What now?" Ken asked. Susan responded, "Take John back to the hospital to get his belongings. Then security will have to drop him off at his sister's place. If she doesn't take him in, then you'll have to take him to the men's shelter. Our hands are tied. We've done all we can." After the others had left, Randy walked over to Susan. "How about going to Miller's Pub? We can get a drink and a bite to eat"

"Sure," replied Susan. "We're both parked here, so why don't we just catch a cab?"

She was nursing her drink when Randy looked at her and asked, "Is something going on? You seem to be pretty preoccupied."

Susan started to get a little teary but quickly wiped her eyes with the back of her hand. "It's been five months since Dr. Denning and I have broken up. Every time I think I'm over it, something comes up; and I think I'll never move on."

Randy asked, "What happened?"

"We came to an impasse," Susan replied. "We both decided that it might be better if we just ended it and remained friends."

"I'm sorry; this must be devastating for both of you."

Susan sipped from her wine. "Well, I can't speak for Mark; but I'm pretty shaken up. I'm happy that my work at the hospital doesn't give me a minute to think; my day goes by quickly. When I get home, I'm too tired to brood. But enough about me, Randy, how is your life going?"

"Things are going okay. I'm finally getting my apartment put together. At least it no longer looks like a frat house. I may even be able to have a party soon. I'm meeting people through work and have met some private practice attorneys who have offices in our building. So, I was thinking of having a kind of mini housewarming at the end of the month. Not that I have a house; but I've been here about six months, and I think it's time to start entertaining."

Susan looked up. "Wow, it just seems like yesterday that we met at commitment court. Do you remember how angry I got when you wouldn't bend the law?"

Randy picked up his wine glass, "Actually we were both right. Your patient needed care, but the law said he couldn't be forced to accept that care. I have to admit there are many times when I would be happier if I lost the case." Susan smiled. "That's what I like about you, Randy. You're a real Mr. Softy."

The waitress brought the check and Randy grabbed it. "It's my turn." Randy leaned across the table, "Susan, I'm so sorry about Mark. I know how painful it can be. I had a relationship that ended before I left Florida, and I'm still smarting. You may not believe it now, but it will get better."

"Thanks," Susan responded. "I appreciate your support, but we'd better get out of here. I see the waitress eyeing us; I think we held her table too long."

* * *

The next week was uneventful. Susan worked down at intake. There were two daily police bus drop offs: one in the morning and one in the early afternoon. Susan intently listened to and watched the person sitting in front of her desk. Many were people picked up off the street and brought into the station because of threatening family members or neighbors. Some, however, were people who were trying to con the system and wanted to have a psychiatric history to keep them out of jail. Others just preferred a warm place and meals at a hospital instead of a shelter. It was Susan's job at intake to determine if the person in front of her required hospitalization. Then she sent the person to the psychiatrist on duty for a final diagnosis and medication orders. Because of the sheer numbers of potential patients, decisions were made in less than fifteen minutes. After listening to several hours of "The Mafia's out to kill me," "My husband is out to kill me," and three Jesus Christ's and one Virgin Mary, Susan left to get some lunch.

Susan joined Maggie and Jenna at lunch. "So, Susan, how many are we getting?" Jenna asked.

"You're getting three of the intakes, and the rest of them are going to the other wards."

Maggie looked up from her plate of spaghetti and meatballs. "Which psychiatrist was on intake with you?"

"Doctor Smith. So that means every new patient today will have a diagnosis of chronic undifferentiated schizophrenia. And everyone will be on Thorazine even if they're manic-depressive and need to be on Lithium. Every time we get a good psychiatrist, they leave for better working conditions and pay."

Jenna looked over at Maggie. "I don't know about you. But after I worked here for a couple of years, I stayed for the pension."

Maggie pushed away her plate. "Well, I'm sure as hell not staying for the food."

Susan laughed. "Come on; I'll race you to the elevator."

"Fat chance of that," Maggie grumbled as she picked up her tray.

Jenna walked back with them. She was an attractive Black woman in her late twenties, about 5'4" with a muscular frame and an aura of power and self-confidence. Jenna had grown up in the Chicago projects and learned that survival required her to always be on guard. One time, Susan had overheard Jenna talking about her little sister and asked how old she was.

"Are you kidding? Don't you know a 'little sister' is a gun! I keep it next to me on the seat of the car. It sees me from the car to my apartment when I have to work the late shift."

As Susan was packing up for the day, the phone rang. "Hi! Susan. It's Randy; I'm just calling to invite you to a party. I finally got all the moving boxes put away and decided to have a house party this coming Saturday. I know its short notice, but I thought I would see if I could get a small crowd. I hope you'll be able to come."

"Yes, I would love to come. Is there anything I can bring?"

"Just your beautiful self, Susan, and I should warn you that the invite list is primarily boring attorneys. I hope you still want to come."

"I sure do, and thanks for the invitation," said Susan. "What time on Saturday?" Susan was beaming as she walked to the parking lot. Finally, she thought, a party with sane people instead of sitting at home with the TV, a glass of wine, and a box of tissues. Thank you, Randy."

CHAPTER 3
MEETING ELLIOTT

That Saturday was a beautiful July night in Chicago. Randy was talking to someone when Susan arrived. He excused himself and came over to greet her. "Welcome! Let me give you the ten-second tour. It's just a three-room apartment, so stand here and slowly turn around. You can see every room from this spot." Randy took Susan by the arm and brought her over to a small group, introduced her, handed her a drink, and then left to greet new arrivals. Susan tried to look more comfortable than she felt; but without knowing anyone but Randy, it was difficult. She glanced across the room and saw an attractive man in his mid-thirties walking toward her. He moved through the crowd in a smooth, competent manner as if he were the host instead of the guest.

The man stopped in front of her, smiled, and held out his hand. He had thick, wavy brown hair; and Susan gazed into the most beautiful blue eyes that she had ever seen. "Hi! My name is Elliott Mason."

"And I'm Susan Carey."

"Are you another public defender?"

"No, I'm a psychiatric social worker."

Elliott took Susan's arm and walked her toward the corner. "Well, a psychiatric social worker is a strange guest in a room full of money-grubbing lawyers."

Susan laughed. "You're right; I feel like I just landed on Mars. Randy and I go to court for two different reasons. He defends his client's right to stay out of the hospital while I try to prove the person still needs treatment. I think Randy invited me here tonight to prove to me that some lawyers are humane and caring people, not vultures."

Elliott looked surprised. "Susan! How could you think otherwise? Randy is right. Behind all this legalese talk is a heart that beats for all humankind."

"Oh, please!" Susan chuckled. "That role is already taken; Mother Teresa beat you to it. But what brings you here? Have you known Randy long?"

"No, I moved here about six months ago. Randy's a newcomer, too. He arrived in Chicago a few weeks after me. We both left the Florida sun for a Chicago winter."

Susan smiled and shook her head. "You know that alone is grounds for a psychiatric commitment."

He laughed. "You're right, but I received a job offer I couldn't turn down; and Randy moved here to be closer to a sick relative." Elliott gave her one of his charming smiles. "Now tell me all about yourself, Susan. Are you madly in love with someone, or are you like me, another lonely person in the big city?"

Susan's face instantly clouded, and Elliott noticed it just as quickly. "I'm sorry. I must have hit a nerve. It's my legal training. I tend to cross-examine people even in social situations."

"No, there is no significant other currently in my life. And tonight I am here to enjoy myself; nothing more, nothing less."

Elliott smiled warmly. "Great, I have the same intentions. There's a terrific view of the city from Randy's balcony. Would you care to share it?"

Susan gave him a skeptical look. "Okay. It's getting pretty smoky in here." Elliott took her hand and led her out to the balcony. "Look at this, what a view of the city! People take beauty for granted. I guess that's why so many relationships fall apart. People take each other's beauty for granted."

That was all it took. Before the evening was over, Susan had told Elliott all about her relationship with Mark and how it had ended. He was sympathetic and understanding. Randy tried to get Susan to come with him to meet other people, but Elliott just brushed him off, finally saying, "Hey, Randy, lay off! I intend to monopolize this lady for the entire night."

When the party started to break up, Elliott offered Susan a ride home. "Thanks, but I brought my car."

"Do you have anything planned for tomorrow?"

Susan hesitated. "No, but . . ."

Elliott put his finger to her lips. "Good, that settles it. We can spend the day together, either at the beach, or the zoo, or the art museum, or where ever you'd like."

Susan hesitated. Mark had never left her mind these last few months, but there was something exciting about this man. "Sure, why not? I find exploring the city is always more fun with a newcomer."

* * *

It was a perfect day. They walked along the beach and spent the afternoon at Lincoln Park zoo watching the animals, who in turn were observing the people. They talked for hours; and when Elliott brought her home, he gently lifted her face to his and gave her a lingering good-night kiss. "Can I call you tomorrow?" he asked.

Susan smiled at him. "Yes, I've had a wonderful time."

Elliott beamed at her and waved goodbye as he headed down the street to his car. The next week they talked every evening for several hours and planned a trip to the Art Institute on Saturday.

* * *

Elliott and Susan spent the morning looking at the Impressionist wing and then took a walk over to Grant Park. Later in the afternoon, Susan shivered as they sat on the edge of the Buckingham Fountain."

"It's cold," said Elliott.

"The wind off Lake Michigan can cause temperatures to drop pretty quickly."

"How about we take a cab to Uno's for pizza?"

"Oh, that sounds good."

When they finished the pizza, and the bottle of wine was empty, Susan looked up and said, "Elliott, I shared so many things about myself, even about my breakup with Mark. You know that I am an only child and that my parents are retired, and recently moved to Arizona. But I don't know anything about you, your parents, or even if you have any siblings."

Elliott looked down at his hands and then said, "That's because it's difficult to talk about. When I was eighteen, both my parents died in an automobile accident. I had no siblings, and my parents never kept up with their families; so I was basically on my own. There was no house to sell, no college money, and no life insurance policy. But my father had a longtime friend who was also wealthy. He gave me a job as his chauffeur. Luckily, I didn't have to wear a uniform as it would have looked pretty stupid on an 18-year-old kid. After my first year of driving this guy around, he decided to send me to college. I owe him everything. There's nothing I wouldn't do for him."

"My God," said Susan, "how sad to lose your parents and not to have any siblings. That must've been so difficult".

"Yes, it was. But it would have been a lot more difficult if I hadn't had this mentor come into my life. It was a long time ago though, and now I'm on a date with a beautiful woman. So let's go get my car, and I'll take you home."

They parked the car and walked up to Susan's apartment. "Would you like to come in for a glass of wine?" Susan asked Elliott.

"Is the Pope Catholic?" he responded.

After a glass of wine, Elliott lifted Susan from the couch and carried her into the bedroom. She was apprehensive, but Elliott was sweet and gentle and quickly made her forget her fears and all of the pain and hurt associated with her breakup with Mark. Susan opened herself to Elliott with an abandonment that scared her. They made love for hours. He was almost obsessed with pleasing her, and soon he had her reaching heights of excitement that she had never known.

* * *

They became inseparable. When they weren't together, they were on the phone with each other. The next few weeks were spent having fun and making love at every opportunity. Susan had broken up with Mark because he wasn't ready to get married, and perhaps he would never be able to commit. Now with Elliott pursuing her every moment, she didn't have time to think of Mark. No thoughts, no pain.

Her relationship with Elliott grew stronger every day while at the same time her friendship with Randy also continued to grow. He never told her to stop seeing Elliott, but Susan sensed it. Sometimes he responded to her relationship with Elliott like the concerned brother, warning her that she didn't know him and how quickly she was falling for him. At other times, Randy seemed to be hiding something, like a family that was concealing some secret from the future bride.

* * *

One day at lunch Maggie started in again about when they were going to meet this Elliott guy. "So, Susan, have you decided to let your friends meet this man or are you going to keep him hidden forever?"

"Okay, I give up. How about dinner at my place this Saturday evening? Elliott and I were planning to go to a movie, but we can do that on Sunday. I'll ask Randy if he's free. It'll be casual, just a salad with spaghetti and meatballs."

Maggie beamed, "I'll bring a bottle of wine."

"And I'll bring a dessert," said Jenna.

Susan made a quick call to Randy and was happy to find out that he also was free for dinner on Saturday. She felt it would be easier for Elliott if there were another guy at the dinner.

That evening when Elliott called, Susan thought he would be happy to hear about meeting her friends; but his voice tensed. She could tell that he was not pleased. When she mentioned that he didn't seem happy about meeting her friends, he responded, "I guess I want you all to myself, but I'm glad that Randy is going to be there. At least it won't be a hen party."

The dinner went well, but Susan sensed uneasiness in the air. Elliott was flirtatious and flattering to both Maggie and Jenna, but Susan could see that both Maggie and Jenna were uneasy. Susan thought the reason behind the uneasiness was because both Elliott and Randy were attorneys, and maybe that was intimidating. However, neither of them had ever shown uneasiness with Randy.

No, she thought—it wasn't Elliott; it was because of their loyalty to Mark.

* * *

At lunch on Monday, Susan asked Maggie and Jenna, "What you think? Isn't he just perfect?"

Jenna quietly responded, "Well, he is certainly handsome and charming as you told us." Susan looked over at Maggie. "What you think, Maggie? Is he a keeper?"

"You're right; he is handsome and charming and seems to be perfect. That's what has me a little worried. All of the perfect people in my life have turned out to be sociopaths. But that's the story of my life, not yours. I have to admit though that I still think the perfect one for you was Dr. Mark."

Susan replied a little too testy, "That's not going to happen, so stop comparing him to Mark."

Maggie quickly retreated, "I'm sorry, forget what I just said. I'm just an old lady shooting off her mouth. I shouldn't be giving advice when it isn't asked for or needed. It's just that I hope you're doing the right thing getting involved so quickly."

Susan took Maggie's hand. "I know you care, but I'm an adult; and everything is going to be fine." Jenna lightly wrapped on the table. "Look, not to change the subject, but I have to be back on the ward in ten minutes; and I want to discuss something. You know, Dr. King was assassinated last April, and then Bobby Kennedy, and now my brother is in Vietnam. There's a protest march against the

Vietnam War downtown this Wednesday. I'm going after work and was hoping you two would come with me."

"Count me in," said Susan.

Maggie took a deep breath. "And the two of you know that my son came back from Vietnam three years ago; and he hasn't stopped having nightmares, drinking, and scaring the shit out of me. So, yes, I want to march; and I may even be tempted to throw one of those Molotov cocktails at the politicians who keep sending boys to fight a senseless war that they can't win."

"Okay, it's been decided. We'll bring a change of clothing and some comfortable shoes on Wednesday, and let the world hear our voices. Let's get back to work."

As Susan was walking past the nurses' station, Helen, the charge nurse, rapped on the window and came to the door. "We just got Mary back on the ward. She was in the acute hospital over the weekend."

"What do you mean? We just discharged her last Friday!" Susan exclaimed.

Helen sighed. "But, Mary got into a fight with her pimp about payment; so he cut off her ear. Acute sewed her up, put her on antibiotics, and sent her back here."

"Oh, my God," Susan responded. "Mary is so sweet and has never been a problem. How could anyone do that to her? She's got to be so upset!"

"Actually no, Mary's her usual self; and she loves the attention.

Look at her out in the day room. The biggest problem is that she's trying to take the bandages off so she can show people where her ear used to be."

Susan sighed. "It's so dangerous to be mentally ill and out on the streets."

"Yes, and we constantly are forced to put more and more sick people on the streets. Let's face it. Unless we get more funding for community mental health centers, patients are going to end up back on the street or in jail. So instead of community mental health centers, we'll have to build more prisons."

"Come on, don't be a pessimist," Susan scolded. "They have a whole new system on paper with community mental health centers and outreach workers. Just give them some time. Having more patients live in the community could turn out to be a good thing."

Helen turned back into the nurses' station and murmured, "Well, that's what I call an optimist."

Susan walked out to the day room. "Okay everybody; let's get these chairs in a circle. We have some new people here. Let's introduce ourselves."

Mary started waving her hand in the air. "I'm Mary, and I'm new again. I left on Friday, and got my ear cut off, and now I'm back."

The rest of the hour passed with most of the patients insisting that Susan let Mary continue talking about all the gory details. "Okay, Mary, but tomorrow you don't speak in group. You let other people take their turn."

* * *

Traffic going home was terrible. Susan turned on the car radio, and the news was all about the hippies in Grant Park. The protesters had come from all over the United States to pitch tents in Grant Park, but City Hall refused to okay the permits. Mayor Daley told the police to get them out of the park and to use whatever force was necessary, even lethal. Susan was getting a little nervous about marching with Jenna and Maggie tomorrow night. Elliott was at a meeting in Florida. After dinner, Susan poured herself a glass of wine; and after reading for a while, turned off the lights and went to bed.

CHAPTER 4

ANTI-VIETNAM WAR MARCH

Chicago, August 28th, 1968

The next day, Maggie and Jenna knocked on Susan's door. "I'm glad to see that we all wore slacks," said Maggie.

"If you two have changed into your marching shoes, let's go!" exclaimed Jenna, "most of the marchers are on Michigan Avenue. We're going to have to drive in that direction, park the car, and walk the rest of the way. I have water in the car."

"Okay," said Susan. "Let's get rolling."

They got as close as they could and parked the car, put water in their purses, and started walking. Within half an hour, they had linked arms with some of the other marchers and started singing, "We Shall Overcome." It was like a love-in until somebody on the street hurled a brick. And some of the group jumped on the hood of a police car and began yelling "fascist pig." All of a sudden Chicago police and National Guards swarmed into the crowd shooting canisters of tear-gas and beating anyone they could reach with their batons. Maggie and Jenna had cowered in the doorway of a boarded-up store and were washing out their eyes with their drinking water. Blinded by the tear gas, Susan was swept away with the crowd. Her arm was grabbed, and she glanced up to see a helmeted soldier. Susan was able to pull away and run down a side street. She ended up sitting on the curb a couple of blocks away. Susan could see the police grabbing people and throwing them into patrol cars and paddy wagons. Weak and sick to her stomach, she managed to get up and walk down another side street. Susan sat on the steps of an apartment building for about five minutes and then started walking toward the car.

"Oh, thank Jesus," shouted Jenna as she ran toward Susan. "We've been worried sick! Thank God you're okay!"

"Come on," said Maggie. "Let's get out of here; the roar is getting louder. They be must be getting closer."

Susan drove to their cars. She put on the brakes and turned to look back at Maggie and Jenna. Their eyes were red, and tears were running down their faces. "I can't believe this is happening in America," Susan muttered. Jenna responded, "Welcome to my America!" There was nothing left to say.

* * *

Susan took off her clothes, looked in the mirror and saw her swollen red eyes, skinned knees, and bruised arm. After a long hot shower, she turned on the late news and found out that while all the politicians were polling and taking votes in the convention hall, cameras had been running revealing the Gestapo tactics employed on the streets. Susan remembered seeing the bloodied heads and faces around her but had no idea of the magnitude. She turned off the news and went to bed, but she had a very fitful night.

* * *

Elliott had been in meetings with Frank and his associates for the last three days. After they had dinner, Frank asked Elliott to meet him in the bar. "Elliott, we are leaving the day after tomorrow, and I wanted to check in with you to see how things were going in Chicago. You have been dating that girl for several months now. I thought by now I'd be invited to an engagement party. Getting you married is my number one priority right now. I hope it's a priority for you. I want you to run for office in the very near future. And it's going to go a lot better if you have a wife. How about we go into that jewelry store off the lobby, and Uncle Frank buys you a beautiful engagement ring for that lovely lady? That way when the right moment comes, you'll be ready. And I'm sure that moment will be very soon."

Elliott didn't protest and half an hour later went up to his room with the jewelry box in his pocket.

* * *

In the morning, Susan took one look at her swollen face, cringed when she tried to move her arm and decided it would be best to take a sick day. Later, Maggie called. "What a night, it looks like all three of us are staying home today. Jenna said the tear gas did a number on her eyes. How are you doing?"

"I've had better days. One of the guards grabbed my arm while trying to pull me into a patrol car. I got away, but he pulled a muscle; and it's pretty sore. I'll survive, but I don't know about all of those people who were getting their heads bashed in. I doubt we accomplished anything, but I'm glad I went. I've learned that being in the middle of something is a lot different than watching it on TV."

"Yeah," Maggie said sarcastically. "I'm sure we made a difference. Take it easy Kiddo; see you tomorrow."

Susan knew that Elliott wouldn't be happy about her going to the march. She didn't mention it when he called that evening. He would be returning from Florida tomorrow afternoon, so Susan asked him to dinner.

* * *

The next day Susan managed to hole up in her office and get some paperwork done. On the way home, she got a couple of steaks and fixings to make a salad. When Susan got to her apartment building, Elliott was sitting on the stairs. He got up and gave her a big hug, took her bag of groceries, and followed Susan upstairs. At the door, she turned to him, "I hope you haven't been waiting here long?"

Elliott replied, "For about an hour; maybe it's time we talked about exchanging keys."

Susan felt a little uneasy but responded, "Sure, maybe we should."

He put the groceries on the kitchen table while Susan went in to change her clothes. A couple of minutes later, Elliott knocked at her bedroom door. "Can I come in and help you get comfortable?"

Susan smiled. "Sure, come on in."

Elliott unbuttoned her blouse, let it drop to the floor, and stared at her arm. "What the hell happened to you? Your arm is black and blue."

"I'll tell you at dinner. It's a long story; but for now, let's finish this part of the story."

They made love for an hour, and then Susan grabbed a robe and went into the kitchen to start dinner.

Elliott started on his salad and looked up at Susan. "So tell me, what happened? Do I have some competition? Was this some rough sex while I was out of town?"

"Maggie, Jenna, and I decided to go to the march the night before last. We just went to show support, and we ended up getting tear-gassed. A National Guard man grabbed my arm, but I managed to pull away."

"What the hell were you thinking? I watched it on television; you guys could've been killed. Why are you supporting some hippie ass-holes that would rather cause trouble than work?"

"Elliott, we weren't marching to support hippies; we were marching in protest of the Vietnam War. This war has been going on since 1955 with no end in sight. You're single; you could get drafted tomorrow!"

Elliott smiled and pulled Susan into his arms. "Not likely; but just in case, I intend to do something about that today." He then reached into his pocket and pulled out a box. Elliott opened the box. "Will you marry me, Susan Carey?"

Susan was speechless.

Elliott repeated, "I love you, Susan. Will you marry me?"

"This is so fast; I just didn't expect it."

"Do you love me?" Elliott asked.

"Yes, but . . ."

"No butts about it," responded Elliott as he picked up Susan and carried her back to the bedroom. "We're getting married."

* * *

Elliott didn't want a long engagement or a formal wedding. He insisted that he had waited long enough to find her. Susan's parents had recently retired to Arizona, and Susan's mother was disappointed that there wasn't going to be a church wedding. However, she forgot her anger after meeting Elliott. They had invited Susan's parents to visit for a long weekend. Elliott was warm and gracious from the moment they picked up her parents at the airport until they saw them off three days later. Susan had a difficult time saying goodbye to her father and mother. She especially missed not having her mother closer, but at least they checked in by phone every Sunday afternoon. A few days after her parents left, Susan and Elliott flew to Las Vegas and married in one of the express wedding chapels. It wasn't the wedding she had dreamed of, and she couldn't understand Elliott's urgency. Although, wasn't it Susan who felt her biological clock ticking? Maggie and Jenna were upset at not being invited to the wedding. But after a week of grumbling, they let it drop.

* * *

A few months later, Susan answered her office phone. "This is Dr. Spelling from Tri-Valley Mental Health Center. I'm getting back to you with the decision of the Board. We have decided to offer you the position that you interviewed for last week."

"That's wonderful! Thank you. I'm excited to start working; it will be a welcome change from inpatient experience. I'm looking forward to working with you and your staff. I enjoyed meeting them."

"Great! I'm happy to hear that. When do you think you'll be able to start? I wish it could be tomorrow."

"I don't think I can start for at least two weeks. I'll get back to you right after I give my resignation to Dr. Denning."

"Fine. But before I sign off, let me be the first to congratulate you on your new position. We'll be looking forward to having you join us."

"Thank you, and thank you for choosing me. I'll be talking to you in a few days." Susan put the phone down and shouted to the empty room, "Hooray! I've got the job."

She took a deep breath and brushed her fingers through her unruly hair. Susan's face flushed with excitement. A few weeks ago she had heard about this position and sent in her resume. But even after Doctor Spelling had called her in for an interview, she was afraid to hope after all those months of wishing. Maybe this was better; now she wasn't running away. She was moving on. It had been difficult working with Mark in the first few months, loving and hating him at the same time. Now Susan had Elliott. He was charming, loving, and most of all, he wanted her in every way. She had a new husband, a new life, and soon a new job.

Susan sat back and thought about the call. Finally, I have a job out in the real world. She smiled to herself. Well, almost the real world. At least her patients wouldn't be living in an institution

Karen and Maggie were sitting at the counter. Susan looked around. "Where are the aides?"

"They are down in admissions with security." Maggie raised her eyebrow. "There's a woman downstairs who weighs over four hundred pounds and is taking everybody on."

"Are you serious?"

Susan looked over and saw Helen nodding her head. "Yes, she is; and guess whose group she's going into?"

Susan put her arm on Maggie's shoulder. "Maggie, how would you like this one in your group, just for a little variety?"

"Hell, no! I'm too old. At my age, when you get knocked on your ass, you end up with a broken hip." Maggie's voice changed to concern. "Listen, you better be careful with this one; she's a hell raiser."

"Have you got any records on her?" asked Karen. "I think she should be in a maximum-security hospital!"

Susan was quickly brought to the present when she looked out of the nurses' station and saw the ward door open. An aide had unlocked the door and was watching the elevator. It was difficult to tell if the Black woman was being pushed out of the elevator or if she was pulling everyone out. Whatever. The biggest woman she had ever seen was moving down the hall toward her. Security guards were trying to control her, but it looked as if she were dragging them along. The woman wore a flowered, cotton shift that must've been homemade because something off the rack would never have fit her enormous body. Susan watched as the nurses, aides, and security guards pushed the woman into one of the rooms and wrestled her into restraints attached to the bed.

She spat out at them, "You bastards, let me loose! Get this shit off of me!"

The woman's eyes bulged as she struggled and soon broke the leather restraints on her arms and legs. A room next to the nurses' station, empty except for a mattress on the floor, was available for such emergencies. Calvin, the chief of security and a group of sweating workers, dragged the thrashing woman into the empty room. It took all of them to hold her down. They looked like a football team trying to stop a short-yardage touchdown. Well prepared, Helen quickly injected a tranquilizer into the woman's hip. The drug took effect within minutes, and soon she went down like a tranquilized elephant.

Even Mary was quiet. For a short time, the patients abandoned their private dream worlds as they watched the frightening scene. Maggie looked out at the day room. "We'd better get out there and calm everyone down, or this whole place will be up for grabs." Susan left the nurses' station with Maggie and Karen right behind.

John was sitting at a table anxiously picking at the scab on his arm. "Come on, John, let's get a couple of people together and play some cards."

Most of the patients were involved in an activity and soon forgot the woman sleeping on the floor of the isolation room.

After several hands of cards, Susan left the day room. She walked down the hall and knocked on the door to Maggie's office.

"Come in."

Maggie was hunched over her desk working on a discharge summary. "I hate writing all this crap about individual, group and milieu therapy. These poor bastards are lucky if they get ten minutes a day of any worth-while therapy. I don't know why they don't just print a form where we can type in a name, an admission date, and a discharge date, because all the rest is just wishful thinking. Well, enough of my complaints. How are things going out there?"

"It's quiet for now, but I need to talk to you about something else. How about sneaking out for lunch before Karen decides to join us?"

Maggie's eyes twinkled. "What's up? I'm the one that usually wants to sneak out for lunch. The food around here is bad enough without having to kiss the Queen's ass between courses."

Susan laughed. "Maggie, I think you've probably bitten her ass more often than you've kissed it."

Susan was ready to burst. She had been waiting all morning to share the news with someone. "I never dreamed I'd get it, but the director of the community mental health center called me this morning with an offer."

Maggie grabbed Susan and gave her a bear hug. "This is terrific! I'm happy for you."

Susan's face clouded. "Oh, Maggie, I've been so excited about getting this job that I forgot I would be leaving you! How am I ever going to function without my surrogate mother?"

"I'm going to miss you too, Kid. But its better you're getting out of here. Look around you. Most of the good people use this place as a training ground." Maggie heaved a long sigh. "Without credentials, I'm stuck here. But you have the education, and you are great with the patients."

Susan put her arm around Maggie's shoulder and quietly said, "Thanks to you!"

Maggie cut in, her face flushed. Giving affection was one thing; receiving it was something else. "And another thing, when your boss is also your ex-lover, it's time to move on. Have you told Doctor Denning about this yet?"

Susan shook her head. "No, I haven't told Mark. I didn't want to tell him until I was sure I had the job. I'll let him know this afternoon."

"Hey, you can tell that it's Friday!" Maggie sniffed at the air. "Smell the clam chowder?"

They were on their way back to the ward when Susan remembered the new patient. "What do you think of the newest addition to the ward?"

Maggie smiled as she shook her head. "It looks like she's going to keep a lot of people on their toes. If that lady's a paranoid-schizoid, she should be more manageable after a few days on meds. But God help us if she's a sociopath. Remember that fellow on Ward Two? He was here about six months ago, the guy with the acne and brown curly hair? I think his name was Hanks, Carl Hanks."

Susan thought for a second. "Yes, I remember him. He was friendly, a real charmer."

Maggie paused at the door of the ward. "By the time they got him off the ward, there was so much internal fighting among staff that the patients were almost forgotten. Sociopaths! They exploit people and then find a way to justify their narcissistic behavior."

For a few seconds, Susan was deep in thought. "You know, Maggie, what's frightening is that so many of the staff fell for his charm and manipulation; and we're supposed to be experts on human behavior."

Maggie gave a little shrug. "But we're also supposed to reach out and be trusting; maybe that's why some slip by. Hey, there's Doctor Kim. I have to get his signature on an off-grounds pass. See you later."

* * *

Back in the office, Susan began to write her letter of resignation. She remembered the many times she had been angry and had imagined herself writing this letter, listing all of her grievances with self-righteous indignation. Here was her golden opportunity. Her day had come, but somehow it didn't matter now. Already this place was becoming just an experience. Maybe that's why most letters of resignation were short and to the point. "So long, it's been nice knowing you . . . ."

Susan put the letter aside and looked at the list of patients approved for weekend home visits. She decided to try again to phone the relatives she hadn't been able to reach. Only one more family agreed to take on a patient for the weekend. Susan picked up the list of patients and stared at each name. Suddenly an uncomfortable feeling of guilt began to surface. She could think of a whole list of reasons why it was good for her to leave. But Susan couldn't think of one reason why it would be good for them. That kind of thinking would have her here until retirement. Susan went out in the ward. She looked in the nurses" station and saw Helen point to the big clock on the wall. It was time for the nursing report to the oncoming shift.

"Come on in, Susan. We've got the admissions write-up on the new patient. The information is rather sketchy, and she isn't exactly a cooperative patient," Helen continued, "Carla Johnson is a twenty-eight-year-old, obese, single, Black, unemployed female, currently living with her maternal grandmother. She was brought to the hospital via the police because of reports from the grandmother of increasingly bizarre behavior. Carla has been hitting people and destroying property. She is considered a danger to herself and others. There are doctor's orders to keep her snowed under for the next 24 hours. I suggest you give Carla whatever it takes to keep her immobilized."

Helen closed the chart. "That's it. Any more information we get will be up to Susan. Her Grandmother didn't come to the hospital, but we have a telephone number."

After a quick rundown of the day's activities, the meeting ended. Susan stood up and squeezed between the counter and the medication cart to leave the room. "If anyone needs me, I'll be in Dr. Denning's office."

CHAPTER 5
RESIGNATION

The elevator was working at the moment, so Susan took it down to the first floor and knocked on Dr. Denning's door. "Mark, its Susan. Do you have a few minutes?"

The door opened, and he was smiling down at her. "Sure, I was looking for an excuse to put aside the budget. I've been working on it for hours and getting nowhere."

Mark stood aside as Susan entered his office. He was thirty-four, but still had a boyish grin that captivated the women around him. His sandy hair, now bleached blonde by the sun, had a little silver in it, enough to change his description from cute to handsome. She noticed his deep tan and wondered if he had company sitting by the pool. Susan remembered reading in a journal that tall, good-looking people get treated as if they were in authority. Maybe that was why she always felt secure around him.

"It's always good to see you, Susan. Anything, in particular, you want to discuss?"

Susan took a deep breath. "Yes, I've received a job offer as a social worker supervisor at a community mental health center; and I've decided to take it."

Mark looked stunned. "I didn't know you were looking!"

"I'm sorry." Susan felt her face flush. "I guess I should have said something earlier. I've been thinking about it for a long time; and when I heard about the opening, I didn't want to pass up the opportunity. They don't come along very often."

Mark sat down on the couch and motioned for Susan to sit next to him. "This is certainly out of the blue. Where are you going?"

"Tri-Valley Mental Health Center." She looked intently up at him, "Please, try to understand, Mark. It was difficult working here with you after we broke up. I would have given anything to find a new job six months ago. But now it's different. I'm married, and my main reason for leaving is to get on with my life."

Mark sat back on the couch, his face somber. "Susan, you're right. I'm not happy about losing a good social worker, especially when there's a hiring freeze; but that's not my main concern." He reached over and took her hand. "I know things have been awkward since we broke up, but are you sure this is the time to make a career change? You've been married barely three months, and now you're going to take on a new job? That's a lot of changes."

"What can I say? You're right on all counts, but sometimes things happen in clusters," Susan smiled weakly. "I know that's not a good answer, but it's the best I can do." Mark shook his head. "No doubt you'll be as headstrong and stubborn about this as you are about most things. Once you've made up your mind, I know there is no turning you back." He smiled at her with resignation. "Susan, I hope everything works out for you. When is all this going to take place?"

"Well, the position is empty, and they want me to fill it as soon as possible; so I'm giving a two-week notice."

Mark frowned. "You certainly don't waste time. Two weeks is going to make it tough on us here at the hospital. Oh well, being understaffed and having good people leave is a chronic condition at Linton. We managed before, and we'll manage now. Don't take any new cases starting Monday."

"What about the patient who came in today, Carla Johnson? She's scheduled for my case list."

"I think you'd better take her. I'm going to have to split your cases between Karen and Maggie, and they'll also be taking on all of the new patients. Why don't you concentrate on getting Carla into a manageable state over the next two weeks? I saw her when the police brought her in. She's a caseload on her own!"

"Thanks, you always did like to see me with the challenge."

Mark moved closer to Susan and put his arm around her. "Can a friend give you a good luck hug?"

"Sure, I can always use a hug from a friend."

He held her close, her short dark curls brushing against his cheek for a moment. Memories a lot stronger than friendship welled up in Susan; and she pulled away, but not before she noticed the hurt in Mark's eyes.

She walked toward the door. "Hey, I better get going. I have to stop back on the ward before I leave. I want you to know, Mark, that I've learned a lot from you these past four years; and I appreciate how you have mentored me. You have a good weekend, and I'll see you on Monday."

He looked at her with his familiar warm smile as she reached for the door. "Sure Kiddo, see you Monday."

She took a deep breath. It was dinner time, and the ward was almost empty when Susan returned. She closed the office door and slumped into her chair. A weight was lifted off her since Mark had taken the news better than she had expected. Leaving the hospital was going to be hard. It felt like quitting a job that was unfinished. This job, however, was never-ending. But leaving Mark was also going to be difficult. He had always been there for her. But now, she would have to stand on her own feet. Enough of this, she told herself. I have a new husband, a new job, and I feel great. She thought of Elliott and could hardly wait to get home to tell him the news.

* * *

Elliott's last client for the day had just left. The law office was high above the city, over-looking Michigan Avenue, with a view that never ceased to amaze him. The streets were trails of illuminated ribbons. Since arriving in Chicago, Elliott had seldom spent an evening alone; and this was easy to understand. He was attractive and possessed a captivating smile. He also worked out regularly at a health club, dressed well, and maintained a standing appointment with a well-known hairstylist. His greatest asset, however, was his charm. He used it to smooze the crowds at a party like a Chicago back-of-the-yards politician paying his respects at an Irish wake. By offering a favor here and free legal advice there, he was gathering IOU's that could be called upon when needed.

Elliott reached for the intercom when he saw the blinking light on this phone. "Barb, tell whoever it is that I left for the day."

"It's your wife, Mr. Mason."

"All right, I'll take it. "Hi! You made it home already?"

"Yes, and I hope you're not going to be late. I've some good news that I'm dying to tell you!"

"It wouldn't have anything to do with that interview you went on last week?"

"Elliott! Don't spoil it; I'll tell you when you get home."

"Okay, I'm leaving as soon as we hang up. By the way, I had lunch with Randy Sloan; and he sends his regards."

Susan smiled as she thought about Randy, the tall, lanky attorney, who always looked like he needed a haircut. He was a special friend to both Susan and Elliott. After all, Randy had bought them together.

* * *

Susan always felt the need for a shower after work. It was a ritual, a compulsive attempt to wash away the smell of sickness and poverty. Susan looked at her reflection in the mirror as she stepped out of the shower and smiled with approval. She ran her hand across her firm stomach; working out with Elliott was beginning to pay off. A membership at a high priced gym was one of his firm's perks. "I'm up here, Honey." Susan was pulling on her robe as Elliott came up the stairs and into the bedroom.

"Hi, looks like my timing gets better every day!"

Susan's voice rose with excitement. "Elliott, I got the job at Tri-Valley Mental Health Center! I can't believe it! It's the first interview I went on."

"That's great! But it doesn't surprise me. You're been wasting your talent at that place. Besides, it's dangerous working with all those low-lives. Now we have something to celebrate when we go out tomorrow night. By the way, how did Mark take to your leaving?"

"Fine; he wished me well even though there's a hiring freeze."

"Tough. That's Mark's problem, not yours. He's another reason why I'll be glad when you're out of there. Who wants his wife working for her ex-lover?"

"Elliott, why are you jealous! You know that Mark and I broke up before you and I ever met." Her face tightened. "And those low-lives you referred to happen to be people I will be working with even at this new job."

"I know, but it won't be the same. At least at a community mental health center, they shouldn't be as crazy."

Susan reached up and loosened Elliott's tie. "Speaking of low-lives, it seems to me that you also deal with a few of them in your job."

He smiled and kissed her forehead. "That's different. I don't get involved, just paid!" He bent lower and playfully gripped her lip with his mouth as he slipped off her robe. Susan felt a warm tingling as Elliott kissed her breast.

With Susan's help, he quickly removed his clothes and pulled her onto the bed. She ran her fingers down the line of hair that started at his navel as Elliott groaned with delight.

They shared in mutual pleasuring, each giving and receiving with heightening agitation until the final pitch of excitement ended in a spasm of ecstasy.

Susan kissed Elliott's cheek and smiled warmly at him as he slumped back into his pillow and reached for a cigarette from the nightstand. "I wonder why sex is always better when a cigarette follows it. I gave up smoking several years ago, but I can't give up this one."

By the time the late news started, Elliott was already nodding off to sleep. He kissed her and stood up with a stretch. "It's been a hectic week; I'm going to call it a night.

"I'll be up after the news."

* * *

Saturday morning was spent running errands. Their last stop was the grocery store. Elliott groaned. "I hate this. When we're rich, we're going to hire a shopping person."

Susan laughed. "You'll need a lot of cases before we're in that league.

He pushed the cart into the checkout line. "Maybe, or maybe not; it just depends on the cases. Some pay better than others."

They had just put the groceries away and were eating lunch when Elliott suddenly put his fork down. "Oh, I forgot; Randy called yesterday and asked us to meet him for cocktails tonight."

Susan finished her sandwich, pleased with the thought of seeing Randy. "Let's go. I haven't seen him in a while. Besides, I want to tell him about my new job."

* * *

When they arrived at the lounge, Elliott held Susan by the arm as he worked their way through the crowd to a table. He quickly sized up everyone they passed, making sure he didn't miss a chance to lay a little charm on somebody he recognized.

"Hey, Randy, how are you?"

"Fine, how are you two?"

"Just great! Three months, and we haven't filed for divorce yet."

"Well, that's good news." Randy turned to Susan and asked a little too earnestly, "Is this guy treating you okay? After all, you met at my place."

She smiled. "Don't worry; we're doing just fine. I have some important news!"

Randy looked alarmed. "Don't tell me you're pregnant?"

"No! Please give us a little time. Now my news is anti-climactic."

He reached over and touched her hand. "I'm sorry, tell me."

Susan smiled again. "I have a new job."

"No kidding? I am indeed surprised! We are you going?"

"Tri-Valley Mental Health Center. I gave my resignation yesterday."

"That's great, but aren't you going to miss the excitement of the hospital?"

"Listen, I've had enough stimulation to last a lifetime. A quiet little clinic with marital discord, delinquent teens, and depressed housewives will suit me just fine."

The waitress came with the drinks. "A toast to Susan: may she find happiness and success in her new job."

"Thank you. How are things going in the public defender's office?"

"Same old, same old. We have caseloads that never end, and salaries that are not worth mentioning. That's why I like to hang out around you, Elliott. Interesting cases and you even get paid for your work."

"Why stay in it?" Elliott asked.

"I stay for the same reason that Susan stays in her field. We complain, but there's not a lot of options. Maybe, it's just a phase we're passing through and we'll soon move on to our profitable stage. What about you, Elliott, what motivates you?"

Elliott smiled, "Greed! I like the good life. But who knows? Maybe it's just a stage, and someday I'll be putting you two guys to shame with my selfless concern for the underdog. However, I hate to break this up; but we have dinner reservations."

Randy glanced at his watch. "And I have a date to pick up."

Outside he shook hands with Elliott and kissed Susan on the cheek. As they left, Randy turned toward Susan. "How about having lunch with me one day next week? Once you become entrenched in that new job, you'll probably never get away."

"Sure, I'd love to. Give me a call soon, and we'll check schedules."

Elliott had made reservations at a restaurant where dinner was more an event than a meal. Afterward, they walked down Rush Street.

"Don't you just love it here? This city is so great!"

"Susan, are you aware that the Windy City got its name from the excessive bragging and boasting of its politicians and citizens?"

"Wait a minute. I only spoke the truth."

Elliott grinned and hugged her. "Okay, I agree. And I must admit, I'm enjoying it much more than I ever expected. But I thought that was due to meeting you. These last few months have been the happiest in my life. Just a minute, I've got something." He reached into his pocket and pulled out a small box. "This is for you-just a little gift I picked up this morning to celebrate your new job. You know, I'm damn proud of you."

Susan reached for the box. "Thank you. I love it!"

"What do you mean? You haven't even opened it yet!"

"It doesn't matter; I love getting gifts. Should I open it now?"

"Yes. That's why I bought it."

She tore at the wrapping while Elliott watched. A pair of

diamond earrings sparkled in the city lights. "Oh, Elliott, they're beautiful. But this is too extravagant!"

"Not for my wife. I'm doing well, and this is just the beginning. We'll work our way up to the bracelet and necklace."

Susan laughed. "If this is what it means to be married to a successful lawyer, then I'm happy with your career choice."

Elliott ran his finger along her cheek. "Make sure you remember that when I'm working long evenings and weekends."

It was after one o'clock before they arrived home and after two o'clock before the tired, but satisfied couple, fell asleep in each other's arms.

* * *

Susan woke up to sunlight and quietly got out of bed without disturbing Elliott. She went downstairs, made coffee, and put on the bacon. Before long its sizzling aroma drifted throughout the house. Elliott stuck his head into the kitchen. "Hey, I heard the cook in this establishment has an insatiable sexual appetite; and for favors rendered, you can get a free breakfast."

Susan shrugged her shoulders and picked up the coffee. "Well, that depends on the favors; but if my memory serves me correctly, you should at least qualify for toast and coffee. Here, have a cup while it's still hot."

Breakfast was just over when Elliott looked up. "Susan, I have to go out. I don't like to work on Sunday, but it's the only time one of our clients is free. And since he pays the firm a rather large retainer fee, we have to oblige him."

Susan was disappointed. "Oh, Elliott, I was hoping we could do something outside this afternoon. It looks like it's going to be a beautiful day."

"Look, I'm sorry, but I don't have a choice. I have to meet this client at one o'clock, but I'll get away as soon as I can."

"Where are you meeting him?"

Elliott's face tensed, "At the man's place of business!" He angrily pushed out of his chair. "Why all of the questions? What is this? I feel like I'm reporting to my mother!"

Susan was surprised at his anger. "Sorry, don't get so defensive. I was just curious."

His tone lowered. "Let's not argue. I'll be back as soon as I can."

"Well, actually your meeting may be a blessing in disguise. I have a lot of paperwork to catch up on if I'm going to get away from the hospital in two weeks." She reached up and touched her diamond earrings. "I remember, no complaints about evenings and weekends."

He got up from the table and kissed her. "How quickly we forget."

"Don't push it, buddy."

Elliott glanced at the wall clock in the kitchen. "It's getting late. I'd better get out of here, or I'll never get home. If I finish early, we can do something together later this afternoon."

She spent three hours working on past-due discharge summaries. She knew that medical records would be calling her about past-due files as soon as they heard she was leaving. Around three o'clock, Susan went into the kitchen. As she started to make a sandwich, the phone rang. "Is Elliott there?"

"I'm sorry; he's not here right now. Can I take a message?"

There was a pause. "This is important. Where can I reach Elliott?"

"I don't have a number to reach him, but I am expecting him back shortly. I'm his wife. Can I help you?"

"This is Frank, an old friend of Elliott's. I've heard a lot about you. I'm looking forward to meeting you. Tell Elliott to call me as soon as he gets in."

Susan opened her mouth to respond, but the phone went dead. A few minutes later Elliott came home.

"You just missed a call. A man named Frank called. He said he was an old friend of yours. I hope you remember him since he hung up before I could get his number."

Elliott looked worried. "I'd better call right away. Frank is a silent partner in the firm."

"I didn't know the firm had silent partners."

"Most firms have silent partners. How about getting us a drink while I make this call?"

Elliott walked past the phone in the living room and went into his office to make a call.

Susan felt resentment well up inside her. Again, Elliott seemed to be purposely excluding her from his work life. She sat down and waited. He reappeared after ten minutes and bent down to kiss her as he reached for his drink, but Susan was quiet and unresponsive.

"What's going on? How come the cold shoulder? You know I couldn't help going out this afternoon."

Susan looked up in annoyance. "It's not that, Elliott."

The phone rang in the office, and Elliott slammed his drink down on the table. It spilled, and he reached for a napkin. "Dammit, that phone never stops." Elliott jumped up to answer it.

He returned a moment later, his composure regained. "Look, Honey, it's not that I'm trying to shut you out. It's just that I feel this part of my life is private. You should be able to understand about privacy matters. Besides, considering some of the scumbags I have to deal with, it's better that you aren't aware of what's going on."

Susan looked over, realizing he was waiting for her response. "You're right. I think I've been too eager to share all of your life. Maybe that's part of learning to live with someone. I'll try to be less intrusive."

Elliott put his drink down and gently pulled her close to him. He kissed her cheek quickly and darted his tongue around her ear. Susan laughed. "Don't you know what that does to me!"

"Of course, I know what that does to you. It gets you so excited I can have my way with you. In fact," he whispered as he slowly kissed her neck, "if I were to keep this up, you'd be begging me to have my way with you."

She felt her frustration drain from her. Elliott was again in control. Later that night Susan quickly fell asleep. Elliott rolled over and looked down at his sleeping wife. Then he dropped back on his pillow and stared up at the ceiling, deep in thought. He had followed orders and was married to a woman, as Frank had put it, with class, education and, beauty. The last attribute had been Elliott's prerequisite. Frank was right; settling down had a lot of pleasant aspects. Elliott thought everything would be perfect if only Susan were a little less principled or a little less bright.

CHAPTER 6
JENNA

Susan braced herself for Monday's onslaught. As she walked down the hall, several patients hurried toward her, each one trying to out-shout the others.

"Wait a minute! I can't hear anyone with all this racket. Look, the group starts in fifteen minutes. Everyone will have a chance to talk; and if anyone needs to speak to me in private, I'll be in my office after the group ends." They seemed satisfied for the moment and stepped aside as Susan continued to the nurses' station.

Helen was writing at the desk when Susan walked in and sat down. "Good morning."

"Hey; I'm charting on your Carla Johnson. I heard she kept the ward in an uproar all weekend."

"I was afraid of that. Who is her assigned aide?"

Helen looked up. "Jenna, she's the only one tougher than Carla!"

After a while, Susan came to realize that it was aides such as Jenna who did the dirty work and carried out most of the patient's treatment plan. For that, they received meager wages and little respect. "Jenna, Carla Johnson is your patient. How did it go this weekend?"

"Girl, she's a mean one. She's hateful to everybody, doesn't matter if you're White or Black. She'll spit at you if you get within five feet. Yesterday we let her out of her room; and ten minutes later, she hit old Thompson because she couldn't see the television. Didn't ask him to move, just popped him upside the head. He's lucky she didn't give him a concussion."

Susan groaned. "It looks like we got a real winner here. At least she doesn't discriminate, hates everybody. Thanks for the run down. Is she going to be let out for the group?"

"Why don't you go meet her? Then decide if you think she's ready for the group."

"Jenna, you're setting me up. But it's already 9:30 A.M., and I'm not yet abused." She walked over to Carla's room and opened the door.

"Bitch, get your fucking White pussy out of this room! Who asked you to come in here?"

Susan looked back and saw Jenna laughing. She turned back to Carla and was again amazed at her size. Carla must've read her mind.

"Why are you staring? Never see a fat Nigga lady before?"

Susan tried to sound friendly. "Carla, my name is Susan Mason; and I'm your social worker."

"I don't need any social worker! I need to get the fuck out of here. Call my Grandmother and tell her to get here now!" She folded her huge arms as best she could and glared at Susan.

"Carla, I have a group to lead right now; but I'll be back to talk later this morning." Susan returned to the day room where her group was waiting. After the meeting was over, Susan went to the nurses' station.

Maggie smiled. "I couldn't help but overhear your conversation with the Amazon queen. She has a terrific vocabulary."

"Are you kidding? Maggie, when it comes to colorful language, you leave her in the dust."

Maggie leaned over and whispered, "Susan, have you told Dr. Denning about your new job?"

"Yes, I told him before I left on Friday."

"How did he take it?"

"Fine."

Maggie grunted. "He's just too proud to let you know how he feels."

She didn't want to get into a discussion about Mark. "He doesn't want me to take any more patients since I'll be leaving in two weeks. But I get to keep Carla; it's my going away present."

"I thought you said he took it well!" Maggie nodded toward the staff in the day room. "Does this mean that the news will be out in the open?"

"Yes, after I tell Karen. I guess she shouldn't hear it from the grapevine."

Maggie grinned. "When are you going to tell her? I want to

watch her face as it turns green with envy!"

"Maggie, I swear you are becoming a vindictive old lady."

"Yes, and I'm enjoying every minute of it!"

Susan smiled. She was going to miss her. "Maggie, one of these days you two are going to end up in a brawl."

"No, she's too smart to tangle with me." Maggie paused. "She knows I fight dirty."

Susan left the station and headed for Karen's office. The door was open, so she stuck her head in the room. "Hi, are you busy?"

Karen smiled her usual pleasant smile as Susan wondered if she meant it. "No, come on in."

"I have some news."

The smile flashed again. "Good news, I hope?"

"Well, I certainly think its good news. I interviewed for a social worker supervisor position at Tri-Valley-Mental Health Center, and they have offered me the job."

For a moment Karen lost her plastic smile but quickly recovered. "Congratulations. I suppose Dr. Denning, being such a good friend of yours, heard about it, and let you put in a bid before the job was open to anyone else."

Susan felt her face flush with anger. "No, as a matter of fact, he didn't even know I was looking. I just wanted to tell you before the patients began talking. I have to get back to my office." Enough of being nice, she decided.

"Well, congratulations again. When are you leaving?"

"Two weeks." Susan backed out of Karen's office and took a deep breath. As she walked down the hall, she noticed Maggie standing outside her office. "You told her already! Dammit, Susan, I wanted to watch her face turn green. I bet she was gritting her teeth behind that phony smile."

"That bitch gets me so angry; she thinks that Mark pulled strings to get the job for me." Susan could see her office down the hall and noticed a line of patients. "See you later, Maggie, my fan club is calling."

Susan unlocked the door and said to the small group behind her, "Okay, whoever was here first, can come in." A sad-looking man with an ugly scab at the end of his nose walked in behind her. "What can I do for you, Leo?"

"Mrs. Mason, the nurse told me to come to you about the doctor's appointment for my nose. I'm supposed to go back."

Patients weren't allowed to have matches on the ward, so electric cigarette lighters were built into the wall. But some of the safety guards had been broken off. Leo had been psychotic the night he was admitted and was pacing around the ward in a daze. He walked up to the wall, stuck his nose into a defective cigarette lighter, and stood there until another patient, smelling the burning flesh, pulled him away.

Susan picked up a pen and started making a list of things to do. "All right, Leo, I'll check your chart and make the appointment."

Leo kept his head down and responded, "I guess I was pretty

crazy when I came here."

She put the pen down and smiled at him. "Yes, you did arrive in a confused state, but you seem to be doing a lot better. Leo, you might want to think about a home visit one of these days."

I don't have any family. Will you call Mrs. Thomas, my boardinghouse lady? See if she'll let me come back when I get out. I don't know, but I think maybe she's mad at me."

"Okay, Leo. I'll give her a call. We'll see if she'll let you come back. On your way out, please let the next person in."

Finally, her last patient left. Susan stood up, stretched, and then went to see Carla.

It was lunch-time, and most patients were in the cafeteria. Carla was sitting on the side of her bed eating her meal from a tray. Susan put on a friendly smile and walked into the room. "Hi, how was lunch?"

"Shit, lady! You can have it!" With that, Carla picked up a carton of milk and threw it at Susan. Some of it splashed on the wall, but Susan felt most of it run down her hair and face and onto her shoulders.

Anger welled up in her; and for a moment, she forgot all she had learned and shouted back. "What do you think you're doing?" Susan quickly realized that she was alone in the room with a woman who could tear her arms from her sockets if she so chose. Carla started to get up from the chair, but with her bulk, it was a slow process. Susan moved toward the door and backed out of the room.

Jenna and another aide had heard the commotion and were coming toward the room in case she needed help. "You okay?"

"Yes, but my hair is going to stink of sour milk in about an hour. Carla's a real sweetheart!"

"Yeah, but it's been worse. We called security three times yesterday. She was coming out on the ward and attacking people. At least today she's staying in a room and only mean mouthing."

Susan put her hand up to her wet hair. "You call this mean mouthing?"

Jenna smiled. "It only counts if you need stitches. Being humiliated is just a routine day!"

As Susan turned and walked away, she saw Mark walking toward her.

"What happened to you? Have an early lunch?"

"Very funny; I was just trying to break the ice with Carla Johnson."

"I think you'd better try another approach or else wear a wetsuit. Susan, I stopped by to ask you to lunch. I'd like to talk to you. There are a lot of loose ends to tie up over the next two weeks."

"I agree that we need to talk, but I don't feel like going out looking like this."

Mark wrinkled his nose. "It's not the look as much as the smell. I know, we'll go to that Chinese restaurant. We can ask for a booth in the back. It has dim lights; and if they make fun of you in Chinese, you'll never know!"

Susan laughed, "You're crazy. But if you're willing to be seen in public with me, I'll go. Give me ten minutes so I can rinse this out of my hair. I'll meet you downstairs. Is your car parked in the front or rear lot?"

"It's in the rear," Mark grinned at her. "Don't you remember? That way people wouldn't see us sneaking out together."

"Yes, I forgot. See you in ten minutes." She left for the washroom feeling uncomfortable. She wished Mark hadn't associated this lunch with the romantic ones in the past.

Susan pushed the rest room door opened and saw Maggie standing in front of the mirror. She smiled at Susan's reflection.

"Hi! Want to go to the cafeteria or would you prefer to finish lunch with Carla?"

"Thanks, Mark asked me to go to lunch. He wants to plan my last two weeks." Susan turned the water on and started to rinse her hair. Maggie handed her a towel. "You know he's going to miss you."

"Come on, Maggie! When are you going to accept that it's over between Mark and me? For God's sake, I got married three months ago. Happily married, I might add."

"Well, you guys were my favorite couple. And you were so right together. I never felt that way about you and Elliott. Sorry, but one of the few benefits of old age is being able to speak your mind."

Susan changed the subject. "It's getting late, and I'm supposed to be downstairs. I shouldn't keep the boss waiting for a business lunch!" As she opened the door she heard Maggie murmur, "I think the lady doth protest too much."

Susan answered back, "Watch it, Maggie, you're not that old!"

Mark was waiting for her by the rear exit. They were both quiet during the short car ride. Except for work, this was the first time they had been alone with each other since the break-up. The familiar place triggered a flood of memories that Susan quickly pushed away. She was thankful for the dim lights. They not only hid her messy hair but, hopefully, the feelings she was afraid to expose.

The waitress stood by the table waiting for the order. Mark glanced at Susan. "Have you discovered something new or do you want your usual?"

She shifted in her seat. Even the words, "Your usual," smacked of intimacy. "No, the ginger shrimp will be fine."

After the waitress left, Mark leaned over and got right down to business. "I just looked at your caseload. Are any of your patients going to be ready for discharge before you leave? Any reduction in the load will help."

She thought for a moment. "Yes, several; and I can start carrying out their discharge plans right away."

"Great."

They spent the next ten minutes going over how her cases should be divided. Then they engaged in awkward small talk. The appearance of the waitress brought relief to both of them. They ate in silence with only occasional comments about the food or a patient. Mark poured Susan a cup of tea; and as he handed it to her, their fingers touched. She looked up, and for a second their eyes met. He looked away and was thoughtful for a moment, but then turned back.

"Susan, there's something I've wanted to say to you for a long time."

"Mark!" Susan tried to interrupt him, afraid to hear what he might say.

He put his fingers to her lips. "No, Susan, let me talk. I've got to tell you how I feel."

A part of her wanted to get up and run; however, a stronger yearning made her lean toward him and listen.

"We separated in anger but managed to behave like casual friends because we still had to work together. I thought I wasn't ready to commit. But I've regretted not taking that risk more than you'll ever know. I realize that you're happy and have made a new life for yourself, and I hope someday I'll be able to do the same." He paused for a moment and shrugged his shoulders. "What I'm trying to say is that I will always care about you. And if you ever need me, call."

Susan was again thankful for the dim shadows. "Mark, I don't know what to say. I also wanted things to be different, but they weren't. I do have a new life, and I'm happy; but I must admit that adjusting to marriage hasn't been easy. It was different for us, Mark; we were friends before we became emotionally involved. I sometimes think that Elliot and I should have taken it a little slower."

He looked concerned. "Are you having problems?"

"No, I didn't mean to imply that! It's just that it's going to take time to adjust. You know. What part of your life remains your own and what part you share."

Mark didn't look convinced. "That was never an issue with us. Susan, promise me that you'll keep in touch. Just give me a call once in a while to let me know how things are going. I don't want to complicate your life; but we had a caring relationship for a long time, and I don't want it to end completely."

"Maybe..." She paused and wondered if he could hear her heart pounding. "Maybe, if I had given you more time instead of an ultimatum, things would have turned out differently. We can't go back and change what happened, but I still care about you, too; and I would like to remain friends."

Mark flashed a grin and squeezed her hand. "Good, now we better be getting back before they put us on the run-a-way list."

That afternoon, in between clients, Susan went over her lunch-time conversation with Mark. Would things have been different if she had given him more time? She had an abundance of patience for small children and her patients, but not a lot for others. That was something she was warned about by Maggie. "Susan, you've got so much going for you, all that energy and concern, but no patience. You'll end up like me. By the time you acquire patience, you will have used all your energy." Perhaps that was what made her, Maggie, and Jenna like each other. They admired the positive things in each other's personalities and excused the shortcomings.

The phone rang. It was Helen.

"Thought you'd want to know Mrs. Johnson, Carla's Grandmother, is here for a visit."

"Good, I couldn't reach her on the phone. Please send her down to my office." Susan stepped out into the corridor to greet her. She looked down the hall and saw a petite, neatly dressed, gray-haired Black woman proudly walking toward her.

"Hello, Mrs. Johnson. I'm Susan Mason, Carla's social worker."

The woman followed her into the office. "Please sit down; I'm anxious to talk with you. Carla hasn't given us much information. I'd appreciate it if you could tell me what was going on with her. Maybe if we knew what brought her here, we could help her to be ready to leave sooner."

Tears welled up in Mrs. Johnson's eyes. "I'll try and help as much as I can. Poor child, the Lord has given her a cross to bear. Her mama was only fifteen when she had Carla; I never could control the girl! She finally ran away and left baby Carla for me to raise. Sweet Jesus knows I tried my best."

Susan leaned over the desk. "It sounds like you've had a rough time taking care of Carla all of these years."

"Yes, but I love the girl. She had such a hard time coming up." Susan saw love and concern in Mrs. Johnson's eyes. "She was always fat, even when she was a little girl. The other kids never stopped teasing her. It turned her mean, Miss Mason. But Carla was smart and got all A's in school. Did you know she won a scholarship to

Mundelein College?"

"No, I didn't know that. You must be very proud."

"I sure am. When Carla graduated the first thing she said was, "Grandma, now I am going to take care of you."

Susan smiled at Mrs. Johnson. "Now we have to help her get better so that she'll be able to do that. Mrs. Johnson, did you ever take Carla to a doctor about her weight?"

"Yes, ma'am; she was always on a new diet. But she'd lose ten pounds and then put on twenty. Last month, Carla went to a hypnotist. He put her in a trance to lose weight, but all she got was a bad case of loose bowels. After that, she just kind of acted crazy."

Susan jotted down a note to ask the doctor to check on Carla's electrolytes. Severe diarrhea could cause a chemical imbalance and that alone could trigger a psychotic episode.

"Mrs. Johnson, did Carla work after she graduated?"

"No, that was the worst disappointment she had to bear." Mrs. Johnson shook her head in despair. "No one would hire her. They said something about the insurance kept them from hiring her. Carla, she got bitter and just stopped trying. She said it was just a waste of car-fare."

Susan reached over and took the woman's hand. "Mrs. Johnson, you've been a big help. The more we understand Carla's problems, the better we will be able to help her. When she's ready for discharge, we'll find a counselor for her at the community mental health center. That way she'll have someone to talk to when she has troubles."

"You mean like I have the Lord?"

"Well, yes, in a way. But I don't think any counselor would fit that bill."

"Praise, Jesus! But you're right. Carla needs a friend, and I'm too old for that. She needs to be around young folks."

"That's true, but she needs you too, Mrs. Johnson. You are her only family. I know that Carla is waiting for you. Unless there is something else you want to tell me, you can visit with her now."

Susan took Mrs. Johnson's outstretched hand and smiled into the tired face. I'll be calling to let you know how Carla is doing; and if you have any questions, please don't hesitate to call me." It was getting close to five o'clock, so Susan quickly made a few more calls and was ready to quit for the day.

CHAPTER 7
CARLA'S SHOWER

Elliott had a late dinner meeting and planned to stay at a downtown hotel. Susan tried not to resent these times and began to call them pampering nights: doing her nails, taking long bubble baths, and catching up on her reading. It wasn't long before she enjoyed his evening meetings as long as they were infrequent.

Susan was turning on the bathwater when the phone rang. The sound invaded a private world, and her voice was irritable when she answered.

"Yes, who is this? Oh, Elliott, I'm sorry my voice was curt. I thought it might be a salesman. How is your meeting going?"

"Fine. We're taking a dinner break now. I can't stay on the phone. I just wanted to check in. I've got to run. Good night, honey. I love you."

"Love you, too." Susan returned to the bathroom. As she slowly slipped into the steaming water, she thought about her lunch with Mark. Susan was glad that Elliott wasn't home; she needed time to get Mark out of her system, again. Susan realized that she still was strongly attracted to him. Part of her felt friendship, but another part felt a tingling excitement that had nothing to do with a platonic relationship. She pushed away thoughts of Mark. After all, in spite of all his words of love, he had responded with silence to her decision to marry Elliott. No, she reasoned, I don't need fantasy. After all, I'm married to a handsome, successful lawyer who loves me and is providing me with a full life and, hopefully, some babies in the future.

Susan finished her bath and snuggled into bed. Her life was happy, safe, and orderly. She had made the right decision. She turned off the light and quickly fell asleep.

* * *

Elliott returned to a table overlooking the marina in Miami. Frank was waiting; his lips turned up in a grin. "Look at you, Elliott, calling into the little woman. You've come a long way."

"Well, it's the small things that keep a woman from becoming suspicious. Besides, I wouldn't want Susan to call the Hilton and find out I wasn't registered."

"She's a suspicious type?"

"No, well actually, I don't know that yet. I'm just beginning to set up the plan. When it goes into effect, there will be a lot going on that won't be any of her business. That's when I'll know how suspicious she can become."

"So when do I get to meet her? I think it's time. She should know you are representing me. Of course, she shouldn't know the extent of our business. One of these days our names may be linked, and it would be better if she already knew that you and I have a business relationship."

"Yes, you're right. How about next Saturday? I'm having a cocktail party for some of our investors. It's a fundraiser for an alderman. And since Susan will be there, you'll be able to meet her by chance instead of design."

"That sounds good. I'll fly in for the event. Let's call it a night, Elliott. I'm tired, and you've got an early flight tomorrow."

"And I'm looking forward to the return flight. These trips to Florida in the winter are great, but I'd forgotten how bad it is in the summer. Going from the airport to the rental car pickup was like walking through a sauna."

Frank frowned. "You young guys want it all. Didn't you ever hear of trade-offs?"

"Only what I've learned from you; never trade off if you can eliminate." The old man smiled and stood up. The meeting had ended.

* * *

Randy settled back in the booth at Denny's and reached for a second cup of coffee. Across from him sat Tom Rivers, his contact from the FBI. Randy set his cup down and leaned forward to listen. "We've come to a standstill. There have been several big shipments in the past two months, but nothing we can link to Mason. The guy acts like he's running for office, spends most of his time making friends with moneyed people, and even picked up a beautiful wife with a holier than thou image."

Randy winced. "And I introduced them. Every time I see Susan, I feel guilty."

Tom waved his hand. "Look, anyone could've introduced them. Hell, they met at a party that happened to be at your place. It's not like you arranged a blind date."

Randy glanced down, a pained expression on his face. "Yeah, I keep telling myself all that, but she's become a friend; and I've watched her get involved with an animal. She's married to a man who is probably a sociopath, and what did I say? Congratulations, and may I kiss the bride!"

Tom lit up a cigarette and slowly exhaled a cloud of smoke. "There are always innocent people who get hurt in this kind of operation. What I don't understand is that if she's a psychiatric social worker, shouldn't she have picked up on this character?"

Randy shook his head. "Beats me. She seems to know what's wrong with her patients. But working in commitment court, I see a lot of crazies; Mason's different, maybe crazy, but not in the same way. Besides, you know what they say about love being blind."

"Exactly, and that's why you can't warn Susan. More than likely, she wouldn't believe you and would probably warn Mason. That would leave us without bait for Frank DiMato."

Randy glanced at his watch. "You're probably right. I'd better get going; I've got a hearing in a half-hour. I'm going to call Susan later this morning and see if she is free for lunch. I want to keep the lines open."

Tom picked up the check. "You better start planting some seeds of discontent about your current job. Something she could mention to her husband. That way Mason won't be surprised when you ask him about job opportunities."

* * *

Susan noticed a difference in the ward when she arrived on Wednesday. The usual morning routine of patients mopping the day room floor, making beds, and cleaning off countertops was gone. Instead, they were lying in their beds; and the day room still had last night's soupy mixture of cigarette butts and spilled coffee littering the floor.

She stopped at the nurses' station before going to her office. "What's up? How come nothing's going on?"

Jenna was preparing morning medications. "I'm glad you're here! There's a bug going around, and half the staff is out sick. Can you give us a hand until we can get some aides from the other wards?"

"Sure. What can I do to help?"

"Take Carla to the showers while I finish setting up meds."

Susan frowned. "Isn't there something else I can do, like mop the floor or wash the counter? I don't know anything about showering anyone."

"Mopping can wait for the housekeeper." Jenna took a deep breath. "Look, Susan, if you want to help, Carla needs a shower now. She's scheduled for a check-up this morning, and that new

Chinese doctor will shit bricks if she goes in there stinking."

"He's Korean, not Chinese."

Jenna shrugged. "Girl, they all look the same to me."

"Okay, I'll do it. But why can't Carla shower herself? She isn't handicapped."

"No, but that lady is so fat she can't even wipe her ass." Jenna started to move the medication cart out of the nurses' station. "Besides, she doesn't fit into the shower stall."

Susan stepped in front of the cart. "What? What am I supposed to do, take her to a carwash?"

"Look, you walk her to the shower room. She stands over the drain in the middle of the room, and you use the hose in the laundry sink to wash her down. It's easy. Now if you'll excuse me, I have to pass meds. There's a plastic apron hanging in the housekeeper's closet; put it on, or you'll spend the rest of the day in wet clothes."

Susan was appalled. "You've got to be kidding! All right, you're not. I'll help her shower. But if you hear screams coming from the bathroom, rescue me. She may try to drown me in the laundry sink."

Jenna left. "Count your blessings. At least she can't bend down far enough to stick your head in the toilet."

"Yeah, thank you, God, for small favors!"

The door was open, and Carla was sitting on the side of her bed. She was now in a regular room. And although she was still hostile, she hadn't been combative for a few days. Susan stood in the doorway for a moment staring at the mountainous patient. She had a pretty face with large brown eyes. Her dark hair, in an Afro, attractively framed her face. Susan smiled as she recalled that trite comment. "She'd be pretty if only she'd lose some weight." Susan cautiously walked into the room.

"Hi, Carla, how are you doing?"

Carla's face clouded. "Shitty. And since you can't do anything about it, get your skinny ass out of here; and leave me alone."

"Carla, I've come to ask you if you'd like some help getting a shower."

"I don't want some White bitch getting her thrills showering me! Just take off lady. Go get fucked or something, and leave me alone."

Determination and impatience took control of Susan. "Look, there's no one else available. You've got a doctor's appointment this morning and either I help you shower, or you go dirty. Which do you want?"

Carla slowly rocked from side to side, her face contorted with the strain of lifting her body from the bed. She finally reached a standing position and paused for a moment to gain her balance. "Okay, let's go."

They slowly walked down the corridor to the shower room. Carla glared at everyone in her path. Mary had turned the corner and was abruptly face-to-face with Carla. Before she could move out of the way, Carla bumped her aside. "Get out of my way, bitch!"

Carla stood in the middle of the shower room and tried to pull her dress over her head. Susan felt uncomfortable and didn't know if she should help her or wait for a request. Susan had never showered anyone, except for a romantic backwash.

After a few moments of watching Carla struggle, she asked, "Do you need a hand?"

Carla gave her a dirty look and spat out, "Just what the fuck are you here for?"

Susan helped put the dress over Carla's head and then regulated the water while Carla pushed her panties till they dropped to the floor.

"Carla, feel the water. Is this temperature okay?"

Susan tried to avoid the appearance of staring as she looked at Carla. It was easy to see why the only reachable parts of her body would be her face, arms, and the front of her torso. Susan smiled at Carla. "Why don't we divide this job: you take the front while I work on the back."

Carla grumbled a response as Susan picked up the hose and wet her down. She stayed busy soaping up the washcloth and washing Carla's back, then her buttocks and legs. She was glad that Carla could not see her facial reaction to the sight of the bather lifting her pendulous breasts to wash the area underneath. Susan was like most thin persons, aware of severely obese people but oblivious to what it was like to live in their body. Carla had stretch marks over her entire body, and her inner thighs were covered with calloused scar tissue. Susan picked up the hose and turned toward Carla. Their eyes met. "Not a pretty sight, is it?"

Susan realized that this was the first time Carla had spoken without her guard up. She looked back at her and answered quietly, "It must be difficult."

She waited for Carla to finish drying the front of her body and then took the single towel and wiped her back. "Have you been to activity therapy yet?"

"No, would you like to make plastic coasters or wallets with those morons?"

"They're not morons, Carla. It's just that some of these patients are functioning at lower levels than others. If the activities are difficult, then some of the people become confused."

"That's great. Usually, I get fucked because of being Black or fat! This is the first time I've had it stuck to me for being intelligent."

Susan helped Carla put a clean dress over her head. "Carla, there's not much I can do about the first two issues; but if you'd like, I will bring a book for you tomorrow."

Carla looked suspicious but had been bored enough to nod an okay.

As they left the washroom, Susan made a mental note to stop in Carla's room in the afternoon to find out what type of books she enjoyed.

Susan left Carla sitting in the day room waiting for an aide to take her to the doctor. At the nurses' station, Maggie sat slouched in a chair with her legs stretched into the middle of the room. Tiny gray ringlets, damp with perspiration, had fallen across her forehead.

"I've had it! This body is getting old. I can't believe that I used to work like this every day."

Maggie was usually full of energy, but today Susan saw that she was indeed getting old, worn out from years of hard labor. She glanced out and saw two aides from another ward. "Maggie, we have help here; why don't you go back to your office and put your feet up for a while?"

"That sounds good to me. Now if I can get my body to move, I'll be on my way. Uh oh, here comes the Dragon Lady. I've just felt a surge of adrenaline. Bye!"

Maggie was halfway down the corridor before Karen got to the nurses' station.

"I heard that you and Maggie were pretty busy this morning. You know, it's not our responsibility to fill in for the aides. I can understand Maggie doing that type of work, considering where she came from and that she's not a professional; but I certainly don't understand why you agreed to do such menial work. It's unprofessional."

For the second time that morning Susan felt anger and impatience. "Professional? Maggie is one of the most professional people I've ever met. She gives more care and concern to these people in one day than you and I do in a month." Susan gripped the arms of her chair and slowly counted to five, realizing that she had stepped over the line. "Now if you'll excuse me, I have some work to do."

Karen's mouth dropped open as Susan walked from the room. One nice feature about leaving a job, she thought as she walked to her office, is that you don't have to hide your feelings anymore. As soon as Susan opened a chart, the phone rang. "Hello. Hi, Randy, it's good to hear from you."

"Do you remember that we planned to have lunch one day this week?" Randy asked.

"Of course, I remembered."

"Well, how about today? I'm going to be in the area. Are you free?"

"Yes, as a matter of fact, I am," Susan replied. "Where do you want to meet?"

"How about going to Riley's?"

"Riley's sounds great; I haven't had a corned beef sandwich in months." Susan glanced at the clock on the wall. "It's eleven o'clock now. I can leave here in a half hour."

"That's fine with me."

"Okay, see you."

Susan put down the receiver and dialed Elliott's office. "Hi Honey, I missed you last night. How did your meeting go?"

"Okay, I got a lot accomplished. Have you had a busy day?"

"Yes, it's been hectic around here. There's a flu bug going around, and we're short staff. But I'm going to get away for a while. Randy just called and asked me to meet him for lunch."

Elliott was silent for several seconds. "That's nice. You can tell me all about it tonight. Susan, I've got someone waiting. You have an enjoyable lunch with Randy, and give him my regards."

"Okay, see you at home later. Bye."

* * *

As Susan walked into the pub, she saw Randy waving to her from a booth in the back. "Hi! You couldn't have picked a better day to call. You don't want to know how I spent my morning. But believe me, I'm glad to be here."

Randy laughed. "I'll take your word for it. I'm glad you could come. I'm going to be in court every day next week, so I thought I'd take a chance that you'd be free today." He looked up. "The waitress is on the way over. Are you going to have a corned beef sandwich or venture into the unknown?"

"I've already tried the unknown today; I think I'll play it safe and have the corned beef."

Randy put his beer down and leaned across the table. "Tell me, Susan, aren't you going to miss the hospital?"

"Yes, probably. It is a job that has plenty of drawbacks, but boredom isn't one of them."

"I bet you'll miss Maggie. I've met her at court, and she's the quintessential mother figure."

"You're right. Maggie's been my teacher and my comfort especially when I broke up with Mark."

"I'm surprised that Elliott let you continue working there. He strikes me as a man who may have a jealous nature."

"Well, let's say he hasn't been happy about it. Elliott has been pushing me to find something else since our engagement. I don't blame him. I'd feel the same way. But, what about you? Are you still happy working at the public defender's office?"

Randy held his breath. Finally, an opening to plant the seed. "Not really. I'm getting tired of being poor, and I'm not happy about my future. I've had my fill of legal, social work. It's time for me to start thinking about myself."

Susan was surprised. "I didn't know you felt that way. You always seem to like your work."

Randy kept his cover. "Well, you know how it is. Poverty gets old fast. Elliott knows that. I admire him for his success."

"Yes, it amazes me how successful he is, and in such a short time." Susan smiled. "I guess cultivating contacts pays off."

Randy smiled. "You'll never know." He became somber. "Susan, we've been good friends this past year. I want you to know that if something ever comes up where you need to talk to somebody, somebody you can trust . . ." He wanted to say more, but stopped. "Enough of the sentimental talk. We're almost out of time, and we haven't started eating."

In the parking lot, Randy hugged Susan. As she walked toward her car, he shouted, "Say hello to Elliot, and tell him I'll give him a call in a few days."

CHAPTER 8

ANGER

Susan arrived back at the ward in time for the discharge meeting. After two hours, she left with a sense of relief knowing that this was the last time she would have to experience the manipulations required to place people nobody wanted.

She went into her office and started making calls to family and community clinics. It was close to five o'clock when Susan remembered her promise to bring a book to Carla. In the day room, she saw Carla sitting off to the side from other patients. Susan sat down next to her, close, but distant enough not to invade Carla space. "How did your doctor's visit go?"

Carla glared at her. "Don't you read the charts? I've seen every asshole in the hospital looking at my charts. This damn place is nothing but a bunch of voyeurs!"

"I read what the nurse said about your doctor's appointment, but I'm more interested in hearing what you think about it."

Carla leaned close to Susan with the conspiratorial half-smile. "The doctor thinks I'm suicidal; he says I'm eating my way to the grave." For a moment she looked as if she were going to cry. "That dumb chink never even asked me how I felt. All he saw was a crazy, fat, Black lady. Suicidal, shit! He missed the boat. I'm homicidal and, that short, yellow creep will be my first victim!" Carla pointed at Susan. "Want to be the second?"

Susan did not move. "Carla, I'm sorry that he didn't listen to you. Unfortunately, some physicians think that doctor is another word for God. By the way, what kind of books are you interested in reading?"

Carla was temporarily disarmed. "I like historical novels."

"Good, I do too. I'll bring you one tomorrow."

Carla's guard went up again. "Sure, that'll be the day!"

"Have a nice evening, Carla. I'll talk to you in the morning."

* * *

Once home, Susan entered the kitchen and rummaged in the freezer. She found a casserole and put it into the oven. She was setting the table when Elliott opened the door. "Welcome home; I'm in the kitchen."

H'mm, something smells good." Elliott whispered in her ear after he kissed her hello. "What are we having?"

"Are you hungry, Elliott, or would you rather have a drink first?"

"Let's relax for a few minutes."

"Fine. Why don't you make us a drink while I finish setting the table?"

Elliott was mixing the drinks when Susan walked into the living room. "This afternoon I had a cancellation, so I took a ride over to a realty office in Crest Hill Estates. The agent gave me information on several homes and, if you're interested, we can go see them."

Susan was surprised. "Elliott, I didn't know we were in the market for a new home. We've only lived here for three months."

"I know we haven't talked about it, but it was just convenient for you to move in here after we got married. It is not like we picked this out for our home."

"There's plenty of room here for the two of us, and this townhouse is in an ideal location. Besides, Crest Hill Estates is out of our league."

"Look, don't worry about the money; I'm doing very well." Elliott kissed her lightly on the cheek. "I've made some good investments before leaving Florida, and they paid off. You know, Susan, you spend your whole day with losers who only have filth and poverty in their lives. There's another world out there filled with the marvelous things money can buy, and I intend to give them to you!" His smile was patronizing, like the grin he turned on to charm his associates.

"Come on, Elliott! Everybody who is mentally ill isn't a loser."

He slammed his fist on the arm of the couch. "Dammit, I can't believe this! I worked hard to surprise you with a beautiful home, and all you can do is go into your social work routine! You're forever trying to turn me into a God damn bleeding heart."

"I'm sorry, Elliott. It's just that I had no idea that we could afford something that expensive. I've had to live on a social worker's salary.

This change in lifestyle is a cultural shock."

Elliott reached over and pulled her close to him, his eyes staring into hers, his tone intimate again. "Honey, I'm sorry. That was totally out of line. I just expected you'd be thrilled. A man wants to give his wife the best."

Susan started to get up from the couch and quickly felt the pain of Elliott's hand tightening on her arm. "Elliott, you're hurting me!"

He smiled sheepishly, releasing his grip on her. "I'm sorry. I guess I don't know my strength. I love you baby, but don't run away from me. It makes me angry." He gently touched her hand and turned to look into her eyes. "I guess maybe I'm just an insecure kid at heart. Look, this was the wrong time to bring up a move. What with you switching jobs and all the other changes, this house thing must have been a shock. We'll forget about it for now. Okay, tell me about your lunch with Randy."

Susan was in shock but not over the prospect of a new house. It was Elliott's unprovoked anger that shocked her. She had never seen that side of him before. Her arm still ached where he had grabbed her. Was the tight grip just an accident or a forewarning?

He reached down and kissed her. "Honey, you're not still mad at me, are you? I thought my temper was a thing of the past, but I see that it still needs work. With some help from my very own therapist, I'll become so perfect no one would be able to stand me."

"Wow, that idea would be terrible. Look, I shouldn't have reacted as I did. But you're right; there are too many changes happening in my life at this time. Let me have a few months to settle in."

"Your wish is my command. Susan, I think I heard the timer go off on the oven."

"The casserole, I forgot all about it. Come on, let's eat."

Halfway through the meal, Elliott asked her again how her lunch with Randy had gone. "Fine," Susan responded. "We had a long talk."

"About your new job?"

"Yes, but mainly about how unhappy Randy is working for peanuts. I didn't think he felt that way. Randy said he admires how successful you've become."

Elliott smiled. "That's nice to hear."

"He's looking for a change. Maybe if you hear of an opening, you can let him know."

Elliott looked up with concern. "Did he ask you to ask me?"

"Of course not," Susan responded. "I think he would die of embarrassment if he thought I was asking you. It's just that Randy brought us together and it would be nice if there were something we could do for him."

"Well," replied Elliott, "I can't promise anything, but I'll keep my ears open. Things come up."

Later that night, Susan looked over at Elliott after he had fallen asleep. The image of his angry face came to mind. She fell back on her pillow and thought about the rage that seemed to come from nowhere. What was I doing, Susan asked herself? The first time she saw that the man was capable of anger, she started to diagnose him. He flew off the handle, that's all. After all, she had a temper too. Stop making a mountain out of a mole-hill. She turned over and put her arm around him, as the moon shone through the bedroom window and rested on a red welt just above her elbow.

* * *

The next morning Elliott showered and dressed while Susan slept. As soon as she awoke and entered the bathroom, he hurried downstairs and nervously tapped his fingers on a small table. Finally, the phone was picked up. "Frank, good morning. I hope I didn't wake you, but I have a favor to ask."

"You didn't wake me. Older people don't sleep late; it just takes us longer to get to the phone. Now, what's this favor you want?"

"I need some information. I have someone in mind for a position in our organization."

"Is he another investor?"

"No, Frank, it's someone who could assist me with some of the legal details in our investment partnership. I'm getting overwhelmed with all the work. We wouldn't want to slip up because of some form we didn't file with the IRS. But first, he'll have to be checked out. Do you have someone up here who can do that?"

"I've got just the person," replied Frank, "are you going to be at your office this morning?"

"Yes, I'll be there all morning."

"Fine, I'll talk to my guy and have him get back to you for the details. What's that attorney's name?"

"Randy, Randy Sloan. If he checks out, you'll meet him on Saturday. I'll invite him to that fundraiser. Then you can let me know if you think he'll fit in the organization."

"Good. Talk to you later, Elliott."

CHAPTER 9
NIGHT SHIFT

The next morning Susan got ready for work while operating on auto-pilot. She looked in the dresser mirror and was jolted out of her mechanical routine by the imprint of Elliott's thumb and forefinger in vibrant colors just above her elbow. She quickly exchanged her blouse for one with long sleeves. She was overwhelmed with a feeling of shame. Susan heard stories of how abused women hid their bruises from family and friends. But this was different, she told herself. It was an accident. Elliott didn't realize his strength. Besides, with the way Maggie felt about him, the last thing she needed was to plant a seed of suspicion. Elliott called up the stairs. "Honey, I'm leaving now. See you this evening."

A couple of minutes later, Susan grabbed her purse and took off for work.

* * *

Mark was waiting at her office. "Got a minute for your boss before the hordes descend upon you?"

He sounded warm and friendly; and for a moment, she felt a

wave of sadness. He noticed immediately. "Is something wrong?"

"No, it's just that my leaving is becoming a reality. I'm going to miss you, boss."

He flashed one of his grins. "Great! I've caught you at a weak moment." Mark's expression became serious. "Susan, this virus going around the hospital has half of our nursing staff off sick, and the rest are worn out from working double shifts. I think the worst is over, but we need backups. Can I give your name to the head nurse just in case we're short staffed tonight?"

"Sure, but I don't know how much help I'll be since I'm not certified to work with medications."

"That's not a problem. The technicians can pass meds. What we need is a body so that there is at least two staff in each ward."

She raised her voice in mock anger. "A body! Thanks a lot! It's nice to know one's skills are appreciated."

"Okay." Susan put her hand up. "No further apologies necessary."

Mark smiled warmly. "Thank you. By the way, if your body, and of course your mind, get called in tonight, take tomorrow off. Coverage during the day hasn't been a problem."

He walked toward the door, stopped, and glanced earnestly back at her. "Oh, one other thing. I heard you're available to help with showers. Is that assistance limited to patients?"

"You've got it, and only to those over four hundred pounds."

He shrugged his shoulders as he left. "There goes my fantasy."

Susan watched him as he walked down the hall and began to

have a fantasy of her own. But she was quickly brought back to reality when she saw the group dragging chairs into a circle. Susan noticed that Carla had, for the first time, pulled her chair into the group instead of sitting outside. She realized why Carla had joined the group as soon as she sat down.

"Well, did you bring the book?" Carla demanded.

Susan smiled at her. "Yes, it's in my office. We can get it after group."

Before Carla could move out of the circle, Susan mentioned to the group that Carla was interested in historical novels. She wasn't sure if Carla stayed because of interest or if it just wasn't worth the effort to move her body outside the circle. Susan realized that it would take Carla half the morning to walk back to her office, as every step she took produced exhaustion and shortness of breath.

"Want to wait here? I'll get the book and be right back."

Carly seemed relieved and for once didn't argue. "Okay, I'll wait here." A couple of minutes later, Susan returned. "Here, I hope you enjoy it."

Carla still had a suspicious look on her face but muttered, "Thanks."

Susan smiled. Finally, a crack in her armor.

Joan, the activity therapist, was making a list of patients going to the ballgame that afternoon. "Susan, how are you?"

"Fine, and you?"

"Well, it could be better. This flu has everyone shorthanded. I feel uneasy about leaving my assistant here to work alone as she still is pretty green. But I hate to close the activity room since only a small number of patients will be going to the baseball game."

Joan tried to persuade Susan to join the excursion. "How about joining us? It's your last chance for a day of fun on the Department of Mental Health bus!"

Susan chuckled. "No way. I have all the memories I'll ever need. Besides, I think I'll take advantage of the quiet to work on charts."

She had just sat down when Maggie knocked on her door. "Why the hell do you have on that long-sleeved blouse?"

Susan felt her face flush. "I didn't get a chance to do my laundry."

Maggie laughed out loud. "You don't have to be embarrassed. It's none of my business that you two spend so much time in bed that you can't do your laundry."

"Please, knock it off! I'm tired of all of these comments about my personal life."

Maggie was taken aback by Susan's outburst. "I'm sorry, I stepped over the line."

"It's okay." Susan put her arm around Maggie. "Maybe I'm starting to go through the change."

"You're stealing my lines."

Nothing more was said. Maggie knew that something was going on; and Susan knew that Maggie was suspicious, but any probing was out of the question. After lunch, Susan put all her energy into charting. Usually, she disliked working alone; but today she welcomed the opportunity to avoid people. It was a little after four when she left her office and went out to the ward. The patients had just returned from the baseball game and were getting their names checked off as they came on the unit. Joan and an aide were standing by the door with an older man whom Susan didn't recognize.

She overheard Joan tell the aide. "Call the other wards. He probably didn't get off the elevator on the right floor."

Susan queried Joan. "What's up?"

"I'm not sure. We took patients from every ward, but I don't remember which ward he came from."

As Susan walked into the nurses' station, the aide put the phone down. "Joan, I think our friend better sit outside for a moment. I need to talk to you."

Susan took the old man by the hand and sat him down in a chair outside the office. He shyly smiled when she said, "Don't worry, I'll be right back to get you."

The aide was talking excitedly. "I'm not kidding; we accounted for every person on each ward. I don't know how you did it, Joan, but you came back with one more patient."

Joan's face went pale. "Oh my God, I worry about a patient escaping but never about someone trying to break in the hospital!"

Susan nodded toward the old man. "How do you think he got here?"

"He must have gotten mixed in with our group when we were leaving the ballpark. Whoever let him on the bus probably thought he was a patient." Joan threw up her hands in frustration. "We turn over patients so fast it's amazing that we can recognize any of them."

Susan looked troubled. "We'd better find out who he is; his family will be looking for him."

"You're right! No one would ever believe that he came here willingly. Susan, you're the social worker. You talk to him and find out who he is."

Susan sat next to the man. He was a frail, white-haired man, who appeared to be in his late seventies; and right now, he looked frightened. "Hello, my name is Susan Mason. I'm a social worker and would like to help you." She took his hand and asked him softly, "Can you tell me how you got here?" He looked over at her as tears welled up in his eyes. "I don't know, Miss. I went to the ballgame. Then this lady came up to me. She said to stay with the group. They made us go on the bus, and it brought me to this place."

Susan tried to reassure him. "Well, there's been a mistake. You don't belong here; and if you tell me your name and someone I can phone, I will make sure that you get back home."

"My daughter is going to be mad at me. I'm not supposed to leave the house unless I tell her where I'm going. She doesn't like me to go to the ballgame." He lowered his head in shame. "Sometimes I get lost and can't find my way home."

Susan gently squeezed his hand. "Look, when I call your daughter, I'll explain what happened and ask her not to be angry with you. I bet she's worried right now."

He hesitated and looked around, staring at one of the patients with his hand down his pants masturbating. "You've been kind to me, Miss; but I don't think this is a nice place." He leaned closer and whispered in Susan's ear, "These people don't act right."

She put her arm around his shoulder. "Yes, it is a little scary here. Let's go inside with the nurses and see what we can do about getting you home."

"My name is John Hendricks; and I live with my daughter, Nora Tindall. I don't remember her telephone number. I forget many things, but I know my address!"

"That's fine, Mr. Hendricks. I'll call Information and get her phone number."

In the nurses' station, Susan related Hendricks' story. She leaned over to Joan and whispered, "I guess they won't be charging you with kidnapping… this time."

"Very funny. Just call his daughter and see how happy she is when she hears that her father is in a mental institution."

Susan made the call and found a very relieved woman. Mr. Hendricks had been missing several hours, and the family had been worried that he might have had an accident. She thanked Susan and said they would be at the hospital within thirty minutes.

"Look, I'm leaving now. If you'd like, I'll take Mr. Hendricks downstairs with me to wait for his daughter. I don't think she should see him in this place."

"Maybe you're right," said Joan. "Now they think we rescued him. But two minutes up here, and they'll think we brought him here for experimentation."

Susan waited in the lobby with Mr. Hendricks until his family arrived. His relieved daughter thanked her; and in spite of Susan's request, immediately began to chastise her father. "Pop, I told you to stay around the house. If you keep wandering away, we'll have to lock you up in this place." A bewildered Mr. Hendricks looked back at the building with wide, frightened eyes.

* * *

As Susan opened the door to the townhouse, she immediately smelled Chinese food. "Hi, I'm home," she called out.

Elliott shouted from the kitchen. "Hello, I'm in here; and dinner is ready."

"You cooked?"

"Nope, I'm saving it for a retirement hobby. Judge Kendall heard my case on time; and since we finished before four, I stopped and picked up dinner. I hope you didn't have anything planned."

"Are you kidding? I just planned to make some BLTs." She kissed him and sniffed the air. "M'm smells good! What did you get?"

"Well," Elliott lifted a white container, "we have eggrolls over here, over there is sweet and sour pork, and that leaky box should be the egg foo young. If you get the drinks, I'll set the table."

"How did your hearing go?" Susan asked.

"Fine, I got my client off. I'll have to bill him while he is still grateful. How was your day?"

"Different. The activity therapist took a group to a ballgame today and came back with an extra patient, an elderly man who had inadvertently joined our group."

Elliott stopped eating. "No kidding! What happened to him?"

"His family picked him up. His daughter didn't realize we had kidnapped him because he often wanders away. As bad as that hospital is for someone who is sick, it has to be a hundred times worse for someone who's sane."

Elliott pointed his fork at Susan. "I'm glad you're getting out of there. Remember Babe, the people who run around with butterfly nets, sometimes end up getting caught."

Susan frowned. "I know. Some of us end up crazier than our patients. I hate to bring this up, but more than likely I'll be called in tonight. There's a virus going around, and we're short of staff."

Elliott pushed his plate away. "I was hoping we could spend this evening together."

Susan reached over and patted his hand. "We'll still have most of the evening. Besides, then I'll get tomorrow off, and we'll have a long weekend."

He was a little peeved. "You'll probably spend the weekend catching up on your sleep, but at least you only have one week left at that psycho's paradise."

Susan was glad she hadn't told Elliott that she had volunteered. They spent the rest of the evening curled up in front of the television. She managed to drift off to sleep for a while before the phone rang and woke her. "I'll get it; it's probably the hospital."

"Susan, it's Dorothy, supervising night nurse. Your name is down as a backup. I wouldn't ask you to come in unless it was necessary. But I've already taken four sick calls tonight, and that's on top of the people already out. At this rate, I'll have to ask for patient volunteers to supervise the wards. Can you make it here before eleven?"

"Sure, I'll be there."

"Good, you'll be working with Jenna. I want to warn you to be extra careful tonight. A trainee was left in charge of the activity room this afternoon, and a patient took a pair of scissors. Security has been searching, but they haven't found them yet. I'll be floating from ward to ward, so I'll see you sometime tonight. Thanks for signing up."

Elliott turned away from the television as Susan hung up the phone. "I gather you'll be going into work?"

"Yes, several people called in sick."

"Is anything wrong? You look worried."

Susan quickly smiled to avoid further questions. If Elliott knew about the missing scissors, there would be an argument. "There's always something going on over there. I better get ready." Susan went upstairs to wash the sleep out of her eyes.

Susan had never been to the hospital at night. Outside of one nurse who circulated between the wards, the building is run by the aides. She was relieved that she would be working with Jenna.

Susan had always been curious about what the ward was like at night, but now her curiosity had been replaced with fear. A part of her wanted to back out, but she didn't know how to do it without feeling foolish. Of course, Susan reasoned, she could tell Elliott and use his anger to excuse herself. But then Susan smiled as she thought of the exhilarating rush she felt whenever she was near danger. You need help, she told herself as she walked down the stairs. This need for excitement has been known to shorten people's lives.

* * *

The ride to the hospital took only half the usual time. That was one benefit from working the night shift-no traffic. The building looked eerie in the moonlight; and with most of the lights off, it seemed deserted. Susan had never noticed before how big the empty parking lot was nor how far it was to the front entrance. She ran toward the building and fumbled with her keys looking for the one that would open the main door. The offices on the first floor were empty, lighted only by fluorescent tubes hanging from the ceiling. Susan pushed the button for the elevator, aware that she was the only person on the first floor. For a moment her imagination conjured up a gory scene in the elevator fighting off a psychotic patient armed with the missing scissors. The doors of the elevator slammed open, and she let out a sigh of relief. It was empty. As Susan pushed the button for her floor, she reminded herself that patients sensed fear. If she didn't get control of her emotions, she would be feeding right into their paranoia.

Jenna was in the nurses' station. "A lot's been going on tonight. Dorothy already told you about the scissors. They haven't found them yet, and the patients are uptight."

Susan listened while two aides ran through a summary of the ward's evening activities before they left. Jenna started to set up medications while Susan sat at the desk and looked out into the day room. She had never felt so vulnerable since it was just her, Jenna, and eighty patients.

Jenna broke into Susan's somber mood. "Here, take the flashlight. We're going to pass meds and take a bed check."

Susan reached for the flashlight. "What do I do with this?"

"I'll take in the medications. You stand by the door with the flashlight and shine it into the room. But don't come in!" Jenna shook her head. "A couple of years ago both of the aides went into a room, and the patient slammed the door shut and beat the crap out of them. Remember, those scissors could be anywhere. So don't turn your back on anyone. And if there's any trouble, get right back to the station and call security."

Susan felt her heart pounding as she followed Jenna down the corridor. They moved from room to room, Susan holding the flashlight while Jenna went in with the medication. There were forty rooms, and any one of them could have someone waiting behind the door with the scissors. Halfway through, she was standing in the doorway of a room watching Jenna when suddenly Susan felt a tap on her shoulder. She jumped and dropped the flashlight.

"Miss Mason, I have to go pee."

Susan picked up the flashlight. "Leo, don't sneak up like that! Just go to the bathroom and get back to bed!"

Jenna pushed the cart out of the room and gave her an angry look. "There are only two of us here, get that? No other help! So, girl, you better start paying attention."

The next three hours went slowly. Dorothy provided the only diversion with a short visit to check on how things were going and to let them know that security was still searching for the scissors. Their task seemed impossible, considering the number of rooms and patients.

Susan hadn't thought about bringing lunch; but she realized that when you're awake, that four-hour feeding cycle continues automatically. Jenna brought out a brown paper bag. "Here, have some soul food. There's plenty; I packed a big lunch. I get hungry when I'm nervous."

"Thanks, I'm starving." Susan reached for a sandwich. She was too hungry to turn down food and too embarrassed to ask Jenna. Susan looked away and hoped she wasn't biting into a "chittlin" sandwich. "Hey, this is a bologna sandwich!"

"Yeah, White folk's soul food. I like ethnic food."

They were almost finished eating when the silence on the ward was shattered with yelling and pounding coming from the men's wing. A fight had started in one of the rooms, and two men were now rolling on the corridor floor trying to choke each other. Several patients came to the doorway of their room, but only to watch. No one attempted to stop the fight. Susan ran to intervene. One man had his teeth into the other's ear. She could see blood running out of his mouth. She was a few feet away when Jenna grabbed her and pulled her back toward the nurses' station.

"What are you doing?" Susan demanded, "We've got to stop them! They'll kill each other." Jenna pushed her into the office, locked the door, and picked up the phone. "Operator, there's an emergency on Ward Two! There's a fight! Send security right away!"

Susan snapped at her. "Why are we locked in here? We should be out there stopping them!"

"Look, girl. I don't know what they pay you; but for a $1.60 an hour, I don't get killed! What good are you with your head split open? You're good to nobody! Those people you're so eager to protect, they'll stand and watch you get the life beat out of you." The anger dissipated, and she looked sad. "Look, I care, but I'm going to survive." Jenna saw security coming down the corridor. "Come on; now we can help."

With four of them, it didn't take long to break up the fight. Security put the instigator into restraints while Susan and Jenna led the other dazed man into the nurses' station to have his ear cleaned.

The whole side of his head was bloody. Jenna picked up a towel and wiped away the blood. "His ear is gone!" She turned to Susan. "Get out there and find it. Maybe they can sew it back on."

Susan just stood there horrified by the bloody stump. Jenna shouted and pointed to a latex glove. "Hurry up! Get out there and find it!"

Susan ran down the hall to where the men had been fighting. She saw the ear lying in the corner. Susan reached down, quickly pulled her hand back and started to gag. Paralyzed with nausea, she closed her eyes. Susan took a deep breath and slowly reached down again and picked up the bloody ear. Trying not to think about what she was holding, she ran back to the nurses' station with her arm outstretched. Susan dropped it into a plastic specimen cup, and security rushed out with the man and his severed ear.

As the guards left the ward, Susan thought about people sleeping through the night and waking up in the morning never aware or even caring about what happened here. "Jenna, thanks for putting up with me tonight. I was probably more of a hindrance than a help."

"You're okay. And if you work hard, someday you might make a good aide."

Susan shook her head. "I don't know about that. It's easy to follow the book and be therapeutic when you have a whole staff behind you. But on the night shift, you're really on your own. Saying that you earn your pay is a joke. What keeps you here?"

"It's a job, and I'm mainly on the day shift. I have a kid to support. But things are looking up. I finished a two-year LPN program last month, and I'm waiting for a position to open up here. But if that doesn't happen, I have something else going. I moonlight on my days off at this private psychiatric hospital some psychiatrist owns. The place caters to the rich White folks who don't want anyone to know that someone in their family is crazy. The pay is good. And maybe it will work out to be a full-time job. Your husband must make a pretty good buck. Why are you putting up with all this shit?"

I don't have anything to keep me at home right now. But maybe one of these days, I'll be chasing after a bunch of kids. Right now, I need to feel like I'm contributing something." Susan chuckled. "Sounds a little high and mighty, doesn't it?"

"Yeah, but I like you. After all, we got tear-gassed together; so I'll forget you said that."

As she left the hospital, Susan remembered the still missing scissors. And her mind was racing with images of a patient getting stabbed in the bathroom or an aide walking past a room only to be pulled in and attacked. She pushed the scene away wanting to get home where she felt safe.

CHAPTER 10
THE COCKTAIL PARTY

Traffic was heavy, and it was after eight before Susan pulled into the driveway. Her body ached, and her eyes burned with fatigue. She had been up for over twenty-four hours and that, coupled with the tension, had drained every ounce of energy from her. Elliott was in the shower. But before he was out of the bathroom, she was undressed and in bed. Susan's eyes were almost closed as he bent over her, patting her head. "What have we here? Is this a dream or are you really home?" "This isn't a dream," she murmured. "It's been a nightmare, and I'm exhausted. I'll call you when I wake up."

Elliott bent over to kiss her goodbye, but Susan was already asleep.

It was two o'clock before Susan called Elliott. "Hi, I'm finally awake. Sorry, I wasn't more responsive this morning; I was exhausted."

"Don't worry about it. It was great having the bathroom to myself. How did it go last night?"

"Horrible! I thought working there during the day was bad, but at night the place is unreal. Remind me to tell you about it sometime. Right now I'd rather forget the whole experience."

"Okay, you can save it for when you write your memoirs. I should be home around five. Susan, don't plan anything for tomorrow night. We have to attend a cocktail party. I know its short notice, but I have to make an appearance. We'll go out to dinner afterward, anywhere you'd like."

"Sounds good to me. Any people I know on the guest list?"

"No, I don't think so. Wait, I talked to Randy Sloan this morning and asked him if he wanted to come. I thought he could use the opportunity to make a few connections."

Susan beamed. "Hey, that's thoughtful of you."

"Well, he's tired of living at the poverty level. Besides, I think the guy has potential. Got to go, Honey, I have another call."

She sat thinking for a moment about how quickly Elliott had responded to Randy's needs and her request. She smiled contentedly to herself. And he calls me a bleeding heart.

* * *

It was about six when the phone rang. "I'll get it! I'm expecting a call." Elliott carried on a muted conversation. After a few moments, he hung up.

Susan asked, "More problems?"

"Yes, I may have to go out. Why don't we eat now in case I have to leave in a hurry?"

She put her arms around him. "You know, I think you're pretty terrific."

"No argument about that."

Susan slapped the dish towel across Elliott's butt. "What an ego!"

He grabbed her and pulled her close. "It matches my sex drive; how long until dinner?"

"That depends on how long it takes to show me that sex drive you're bragging about." Susan grabbed his hand and giggled all the way to the bedroom.

They were finishing dinner when Elliott took another phone call. "Okay, I'll be there in a half hour." On the way out, Elliott quickly brushed Susan's cheek with his lips. "Don't wait up. I don't know how long this will take."

Susan couldn't help but wonder why he was so mysterious. Were all lawyers so secretive with their clients? Of course, she could never share all her work with Elliott either. He'd laugh or never believe it. She knew it was late when Elliott returned since she woke several times and found the bed empty. He slept until noon Saturday morning while Susan did some paperwork. As soon as she heard Elliott coming down the stairs, she poured coffee and put bread in the toaster.

"Good afternoon, Hon. What happened last night? You didn't get back until after two. I was getting worried."

Elliott sipped his coffee. "Remember when I asked you how things went Thursday night? You told me you just wanted to forget about it. Well, that's exactly how I feel. Work is work, and home is home. I don't want to mix the two." He looked at her. "Let's make a pack. I won't ask for details about your job, and you don't ask me. We both work at professions that produce a lot of headaches. Let's leave them at the office."

"That's true. Between your clients and my patients, we could spend all our time dealing with their problems."

Elliott put his empty cup in the sink. "How about bundling up and taking a walk along the lake?"

"Terrific! Just give me a few minutes to get ready."

The crowd on the beach began to thin. Elliott and Susan were sitting on the breakers watching the waves crash into the concrete wall. "Susan, you've been quiet. What are you thinking about?"

She leaned close to Elliott and smiled into his blue eyes. "I was just thinking about babies."

"Babies, Susan? You're the one who said we should wait a year."

"I know. It's just that seeing these bundled up little kids waddling on the beach made me want one more than ever."

He laughed as he put his arms around her. "Fantastic! Shall we start on one right now?"

"No way," said Susan. "We'll get arrested! Besides, it's not the right time, not really. Give me a few months to get settled in my new job, and then we could create a beautiful little boy or girl with your blue eyes."

Elliott hugged her and looked down at his watch. "Well, we'll have to decide on the details later. It's five o'clock, and we still have to get ready for tonight."

* * *

Pulling into the parking garage off Rush Street, Susan asked, "Who's throwing the party?"

Elliott replied, "Judge Morris. I contributed to his campaign. That's why we got an invitation. But the contacts I make will more than offset the expense of the donation."

A worried look crossed her face. "I wish I wasn't so politically naïve. Except for issues affecting mental health, I don't keep up with what's happening in the political arena."

"Believe me, politics in Chicago is a three ring circus! Just enjoy the show and be charming for forty-five minutes. Then we'll skip out and have dinner."

There were about fifty people in the large hotel suite. Elliott and Susan were the most attractive couple in the room. A Black man was playing the piano in one corner while several middle-aged women, who had drunk too much, vied for his attention. At the other end of the room was a portable bar and buffet table.

Elliott looked around the group and saw a familiar face. "Why don't you go over and sampled the buffet? I'll join you after I pay homage to a few people unless you want to come along."

"No thanks, I have to listen to delusions of grandeur all day. I'll leave the politicians to you." Susan was picking through the hors d'oeuvres when she heard a voice behind her. "Hello, anything interesting?"

"I was hoping there might be something different to eat, but it's the same thing you see at every party." She turned around and looked into the face of an elderly man dressed in an expensive gray silk suit. The man looked vaguely familiar.

He pointed to the table. "You're right; in fact, I think I saw that meatball at a cocktail party last Wednesday."

Susan smiled at him just as Elliott returned. "Frank, I see you met my wife."

Frank gave a courtly bow. "Not officially."

"Well, let me make it official. Susan, this is Frank DiMato. He lives in Florida but has retained our legal firm to handle his Chicago business ventures."

"I've heard a lot about you from Elliott. But he neglected to inform me of your beauty. He's a lucky man!"

She smiled up at Elliott. "Not as lucky as I, Mr. DiMato. Are you in town for this party?"

"Yes, and I have business with your husband. Speaking of which, Elliott, I see someone we need to talk to. Susan, would you excuse us for a moment?"

Elliott accepted a glass of wine from the tray of a passing waiter. "Susan, have a drink. I'll be back in a few minutes."

She watched as the two men sought out a distinguished-looking middle-aged man. The three men stepped over to the side of the room and engaged in an intense discussion. When Randy arrived, Elliott waved him over and introduced him to the other men. Susan finished her drink and picked at the hors d'oeuvres on her plate, trying to remember where it was that she had seen Mr. Frank DiMato. Both his face and name were familiar, but she couldn't place him. Susan glanced around the room and saw Elliott trying to get her attention. She walked over, and he took her arm.

"Honey, you already know Randy. But I want you to meet Dr. Rhoades. He's someone in this room you should be able to identify with; Dr. Rhoades is the director of a private psychiatric hospital." Dr. Rhoades smiled warmly and held out his hand. "Susan, I've heard a lot about you. I'm happy we're finally meeting."

"Thank you; it's nice to meet you, too."

"Elliott has represented my hospital several times in the past few months. We're lucky to have him. Susan, I wish I could get to know you better, but unfortunately, I have an emergency patient back at the hospital that I have to admit."

Frank DiMato reached out and took her hand. "Susan, meeting you was the highlight of the evening; but now I have a plane to catch. Elliott, thank you for introducing me to your friend, Mr. Sloan. It has been a pleasure talking to him. Dr. Rhoades, may I walk out with you?"

After they were out of ear-shot, Susan turned to Elliott. "What's their connection with Judge Morris?"

"Let's just say that in one way or another they have made their contribution."

Randy thanked Elliott for the invitation and left right after Mr. DiMato and Dr. Rhoades. Susan looked puzzled. "I know that

Mr. DiMato, but I can't place him. Oh well, it will come to me." Suddenly her face lit up. "I know who he is! I've seen his picture in the paper. Isn't he involved with organized crime?"

Elliott's face tightened. "We made our appearance, let's go. We have dinner reservations."

As they waited for the elevator, Susan leaned close to Elliott and whispered, "This has been an interesting evening. What a strange group of bedfellows! You have a much wider circle of friends than I ever imagined."

He smiled down at her. "That's part of the game. Everybody's entitled to representation, from the president on down to the scum you scrape off your shoes. You wouldn't turn away someone coming to you for help if you didn't approve of their lifestyle. Would you?"

"No, but I think it's a little different."

He hit the elevator button with his fist. "Let's not get into an argument. Besides, I'm famished. I didn't have time to check out the buffet table."

"You didn't miss much. Where do we have reservations?"

Elliott looked annoyed. "It better be a restaurant where married couples are not allowed to discuss work!"

The conversation was now strained. Susan couldn't forget the incident at the elevator. It was the rage. Rage brought about by a simple comment, and the bruise on her arm was another example of his anger. Why wasn't she confronting him? If a patient expressed anger like that, she'd be the first to point it out. What was happening? Was she afraid of him? For God's sake, a few hours ago they were talking about making babies!

"Susan, you look like you're a million miles away."

She looked up. "Elliott, is something troubling you?"

His face clouded. "Why, what's wrong?"

"I don't know. That's why I'm asking you. The last two days you seemed tense and angry."

"I've been under a lot of pressure at work. I'm in the middle of a project that has a lot of money hinging on the right outcome. Just be patient, Hon. The pressure will be off soon, and then I won't be so uptight." His hand pressed hers.

Susan felt mellowed a little. Elliott was out there in the real world where the bottom line counted. And he was right; everyone should be entitled to representation. Elliott was then so attentive that Susan enjoyed the rest of the evening

* * *

Sunday flew by. Elliott put on a jacket and grilled burgers on the patio while Susan did laundry. It wasn't long before she was preparing for bed, wondering where the weekend had gone. Elliott stepped out of the bathroom as Susan was sitting on the edge of the bed brushing her hair. He sat next to her and ruffled her hair. She smiled up at him as he commented, "By the way, I called the phone company today and arranged for a business line. That way our phone won't be tied up; and with the recorder attached, I won't miss business calls when we're out."

"Where are you going to put it?"

"I was thinking about the den."

Susan agreed. It certainly sounded logical.

* * *

In her office the next morning, Susan checked for messages. She then left for the nurses' station with a lighter step than usual. It was her last week coming to the hospital. She held her breath and navigated the foul-smelling corridor. She saw a small dark mass in the middle of the floor, but her stomach relaxed as she got closer and saw that it was just a chewed cigar butt. The hospital had only a skeleton crew working the weekends. Consequently, on Monday mornings the place looked like Grant Park after a Fourth of July celebration.

At the nurses' station, Maggie looked up from the logbook. "Well, hello there stranger. Did you enjoy your three day weekend?"

Susan beamed. "I sure did. But it would've been better if I could have skipped work on Thursday night." Susan's expression turned serious. "We had quite a night, but it was worse for the patients. At least we could escape to the nurses' station. I still feel guilty about running there for protection."

"Considering what was going on, it sounded like getting help was the best thing you and Jenna could have done." Maggie smiled at her. "Well, if nothing else, at least you learned not to get committed!"

Susan gasped. "What a horrible thought!" She looked into the day room and saw the patients dragging chairs into several circles.

"See you later, Maggie. The breakfast club has gathered."

As she approached the group, she heard Carla ask John. "Why do you cut yourself? That's a dumb ass thing!"

John sneered back at Carla. "Why do you eat like a pig? That's a dumb ass thing, too!"

Susan intervened. "Hey, we're here to help each other. Carla, did you want to ask John if he kn0ws why he cuts himself?"

Carla looked a little sheepish as she answered. "Yes."

"I'm not sure," John mumbled. "I know that it's stupid; but sometimes I feel bad, and it makes me feel better … at least for a while."

Carla responded. "Yeah, I know how you feel. I don't want to eat like this, and I tell myself I'm not going to. But every time something goes wrong, I go to the refrigerator. And then I feel worse because I've pigged out."

Forty-five minutes later, Susan finished the meeting. "It sounds like we all need something to help us cope with stress. Let's think about that and see what ideas we can bring back to the group tomorrow. Okay, that's it for today. If anyone wants to talk to me, I'll be in my office for the next hour."

Susan stopped at the nurses' station; Karen was the only person in the station. "Hi, how are you doing? Susan asked.

Karen frowned. "Fine for now; but thanks to you, it won't be for long."

Susan looked puzzled. "What are you talking about?"

"I'm talking about the fact that the last thing you did before leaving this place was to volunteer for an aide's job on the night shift, and now you've set a precedent!" Karen slammed the logbook down on the counter. "Now we'll be expected to fill in every time one of them calls in sick!"

Susan picked up her cup of coffee and walked to the door. "Think of that as my going away gift to you." As Karen glared at her, Susan smiled and walked from the station.

She was working on a discharge summary when a knock on the door interrupted her.

"Come on in."

The door opened, and Carla was standing there with a sheet of paper in her hand. She squeezed through the doorway and leaned on Susan's desk. "You said you had some time. I'm enjoying the book you lent me, and I want to thank you. It's not much, but I sketch a little."

The likeness was unmistakable. "Why, it's me! Thank you. Hey, this is my first portrait. I'm flattered. I can hang it my new office." She beamed at Carla. "I didn't know you had this talent. Social histories have a knack for ignoring people's assets. Carla, would you like to talk for a while?"

"Yeah, I would. I was so upset when I first came here I didn't want to talk to anybody. But now I feel a lot better. The medicine must be helping. I've been thinking about what was said in the group this morning. Maybe there's a better way for me to handle my problems. You're only going to be here for a week, so I guess I better start talking."

"I'm glad you came, Carla, but you should know that this is just the beginning. It takes time and hard work to break old habits. When I leave, someone else will work with you. And after discharge, I hope you will continue to work with a therapist at a community mental health center."

Carla shifted in the chair. "I don't like this! As soon as I feel comfortable with you, you take off; and someone else steps in. Then I get discharged and have to learn to trust another person."

"I know," said Susan. "But believe me, Carla, once you start to trust, it gets easier. And who knows, you may find therapy worthwhile. How about giving it a try?"

Carla's eyes welled up. "The way I came in here, you can't get much lower than that; so I guess I don't have anything to lose. All my life I've never had a friend. Fat people are supposed to be jolly and have a lot of friends. I hated the other kids for being thin and pretty, and I hated myself for being fat and ugly. Do you know what it's like to never have a friend?" Susan reached over and touched Carla's hand; her heart ached for the pain she saw in Carla's eyes. "What about your Grandmother? What kind of a relationship do you have with her?"

Carla pulled a tissue from the box on Susan's desk and wiped her eyes. "Oh, Grandmother is a good Christian woman. She took care of me when my Mother dumped me. Every day she told me to praise the Lord, turn the other cheek, and that God would reward me in heaven. I love her, but sometimes I think I hate her, too. My Grandmother never understood how hurt and angry I felt. She fed me whenever anything went wrong: ice cream if the girl next door ignored me, cake if I fell and skinned my knee, a chocolate fudge sundae if things were bad."

"I met your Grandmother last week. I think she loves you very much, Carla, but it sounds like she has trouble handling problems. Did you see your Mother very much?"

"Just once in a while, she'd come by and tell me how fat I was and how embarrassed she was to be seen in public with me. I don't understand why she's thin. Maybe my Grandmother didn't feed her as she fed me."

"Perhaps with your Grandfather dead and being older herself, she felt she couldn't cope with the problems a child brings. Remember this morning? We talked about how people don't always pick the best way to deal with stress."

Susan saw that Carla was beginning to look uncomfortable, and she didn't want to scare her away. If she exposed too much, Carla would be afraid to return. "Carla? Do you think you've had enough for today?"

"Yeah, this makes me nervous."

"I want to thank you for sharing your feelings. I know it took a lot of courage to knock on my door. If you'd like, I'm free tomorrow after group; and we could talk again."

Carla stood up using Susan's desk for leverage. "Sure, I'll come back. I guess it wasn't that bad."

Maggie came to the door just as Carla was leaving. "Hi Carla, how's it going?"

"Okay, I think it's going to be okay."

Maggie walked into the office and closed the door, "I can't believe it! She isn't snarling. She sounds human!"

"Yes, she's finally starting to open up. I'm almost sorry I've resigned. It looks like Carla may be one of the rare patients around here that can respond to therapy. She's bright, verbal, and beginning to trust."

Susan picked up the drawing. "I want you to see this. Carla drew my picture. It's good, and it looks like me; but there's something off."

Maggie reached for it, studied the drawing for several seconds, and then looked up with a smile on her face. "Do you remember the first few days Carla was here and how she hollered about not having a Black social worker? She said she couldn't talk to a honky. Well, I think Carla solved her problem. Look at the drawing again."

Susan gazed intently at the figure in the drawing. "I can't believe it! I'm passing. Look at this. She made subtle changes in my features, just enough to make it appear that I have some Black genes in this White body. Pretty good! I guess that's one way to solve the problem."

"You're right, Susan. Carla is beginning to sound very interesting."

"Good, I'm glad you feel that way, Maggie, because I'd like to recommend that you take over her case when I leave. I know how busy you are, but you're going to get half of them anyway. And you know how quickly Karen would undo whatever progress Carla made this week."

Maggie slowly shook her head. "I don't know, Susan, maybe she would resent the fact that I don't have a degree. After all, she's not the usual patient we get here. She's earned a college degree and might feel she's being discriminated against if I'm her therapist."

"But she needs someone she can trust, someone who can teach her to care about herself. You're the best person for that job."

Maggie threw up her arms in mock surrender. "Okay, who can resist such flattery? But let's get out of here before you talk me into taking over your whole caseload. Shall we try the cafeteria?"

"Sure, why not?"

CHAPTER 11
LAST DAY AT LINTON

The The staff meeting had already started when Susan slipped into the conference room. As the meeting dragged on, her mind wandered. Now that she was leaving, it was hard for her to feel fully involved. Images of last Saturday night's cocktail party began to flood her mind. There was a lot of power in that room-some of it legitimate and some of it very questionable.

"Susan, are you with us?"

"I'm sorry. What did you say?"

One of the staff doctors smiled at her. "Three more days to go. In the meantime, I still value your opinion. What do you think about discharging Ben Halter?"

"He certainly seems to be doing well. He's participating in ward meetings, and he told me he had a good home visit."

"Good. Then if no one objects, let's put Ben's name on the discharge list."

***

Elliott had another evening meeting. Susan kicked off her shoes, turned on the television, and tried to push away her nagging thoughts. Why did Elliott have such strange working hours? Why was he so secretive? Did his ambition have limits? And no matter how hard she tried, she couldn't stop thinking about that DiMato character. If Elliott worked for him, wasn't he, therefore, connected to him? And most of all, why did he always brush off her questions? Was she that naïve about the business world? Or should she be worried? Finally, Susan turned off the television and made her way upstairs, bleary-eyed; and sleep came quickly.

* * *

The next morning Susan was waiting for the elevator when she noticed Mark hurrying toward her. "Susan, wait! If you have a minute, I'd like to talk to you."

"Sure."

"Come on, let's go into my office." Mark closed the door behind them. "Is there anything I can do to get you to stay?" He smiled at her and shook his head. "No, I'm kidding. I know your mind is made up, but I thought I'd give it one last try. You're going to be missed around here."

"Thanks. There are also a lot of people that I'm going to miss."

Mark sat down on the couch and motioned for Susan to join him. "I want to thank you for helping out last Thursday night. I heard it was rough."

"That's putting it mildly," Susan replied. "But the ward is calm now, and I have only three patients left from my caseload."

"It sounds like everything is in good shape."

"The only patient I hate to leave is Carla. She has made so much progress that I wish I could continue working with her. But at least I'll be leaving here feeling like a successful therapist."

"Just wait, Susan, in a few weeks you will be working with many more like Carla."

"I hope so, but she'll always be someone special." Susan looked up at Mark. "Kind of like your first love."

He gently covered her hand with his. "You're right. That's very special."

Susan got up and walked to the door. "I have to get upstairs, but I'd like to ask you something before I leave."

"Ask away."

"Do you know a psychiatrist by the name of Dr. Rhoades?"

An annoyed look came over Mark's face. "Yes, he owns a private for-profit hospital. Everyone admitted is miraculously cured the date their insurance runs out. If you have ten-day coverage, you stay ten days. If you have six months coverage, then five months and thirty days later you're discharged. He also has a reputation for using excessive electro-shock treatments. Patients come in depressed and leave with a fried brain. He appeals to wealthy people who are impressed with his charm and the hospital's country club atmosphere. Why are you asking about him?"

"I met him at a party last Saturday. He's one of Elliott's clients."

Mark raised his eyebrows. "Well, I'm sure he will keep Elliott busy. I wouldn't want to represent him. But then again, I'm not a lawyer."

"Thanks for the information." Susan looked troubled. "I almost wish I hadn't asked you. I have this fantasy about Elliott defending the downtrodden, but I guess one of us has to think about making money."

"It helps," said Mark. "Maybe that's why we're not together. We would've starved." Susan gave a halfhearted laugh. "Well, that's one reason. I won't keep you any longer. Thanks for the information."

The morning flew by with a longer than usual group meeting and a productive therapy session with Carla. After lunch, Susan went over to check with personnel. It was final; by tomorrow afternoon, she would be a former employee.

Susan walked back to her building. As she waited for the elevator, a security guard came up with a man in leather cuffs, a tall, muscular man with black hair. Susan turned away as he stared at her. The only time she had seen eyes that blood-shot was when the patient had gone into such a rage that the small blood vessels in his eyes burst. The elevator door opened.

Her instinct was to stand back and let the guard and patient have the elevator to themselves. But the guard held the door open, so she smiled feebly and walked in. The door shut, and the elevator started to move. Without warning, the man's face turned red. He let out a karate yell and smashed his cuffed fist against the head of the surprised guard. The force of the blow banged his head against the metal wall and split his cheek open. Susan's pants-suit was splattered with bright red specks of blood. The guard lost consciousness and slid to the floor while she stood terrified with her back pressed rigidly against the elevator wall.

The man stood across from Susan staring at her with a vacant look in his eyes. He started to move toward her, and she put her hands up for protection. But then the elevator stopped, and the doors opened to the third floor.

"Excuse me, ma'am, but is this our floor?"

Susan nodded and watched as the man stepped out, oblivious to what he had just done. She left the elevator and slowly walked behind the man. He waited at the ward door while Susan, with her hands shaking, unlocked the door. She wanted to shout for someone to come and help the guard but was afraid that it might set the man off again. As she stepped inside the nurses' station, the man walked to the day room and sat down calmly watching television.

"Call security! We need an ambulance. That man sitting in the day-room just knocked out a guard. He's lying unconscious on the floor of the elevator."

The nurse jumped up. "Donna, make the call. And, keep an eye on the patient. Try to keep the other patients away from him. Come on, Susan. Let's get back to the guard."

The man was dazed and sitting on the elevator floor when they got there. The nurse dropped to her knees. "Don't try to get up."

"I won't," replied the man. "My head feels like it's the size of a watermelon. What happened? One minute I was standing in the elevator, and the next thing I remember was waking up on the floor with blood all over me!"

Susan knelt. "The patient you were bringing up to the ward knocked you out."

The nurse held the towel on the split cheek. Blood was still pouring, and half of the guard's face was swollen and starting to bruise.

"We called an ambulance. It looks like you'll need stitches in your cheek. You're going to have a headache like you haven't felt since your first hangover."

After the ambulance removed the guard, Susan gave an incident report to security and then returned to her ward. When she walked into the nurses' station, Jenna looked up at her and immediately noticed the blood splattered suit.

"What the hell happened to you?"

"I was in the elevator when a new patient attacked a guard. I was lucky; the patient didn't pay any attention to me. He was polite. God help the people on Ward Three!"

"Don't worry," said Jenna, "they'll keep him snowed under. You better rinse out those bloodstains before they set."

"Yes, and then I'm going home. See you tomorrow, Jenna."

* * *

Susan was looking in the refrigerator for something for dinner when Elliott walked in. "Hi, anything interesting in there?"

"No, not really." Susan took a bottle of red wine from the counter. "How about ordering a pizza tonight?"

"It sounds good to me. Susan, you look beat. Did you have a

rough day?"

"Yes, it was a rather exciting day. Want some wine?"

"Sure," replied Elliott. "Well, in a couple of days you can forget about that place."

Susan grabbed a couple of glasses and sat next to Elliott. "Oh, it wasn't all bad today. There's a patient on the ward that I hate to leave. She's an interesting person, and we have a lot of similar interests. And she's responding so well to therapy that for the first time I feel like a professional."

Elliott looked annoyed. "Christ, you sound like you're involved with her. I thought therapists were supposed to stay detached from their patients."

"Elliott, I don't know how you cannot get attached in some way!"

"Well, I care about winning my cases. That's good enough for me, and it better be good enough for my clients."

The phone rang, and Elliott stood up. "I'll get it. It's my business phone." He bent down and kissed her. "I'll be back, Florence Nightingale."

Susan tried to reassure herself that it would just take more time, but she doubted that he would ever regard her work as valuable.

After a few moments, Elliott returned from the den. "I'm starved. When is the pizza coming?"

"I'll call now. Do you want the combo?"

"Yeah, I can smell it now: onions, peppers, mushrooms, sausage, olives, and cheese!"

"Stop it! You're drooling, and it won't be here for an hour."

The phone rang several times that night. Elliott went in and closed the door to the den with each call. Susan smiled as she realized that his plan to keep business separate from home was backfiring. With these numerous calls and his need for privacy, Susan was becoming more curious about his work. But then she reasoned, Elliott's clients were entitled to confidentiality.

* * *

Today was Susan's last day, and Carla was waiting for her on the other side of the ward door. "Good morning, Mrs. Mason."

"Good morning to you, Carla. I don't have a group this morning, so we can start earlier."

Carla leaned her bulky body against the wall for support. "Okay, but it'll take me a while to walk to your office. I'll meet you there in a few minutes."

"Fine. We've got a lot to accomplish today. See you in a few minutes."

As Susan walked down the hall, she noticed the door to her office was open. She cringed when she looked in and saw Karen sitting at her desk.

"Did you come to say goodbye?"

"Not exactly. I'm here to tell you that I'm going to be taking over Carla's case. I heard that you went behind my back and asked Maggie to take her, but you're not giving orders around here. You seem to forget that I am Maggie's supervisor and I decide who is on her patient list. And it's going to take a skilled therapist to undo the harm you've done! Carla is a compulsive, self-indulgent woman who has manipulated you. Just because she has an education, Carla thinks that she's better than the other patients. But she's no different from the rest. That woman needs someone with authority to take control of her life and give her firm guidelines. Besides, she can't be trusted to make her own decisions until she's changed that arrogant attitude of hers."

Susan had heard enough. She leaned across the desk and shouted into Karen's face. "Get out of my chair! This is still my office, and Carla is my patient! And if it's the last thing I do, I am going to make sure you stay away from her. You call yourself a professional, but you're nothing but a rotten excuse for a human being!"

Carla had finally made it to Susan's office and was standing in front of the open door listening to the argument. Suddenly, Karen spotted her. "You miserable sneak! What are you doing eavesdropping on us? Get away from that door! Mrs. Mason may think you're special, but I know different. You're no better than any of the other patients here. And the sooner you accept that, the better off you'll be!"

Susan shouted, "That's enough! Get out of here right now!"

Karen rushed toward the door and reached to push Carla out of the way, but Carla grabbed Karen's arm and slammed her against the wall. "Get your fucking hands off of me! Touch me again, and I'll tear your arms off!"

When Karen regained her breath, she started screaming. "Help me! Help me! She's killing me! Call security!"

Carla's whole body shook with rage. She lunged toward Karen; but in mid-step, she abruptly slumped to the floor gasping for air.

Susan pushed Karen aside and dropped to the floor. "Carla, what's wrong?"

"I can't breathe! My chest hurts." Before Susan could react, Carla gasped and then stopped breathing.

Susan's expression turned to horror. She looked up as the nurse arrived in response to Karen's screams.

Helen shouted to call an ambulance, and then knelt, and began giving Carla cardiopulmonary resuscitation. Within a few moments, Mark was soon there helping Helen with the CPR; but Carla never regained consciousness. The paramedics arrived on the ward and continued the CPR effort for another ten minutes, but there was no response. Carla was dead.

Security was summoned to help get Carla's body onto a gurney. Six of them struggled with the heavy body. Susan looked on in horror as they tugged and pushed Carla as if they were loading a carcass of meat onto a butcher's table. She turned her face away, unable to bear the sight of this final indignity. After they wheeled Carla's body away, Susan looked around for Karen who had sneaked away during the commotion. Mark put his arm around Susan and led her back into the office. "I'm sorry. I know how much you cared about Carla. But with all the weight she was carrying around, this was inevitable."

"No, it was Karen. She killed her!"

Mark looked puzzled. "What are you saying?"

"Karen deliberately started an argument with Carla and then shouted for security. Carla became so angry and excited that her heart couldn't take it."

Mark pulled a chair next to Susan and sat down. "Susan, I know that Karen has more than her share of faults; but she's not a murderer. She would never purposely try to kill Carla. I want a full report from you about the whole incident, and I promise you that I'll follow through with it. But believe me, this was a tragedy just waiting to happen. Carla had an enlarged heart, and it was just a matter of time before it gave out. Mourn her, Susan, but don't turn this into something worse than it is already."

Tears welled up in Susan's eyes. "Mark, it's not fair. Why now, just when her life was starting to change for the better?"

Mark leaned closer to Susan "I know, but death is never fair. Ask a parent who loses a child. Susan, you're upset now. Just remember that you helped her to feel better about herself these last few days. At least she didn't die full of self-loathing."

Susan asked, "Where did they take her?"

"To the morgue; the coroner's office has to do an autopsy. It appears to be a heart attack, but they have to be sure."

Susan took a deep breath. "Who's going to let her Grandmother know?"

"Do you want to tell her?"

"No! Considering that I believe Carla's death had been provoked, it would not be wise to have me talk to her Grandmother."

"I understand." Mark started to walk toward the door. "Carla must have been someone special. I've never seen you so excited about your work. It's hard to be a part of a person turning around their life, only to see it end like this."

Susan smiled. "You know, Dr. Denning, it's going to be difficult working without you. Having you close has been like having my living, breathing security blanket. I'm going to miss you!"

"No more than I'm going to miss you, Susan. I have to get downstairs. Are you going to be okay?"

"I'm fine. Go on. I know you're busy."

"Okay. I have to prepare a report on Carla's death, and I'll also need an incident report from you."

"Don't worry. I intend to start it right now. I'll leave it with Helen."

Mark had just left when she heard a knock on the door. "Come on in."

Maggie stepped into the office. "I just wanted to tell you how sorry I am about Carla. I know this sounds crass, but at least the woman died with a few friends. Two weeks ago, everyone except for her Grandmother, would have said 'good riddance'. I was looking forward to working with her."

Tears welled up in Susan's eyes. "Maggie, you weren't going to work with her. Karen was here when I arrived this morning, and she informed me that she was going to take Carla's case. We got into an ugly argument. Carla was standing outside my door and heard everything. Then Karen started on Carla and got her so agitated that she just collapsed from the stress. I'm going to give Mark a written report."

Maggie shook her head. "There's nothing Mark can do except make life miserable for Karen and hope she leaves. Karen knows how to use the system. It will end up being your word against hers." Maggie leaned back in the chair. "The only thing I can say is 'what goes around, comes around'; and that woman will get what she deserves."

Susan managed a faint smile. "You're right, Maggie, but you'd think it would hurt if I tried to hurry her day along?"

"Hell, no; she's way past due."

"In that case, I'd better get busy writing this report."

Maggie got up and walked toward the door. "I'm sorry your last day here turned out to be such a bummer. It was supposed to be a happy send-off."

After Maggie left her office, Susan spent the next hour and a half writing and rewriting her report. She pushed aside the final revision and picked up the phone.

Elliott was in his office. "Hi, what's up?"

"Do you remember that woman I was telling you about last night, the one I was so excited about working with?"

"Yes, don't tell me, she won the Miss Mental Health Award!" Susan felt anger and disappointment. "No, I called to tell you that she died this morning. She had a heart attack right inside my office. It was terrible. I just wanted to talk to you."

"I'm sorry, honey, but it was probably for the best. More than likely the woman would've spent her life in and out of hospitals just like the rest of those people. Look, I have to go. I'm due in court in twenty minutes. Bye now."

Susan hung up the phone feeling worse than she had before making the call. Where was his empathy? It was as if Elliott didn't have feelings! She tried to put the morning out of her mind as she emptied the last of her personal belongings from her desk.

There was a faint knock on the door. Joan, the activity therapist, stuck her head into the office. "Susan, got a minute? I want to say goodbye, and I have something for you. Carla came in for the first time yesterday and told me she was making this for you."

Joan handed her the drawing and left the office. Susan looked at the paper and smiled as the tears ran down her cheeks. Carla had drawn a picture of Susan and Carla flying hand-in-hand over a cavern, leaving a desolate plateau behind and heading toward a lush, beautiful land. Under the picture she had printed, "You Helped Me Soar!"

Susan sat for a few minutes taking in every detail of the drawing. Finally, she opened her briefcase and carefully slipped the drawing inside. She sadly took one last look around the office and wondered how she ever managed to show optimism in such a depressing environment. After handing Helen the final report and saying goodbye, Susan walked to the door by the elevator and unlocked it, letting in several waiting patients. As she drove from the hospital, she felt a tremendous pressure lifting from her. Susan thought about the four years she had spent here and was glad for the experience. But lately, it had become a depressing and unrewarding job. It was time to move on. She couldn't help comparing how differently Mark and Elliot had reacted to her grief. She now found herself overwhelmed with sadness unrelated to Carla's death.

CHAPTER 12
NEW JOB

Susan was surprised to see Elliott's car in the driveway. He opened the front door as she hurried up the stairs. "Hi, come on in! I've got a surprise for you." He grabbed her and kissed her. "Go upstairs and pack a bag! It's unseasonably warm, and we got lucky. I was able to get reservations at the Abbey Resort in Lake Geneva. You deserve a break before you start the new job."

"Oh, you have no idea how much I need to get away! Give me a half hour, and I'll be ready for the road." She forgot her morning disappointment with Elliott and got ready to leave for the weekend.

* * *

They arrived at the Abbey late Friday night, tired but happy to be away. While Susan was in the bathroom getting ready for bed, Elliott went down to the lobby. He walked over to the front desk and asked for a morning wake-up call.

The next morning the phone rang only once before Elliott picked it up and mumbled a sleepy "thank you". Susan rolled over and continued to sleep while Elliott dressed in the early morning light. He scribbled a quick note and quietly closed the door behind him as he left the room.

Several minutes later, he was on the golf course. After parring two holes and scoring a bogey on the third, Elliott set his ball on the fourth tee and made a few practice swings with the driver. He then connected; and the ball flew over the fairway, narrowly skirting a bunkered sand trap, while Frank watched from the golf cart. His bodyguards were a short distance away. Elliott stepped into the cart and started to drive toward the next hole. "No, wait, Elliott," said Frank. "We can talk here. I don't see anyone behind us. If someone comes up, they can play through. This is my last trip to Chicago for a while; the Feds have been tailing me more than usual. Is everything set up on your end?" Frank lit his cigarette and waited for Elliott's response.

"So far things are going perfectly. We've got over thirty investors ready to come up with at least the minimum investment. Everything is going well with my buddies here in Chicago. I found a distributor who is working out well. He was highly recommended by some of your associates, and we've used him on some small jobs for the past few months. The first big delivery has been scheduled for next week."

"Are you sure you can trust him?" asked Frank. "That's a lot of money he'll be taking to Florida. And what about the stuff he'll be bringing back? I hope he won't be getting ideas about setting up his own business with our inventory!"

Elliott gave a little laugh. "Bill may think about it, but that's as far as it will go. You have a reputation as a fair man, Frank; you reward those who are loyal and destroy those who are stupid enough to cross you."

Frank shrugged his shoulders. "I do what I have to do. That's what keeps me alive. Let me say, Elliott, that you have one classy and beautiful wife." He took a long drag from his cigarette. "But tell me, does she have any idea what you do for a living?"

Elliott shifted around in the cart. His discomfort was evident. "Yes, I'm a lawyer. I represent clients and advise for a fee. If you're referring to our business deals, no, she doesn't know about them. And they're none of her damn business."

Frank reached out and put his hand on Elliott's arm. "What if she makes it her business?"

Elliott smiled reassuringly. "Don't worry; she's my wife!"

Frank didn't return the smile. "Do you remember when we had that talk about you finding a wife?"

Elliott thought back to that day in Florida last January. "I sure do."

"I think I left a few words of wisdom out of our little talk. I told you to marry an educated girl with class and forget about the whores. But I didn't tell you to marry a beauty. In all fairness, I didn't tell you to marry an ugly girl either."

Elliott looked puzzled. "What's wrong, Frank? Don't you like Susan?"

"Of course, what's not to like? But I'm concerned." Frank took a deep breath. "You see, if you had married a whore or an ugly girl, she would have been grateful! And a grateful woman makes a loyal wife. You went out and married a girl that has brains, looks, and class. Why should she be grateful? What if she finds out something? Will she be loyal to you or some lofty ideal? Christ, she's a social worker!"

Elliott smiled and patted Frank's knee. "Not for long. Susan wants to start a family in a couple of months."

Frank looked somewhat relieved. "Great, give her a baby every year. That will keep her so busy she won't have time or energy to even ask about your work. Yes, with a lot of kids and a lifestyle Susan can't afford on her own, see how loyal she'll become. In the meantime, make sure she doesn't find out about our deals. You got a separate phone line for business?"

"Yes, I'll give you the number. But for now, I don't think Susan should see us together."

Frank nodded his head. "I could see by the look on her face that she recognized me from the papers. They look for dirt. One wrong thing you do, and it's on the front page. One hundred charities you gift and never a word. You're right; the less Susan knows, the better it will be. I'm checking out before noon. Keep her out of the lobby until I'm gone. Let's finish this nine; I'm getting tired."

They quickly finished playing the front nine and headed back to the clubhouse. Elliott stepped out of the cart, but he stopped as Frank spoke. "One more thing. Elliott, remember that Susan's your wife, and you're responsible for her. You keep her in line, you understand?"

Elliott nodded. He understood.

* * *

Susan stirred and reached out for Elliott. The bed was empty. She sat up and looked around. He wasn't there! Susan threw the covers back, stepped out of bed, and then noticed the note on the dresser. "Going to play some golf. See you around ten." She didn't know that Elliott played, and why didn't he mention last night that he was going to play this morning? Twenty minutes later she was out of the shower and getting dressed. Susan stood in front of the window and watched for Elliott. It wasn't long before she saw him and an older man coming up the walk. As the men got closer, Susan recognized the man with Elliott. It was that Mr. DiMato. Elliott never mentioned that he would be here. This trip was supposed to be a spur of the moment. A few minutes later, Elliott walked into the room.

"Hi," said Susan. "I didn't know that Mr. DiMato was going to be here."

Elliott smiled at her." He isn't. What are you talking about?"

Susan looked confused. "But I thought I saw him walking up the road with you."

He shook his head. "No, I was walking with a guy that left the clubhouse with me. You know every old man that looks Italian is not Frank DiMato. Come on. Let's go into town and browse through the antique shops."

Susan picked up her purse and took one last look out the window. She was certain that man was Frank DiMato. Why did Elliott lie?

* * *

It had been a glorious weekend, a fantasy getaway. Elliott was the ideal loving husband. Susan felt renewed. And now the hospital was relegated to the list of past experiences on her resume. The memory of Carla was something else. It was still painful to even think about her death; but Susan knew that eventually, those feelings would diminish. Now she must concentrate on the present.

* * *

Susan shifted into park and sat in the car for a few minutes looking at the Tri-Valley Mental Health Center. Unlike the cold, forbidding, concrete block construction of the hospital, the center was a warm, inviting one-story red brick building. It was similar to the newer professional buildings found across the country. Susan turned off the engine and said softly, "I think I'm going to like it here."

The entrance was unlocked, a joy after all those years of locked doors. The waiting room had been painted a pale yellow, and the carpeting was dark beige. Bright blue plastic chairs lined the walls. Several occasional tables stood around the room, holding magazines and ashtrays. In one corner was a yellow child's plastic table and chair set. Sitting beside it was a box, overflowing with used and abused toys. There was a counter where patients signed in and made appointments. On each side of the room, a door led to a wing containing offices of the doctors and therapists. Susan stood there for a moment before the secretary noticed her.

"Hello, may I help you? Oh, Mrs. Mason, we're all expecting you. If you go to your left, I'll meet you."

Susan pushed the door open and saw the secretary, an attractive woman about forty, coming toward her with her hand outstretched. "Hello, I was out of the office when you were here for your interview. My name is Diane. I'm sorry, Mrs. Mason; Dr. Spelling had a board meeting this morning. He was disappointed that he couldn't be here to greet you, but he should be back in two hours."

Susan followed Diane as she walked down the corridor. "We have two conference rooms: one for group and family therapy, and the other is for staff meetings, coffee, and lunch breaks. I think the staff is in there now."

Four people were sitting around the table talking and sipping coffee. They looked up when Diane walked in with Susan. She remembered meeting them at her interview. Jan Fleming did her social work internship here last year, and Dr. Spelling hired her when she graduated. Tony Henry was another social worker. Dr. Beth Jordan was the psychologist, and Dr. Marshall was the psychiatrist.

Beth smiled up at Susan. "Sit down, Susan. How do you like your coffee?"

"Black please, and the stronger, the better."

Dr. Marshall smiled at Susan. "I remember that you worked at

Linton State Hospital. Some of my colleagues have been on staff there. It's a rough place."

"Yes, it's the kind of experience that prepares you for all the worst things in life."

"You're not kidding!" Jan said intently. "I hate to go there, even for staffings. It gives me the creeps. But I think I missed out by not working at Linton. I bet you've seen every diagnosis in the book."

"Well, it was a good training ground. Right now, I'm looking forward to working with patients who actually might get better."

Beth laughed. "Don't expect too much, Susan. After all, the patients discharged from the state hospital get referred to the community mental health centers. And with the political push to reduce the number of patients at state hospitals, we get some very sick people coming in here."

Tony spoke up. "Welcome to Tri-Valley, Susan. I hate to interrupt, but I have to ask Beth about the results of an MMPI she did on a patient that's my first appointment today."

Susan was going through charts when Dr. Spelling returned to the office. He went directly through the side door and back to the secretary's office where Susan was sitting.

"Susan, welcome; sorry, I couldn't be here when you arrived. Come on into my office. Let's talk a while."

Dr. Spelling's office was bigger than the others, and every available space had been filled. The top of the desk and couch were covered with books, articles, and stacks of computer printouts. He pointed to an empty chair. "Better grab it before Diane brings in another report. It's so cluttered in here; soon I'll have to see people in the waiting room."

Susan sat down and waited while Dr. Spelling walked around the desk. "Did Diane show you around?"

"Yes."

"Good, then we can get down to business. We've already talked about the philosophy of the clinic when you were here for your interview. So now we need to talk about the practical side. As you may have already noticed, there's an abundance of forms and paperwork." He threw up his hands. "It's a pain, but we have to do it; and most of the work falls on the social workers. We have to fill out forms for how we spend the entire day. There are forms for opening cases, closing cases, and everything in between. It's called accountability, a necessity to qualify for federal and state funds. The other reason is to cover ourselves in this age of lawsuits. And the only way to protect yourself and the clinic is to keep proper records. Of course, it's a given that you will also use good judgment. Susan, you'll be supervising so I expect you to carry half a caseload. I'll give you a free hand as long as you stay within the guidelines that we've already discussed, but I want you to come to me if there's a problem. Things can be unpredictable. If there's trouble, make sure you keep me abreast of it. I don't expect to be the last one to know. Any questions?"

Susan shook her head. "Not at the moment. But I'm sure that

after I've been here a few days, I'll have plenty."

Dr. Spelling smiled warmly. "Susan, I'm glad you decided to work here. There are a lot of skills you'll be bringing here that you acquired at the hospital. But you'll also discover a whole new set of problems. For instance, you'll have to be exceptionally sensitive to trouble. There are no security guards here, just a small staff. If someone becomes violent, it's already too late. As bad as the hospital was, at least you had some protection. I'm not trying to scare you. I want you to be aware of the danger; and most importantly, I don't want any of my people to get hurt."

"I appreciate your warning. And if there's any problem, you'll be the first to know."

Dr. Spelling stood up, signaling the end of their meeting. "Don't get overly concerned; agitated or dangerous patients are the exception rather than the rule. I have another appointment now, so why don't you take time to get comfortable with our routine? If you have any questions, I'm available."

"Thank you."

Once outside Dr. Spelling's office Susan took a deep breath and said to herself, 'Mark, only three hours on the job, and I miss you already'. She stepped into the secretary's office and realized that she still hadn't seen her own office.

"Diane, I know you're busy right now, but if you can spare a minute before lunch. Dr. Spelling said you would show me my office."

"Sure, let's do it now. Your office is the first one as you come in the door."

Susan looked around her new office and compared to her last workspace, it looked like a designer's dream.

Diane continued. "I'll go over the phone system with you, and then I have to get back to my desk. If you don't have any plans for lunch, there's a carry-out place right here in the plaza. The food's not terrific, but it's handy; and they're fast."

"Thanks," replied Susan.

After Diane left, Susan sat back behind her desk, opened drawers, and puttered around the room. While she was basking in her new environment, the phone rang.

"Susan, it's your husband."

"Hi, how is everything going?"

"Great, I've met everybody. Nice people. Dr. Spelling is letting me take it easy this week, but I think he's going to be a tough task-master."

"Well, I don't want to imply that having your ex-boyfriend for your boss had some advantages; but welcome to the real world."

"Normally, I would be angry at such a statement. But I think you may be right. Anyway, I'll survive; I may do a lot more than survive."

"I'm sure you will; but I can't stay on, Honey. I just wanted to see how things were going your first day. I've got to run. I'm having lunch with Randy."

"Say hello for me. It's nice that you fellows manage to get

together so often."

"Well, you've got to keep up with your friends. Bye, see you tonight."

Susan was pleased that Elliott was seeing Randy. Maybe she had been mistaken about seeing Mr. DiMato last Sunday. After all, it wasn't like she was standing close to them.

Susan joined Tony and Diane in the conference room for lunch. The conversation was relaxing, and Susan enjoyed the change of pace. She planned to spend the afternoon reading charts, making appointments to visit with staff at St. Stephen's psychiatric ward, and setting up a time for regular staff meetings with Tony and Jan.

CHAPTER 13
BILL

Elliott had finished one drink and was ordering another when Randy arrived. "Sorry, I'm late. The judge droned on and on. I'm sick of all the shit. How are things going for you?"

"Fine. I'm getting richer by the day."

"Ouch! That hurts. My current remuneration matches the enthusiasm I have for my dead-end job."

"That's why I asked you to have lunch today. My work is getting to be more than I can handle comfortably, and the firm is considering hiring someone to reduce my load. If you're interested, I'll keep you in mind. There's a lot demanded from the people who hire us, but the rewards justify the extra effort. What do you think?"

Randy beamed. "I think that's the best piece of news I've heard in months. No! Make that years. I've been hoping for this kind of opportunity. I'll do anything to get out of this rut. I don't know what possessed me to get into legal, social services in the first place."

Elliott laughed. "At least it was a temporary illness for you. Susan has a chronic condition. I don't think she's ever in touch with reality." He lifted his glass to Randy. "May she earn a heavenly reward for all three of us!"

Randy lifted his glass and forced a weak smile.

* * *

Susan let the phone ring several times before someone answered. "Mark, I was just going to give up."

"I'm glad you're persistent; I was across the hall in admissions when I heard my phone. I've been thinking about you all week. How's the new job going?"

"Great. I spent my first week just getting a feel for the place. I'll be taking all the new clients next week, but Dr. Spelling wants me to carry just half a caseload."

Mark paused for a second. "You sound happy, Susan. I guess getting out of here was the right decision for you after all."

"The pace is slower here. And I will be able to do some in-depth therapy. My only complaint is that I miss my friends."

"If you can tear yourself away from that paradise, how about having lunch one day next week?"

"I was hoping you'd suggest that. Are you free next Thursday?"

"How about meeting at Marlowe's? It's half-way for both of us."

"Sounds good, Mark. See you there at noon."

Susan sat thinking about Mark. Was she confusing friendship with old emotions? But she quickly moved on and picked up the chart of her first patient.

After lunch, Susan took off for a tour of St. Stephen's. The first thing she noticed was how different it was from Linton state hospital. The patients looked as if they could afford insurance. The rooms were clean, and the dayroom was cheerful. But when all was said and done, there were locks on the doors, people were in restraints, and a sheet in the nurses' station listed the patients scheduled for electro-shock therapy. It was still a world where one lost control over everyday decisions, sometimes voluntarily and at other times because of a court commitment.

After the tour, she met with social service director, Richard Malcolm. Susan spent an hour becoming acquainted with admitting procedures. She also inquired about treatment plans and the patient's daily routine. Now if someone needed hospitalization, Susan would be able to tell the patient and the family something about the place. She was delighted to find that the state funded a certain number of beds for uninsured patients. It was a productive afternoon.

* * *

Randy smiled with satisfaction as he related his conversation with Elliott to his DOJ supervisor, Tom Rivers. He cupped his hand over the phone as someone walked up to his desk. "I have to go now. Check in later. Yeah, I agree; it's just the break we've been waiting for." The secretary dropped the list of tomorrow's commitment hearings on his desk. It looked like that would be a light day. He checked over the list for his name on the attorney side and then quickly scanned the names of clients. It was silly, but he always checked to see if anyone he had committed in the past was coming back for a rerun. Randy set the sheet back on his desk, leaned back in his chair, and ran his fingers through his hair. I'll need a haircut if I'm going to work for Elliott.

* * *

The telephone was ringing, and Susan ran into the den, thinking that Elliot must have forgotten to activate his answering machine.

"Hello, Elliott Mason's office. May I help you?"

"Is he there?"

"Elliott is out right now, but he should be back in about an hour. This is his wife. May I take a message?"

"Yes, when he gets back have him call Bill."

"Can I please have your last name and telephone number?"

His voice became tense. "That's not necessary. Just tell him to call Bill."

"All right. I'll give him the message as soon as he gets back."

As Susan put the phone down, she noticed that Elliot had forgotten to put the new number in the slot and that the den needed a woman's touch, preferably a cleaning lady's. For some reason, the housekeeper must have skipped this room. Susan was vacuuming and didn't hear Elliott come into the room.

"What are you doing in here?"

"I'm cleaning up. The housekeeper didn't touch this room."

Elliott threw his keys on the desk. "I'll tell you why! I told her to stay out of this room! The office is mine, and I don't want anyone in here! That's why I have the answering machine. We talked about this before. I intend to keep my business life separate from our personal life."

"Well, you don't have to get so nasty about it! I was trying to help. I came in here to answer the phone, and I noticed the room wasn't cleaned."

Elliott raged. "What the hell do you mean you answered the phone? I told you to ignore it when I'm not here. I just forgot to turn on the answering machine. Dammit anyway, Susan! Stay the fuck out of here!"

"Why are you getting so upset about this? You act as if you've got something to hide. Just what's going on?"

Elliott grabbed Susan's arm and pulled her close to him. "Not a fucking thing! What kind of marriage is this if I can't have a little privacy? You're the one who's always talking about respecting rights."

Susan fought back the tears as she left the room turning around to shout, "All right, Elliott. I'll keep my nose out of your damn office! But if you ask me, you're going overboard about this privacy thing!" She took a breath. "By the way, the call was from someone named Bill. He said you had his number." Susan was shaking with anger. She went into the kitchen and started to keep busy so she could avoid Elliott. After a while, he came into the room, his rage now under control.

"Honey, I'm sorry I blew up at you. I'm only trying to protect you from my business."

"What you mean to protect me from your business? You sound like you're working for the CIA!"

His face tightened. "I told you before, Susan, I have to deal with all sorts of scum. I don't want you to get involved. I'm a criminal lawyer. I don't spend my time advising corporations or writing wills!"

"Elliott, I'm not exactly living a cloistered life. What the hell could I hear that I haven't already heard?"

"Let's not argue. I don't want you involved in my business. Is that clear? My office is off-limits!"

The rest of the day Elliott acted his charming self and for the remainder of the week, and he behaved as if nothing had happened. Susan didn't bring up the episode again, but she vowed never to go into the den. To her, the closed door was becoming a symbol of their relationship.

* * *

When Susan made her Sunday call to her Mother, her mood must've been evident for her mother quickly asked if anything was wrong. She didn't want to go into detail. Besides, it sounded kind of silly complaining that your husband didn't want you to be involved in his business. Susan forced herself to be cheerful as her Mother described the retirement trip she and Susan's Father had planned. They were leaving next week for a two-month European cruise.

"I'm happy for you and Dad. Its time you two did something for yourselves. I'll take a long weekend to visit when you get back.

Give Daddy my love."

"Susan, your Father wants to say hello."

"Hi, Honey, how's married life?"

"Just fine, Dad, just fine. You and Mom have a wonderful trip. I miss you guys; and as soon as you return, I'm coming for a visit."

"That's great. Are you going to bring that new husband of yours?"

"It depends on how well he behaves himself."

There was a moment of silence. "Susan, is everything okay?"

"Sure, I was kidding. Of course, I'm hoping Elliott will come. It's just that he's pretty busy and may not have the time."

"Are you sure everything's okay? You don't sound all right."

"Dad, you say that every time I call. Yes, I'm fine. You and Mom have a wonderful trip and take lots of pictures. Love you"

"Love you too, Baby."

Susan hung up the phone and thought about her parent's relationship. They had their arguments over the years, and there had been rocky times. But she had never seen the anger in her Father that she had already seen many times in Elliott.

* * *

Susan arrived at work on Monday and stopped at the counter. She saw that she was on intake, but only had one appointment. If intakes were light this week, she planned to visit some of the other social service agencies in the area while she still had free time.

Beth, Jan, and Tony were in the conference room when Susan

entered. Beth turned to Susan. "You're married, aren't you, Susan?"

Susan was usually happy to discuss her marriage, ready to bubble over with unsolicited information whenever asked. But today she resented the question. Before Susan could respond with more than a curt "yes", the phone in the conference room rang. Tony picked it up and quickly handed it to her.

"It's Diane with an intake."

"Sorry, Susan, it's starting already. There's an intake on line 304. He sounds shaky and won't give me his name. I'll transfer the call to your office."

"Thanks, Diane. I'll get it right away."

The rest of the day was quiet, only two intakes. Susan had time to think about Elliott's outburst last Saturday. The more she thought about it, the more bizarre the episode seemed. Either Elliott was going through a rough adjustment, or their marriage was in serious trouble. Susan sighed. The honeymoon was over. It was five o'clock, and she dreaded going home.

* * *

The next day started with Diane letting Susan know that a woman called and said she needed to talk to someone about her husband.

"I didn't get much out of her, but she sounded frightened. Her number is in your message box."

"Thanks. I'll call her right away."

Susan looked at the number on the memo and picked up the phone. She glanced down at the name on the paper.

"Hello, is this Tina Collins? I'm Susan Mason from Tri-Valley Mental Health Center. I have a message that you wanted to talk to a therapist. May I help you?"

A shaky voice responded. "I don't know. I don't even know if I should be calling you. My husband is acting strangely. He's not in the room right now, so I can talk for a few minutes."

"Tina, just what is your husband doing?"

"He thinks he has special powers. He says he has a third eye and that it seeks out the devil."

"Tina, do you think you'll be able to get your husband to come into the office?"

"I think so. I asked Bill before I called, and he said he would show the doctor his powers."

"If he's agreed to come, then you should come before he changes his mind. Tina, what's your husband's name?"

"It's William, William Collins. We can be there in about an hour."

"Fine. I'll be waiting."

Dr. Spelling was out for the day, and Dr. Marshall had taken two days off for a continuing education course. That meant Susan would have to make decisions without the benefit of a psychiatrist consultation.

Beth was on the way to her office and stopped in front of Susan's open door. "Busy?"

"No, I'm waiting for an intake. Come on in."

"How are things going for you? I know the first few weeks on the job are always difficult."

Susan nodded in agreement. "I underestimated how much more responsibility would come with the territory; but on the whole, it's going pretty well."

Beth sat down in the chair opposite Susan. "You're luckier than most of us. With your background, you know what to expect from the patients. I still feel guilty every time I think of those poor patients I cut my professional teeth on!" She smiled at Susan. "Well, I just wanted to stop in to say that I'm glad you're here. And if you have any questions or need any help, just let me know."

"Thanks, I'm feeling more comfortable every day; and I'm going to take you up on that offer. I want to talk to you about a telephone intake I just received."

"Sure, go ahead."

"I spoke to the man's wife for only a few minutes. But from what she said, it sounds like he's psychotic and needs hospitalization. I'm hoping he may have insurance, but I'm not sure. Do you know what the bed situation is at St. Stephen's?"

Beth's response was not encouraging. "I hope the guy has insurance. I talked to Richard Malcolm this morning, and there are no grant beds available. Unfortunately, if a patient can't get into St. Stephen's, they must go to Brighton State Hospital."

"Is it difficult to get someone admitted to Brighton?"

Beth smiled weakly. "Susan, far be it from me to negatively influence you. However, if you have a patient that's threatening to hang himself and you have to send him to Brighton, I suggest you send him with the rope tied around his neck!"

The intercom buzzed. Susan pushed down the button. "Okay, Diane, I'll be right out."

Beth walked out with Susan. "If it's necessary, try Richard Malcolm again. Maybe someone will be discharged today."

Several people were sitting in the waiting room. Off to the side was a pretty woman with blond hair who was around twenty-seven years old. She was sitting next to a man who looked to be about thirty. He was dressed in an expensive, but rumpled, suit and was busy muttering to himself. Susan walked up to them and smiled.

"Hello, my name is Susan Mason. Are you Mr. and Mrs. Collins?"

The woman hesitated for a moment then responded, "Yes, I'm Tina; and this is my husband, William."

"Shall we talk in my office?"

Tina got up, but William just sat and stared at Susan. She smiled confidently at him. "William, your wife was telling me that you have some special powers. I'd be interested in hearing about them."

The man grinned smugly in the direction of his wife. "See, I told you the world has been waiting for me." He got up and followed Susan and his wife into the office.

"William, do you want to tell me what has been happening to you?"

"Yes, call me Bill." he smiled at Susan. "It's great; God has visited me! He implanted a golden chip in my brain." He smiled at Susan again. "I shouldn't brag, but gold is just for His special friends. Now, this chip activates my third eye, and with it, I can see the devil in people." Bill sat back in the chair with a smug look on his face. "Well, what do you think about that?"

Susan gave him an admiring look. "I must admit, I am impressed! Do you mind if I ask your wife a few questions? She's probably wondering what's been happening this past week with all the changes you've been through."

Bill glanced over at Tina. She cringed from the strange grin. "Yes, I think Tina's upset. She's been acting strange lately. Maybe you can help her."

"Well, I'll try. Tina, can you tell me what's been going on?"

The woman reluctantly joined the bizarre conversation. "It started about a week ago. Bill changed. He went out and bought a Bible and started to read the Scriptures out loud. He was reading them day and night. Bill kept telling me to get down on my knees and repent. Then two days ago he said that God had given him instructions to rid the world of evil." Tina looked at Susan with a frightened expression. "He thinks he has this invisible eye that finds the devil. This morning he said he saw the devil in me and that he would have to destroy it. That's when I called here."

"Bill, is that what happened?"

"Yes, it's true. As Tina said, I have the power."

Susan leaned closer to him. "I think this is an important discovery, and maybe it would be better if you talked to a doctor about this. If I can arrange to have you see a doctor at the hospital, would you be willing to go there?"

He slapped the arm of the chair and smiled at Susan. "Yes, I know I'm important, too; and I should let them study me!"

"That's good of you, Bill. Besides, you must be tired; and they can give you something to help you sleep. You go back to the waiting room; I'll have your wife give me insurance information. And then I'll make arrangements at the hospital."

"Okay, I'll wait. Do you have a Bible I can read?"

No, but I think someone left some religious pamphlets on the counter. Just help yourself."

With Bill out of the room, Susan turned to Tina. "Is there anything else you want to tell me?"

Tears ran down Tina's cheeks. "Yes, I'm scared of him. He thinks I'm the devil. And you heard him-he said I should be destroyed!"

"Tina, I don't want to frighten you more than you already are, but Bill could be dangerous. And he's unpredictable. It's important not to challenge him. He believes the things that he is saying, and you can't argue with a delusion. I believe taking him to the hospital would be best for both of you. The secretary had you fill out a form when you came in, and I noticed that you left employment and insurance blank."

Susan handed Tina a tissue. She wiped her eyes, taking a moment to answer. "Yes, Bill is self-employed. He does freelance jobs. I don't know much about it. He has been doing very well, so

I quit my job a couple of months ago. We signed up for new health insurance last month, but it doesn't go into effect for another three weeks. We have some cash; only I don't know where Bill has his account. He takes care of the money."

Susan look concerned. "We have a grant at St. Stephen's, but I think the beds are full. We may have to put him in Brighton State Hospital. I'll call and see what I can do."

Susan flipped the Rolodex and pulled out a card with Richard Malcolm's number. She crossed her fingers as the phone rang. "Richard, this is Susan Mason from Tri-Valley. I have a man in my office that I believe needs hospitalization, but he doesn't have insurance. By any chance do you have a bed? I heard from Beth this morning that the beds are pretty tight."

"Sorry, Susan, I hate to turn down your first request; but we don't have an empty bed. Even the ones we keep available for emergencies have been filled."

"I'm sorry, too. It looks like I'll have to send this patient to Brighton. Thanks anyway, Richard."

"I hope I'll be able to be more helpful next time."

Susan looked sadly at Tina as she put the receiver down.

"They're filled up. I'm sorry, but we'll have to send Bill to Brighton. I'll give them a call now." She pulled another card out of the Rolodex. This time Susan reluctantly pushed the numbers. "Admissions please," she nervously swung her foot as she waited. "Hello, this is Susan Mason, social worker supervisor from Tri-Valley Mental Health Center. I'm calling to let you know that Mr. William Collins will be coming in for an evaluation."

Susan listened for a few minutes with a disgusted look on her face. "No, I'm not a doctor; but I would not be sending him unless I thought hospitalization was necessary. Yes, I've already tried St. Stephen's. They don't have any beds. Mr. and Mrs. Collins should be there within an hour. I'll send a copy of my evaluation with Mrs. Collins. Thank you. Please call me if I can be of any help."

She put the phone down and turned to Tina. "Please call and let me know as soon as Bill is admitted."

Tina looked a little relieved as she stood up. "Thanks for helping Bill. I didn't know what to do! I'll call back this afternoon."

Susan walked out to the waiting room with Tina and sat down on a chair next to Bill. "I've made arrangements for you to talk to a doctor at Brighton Hospital."

"All right. But she's the devil, you know, and one of these days she has to be destroyed." Bill smiled and shook his finger. "But not today; her time has not yet come."

As they left the center, Tina glanced back with a frightened look. Susan mouthed the words, "Call me."

She worried about Bill and Tina for the rest of the day. She called Brighton at four-thirty, and the clerk told her that William was still waiting for an evaluation. At five o'clock Susan went home, relieved that at least he was at the hospital.

CHAPTER 14
NO LONGER FRIENDS

Susan was browning beef when Elliot arrived home. "I thought a taco salad would taste good."

"Sounds good to me; want me to help grate the cheese?"

"Sure, the grater is in the top drawer by the sink. Are you going to be home this evening?"

"I hope to be, but I may have to take care of some business."

"Oh, not again," said Susan. As she pulled the spoon across the bottom of the skillet, a chunk of hot greasy beef flew up and landed on her wrist. "Ouch!"

Elliott dropped the grater and stepped over to Susan. "Here, let me see. Oh, Honey, you've got a burn." He steered her toward the sink and ran cold water over her wrist. After several minutes, he gently dried her arm with a towel and lightly kissed the red mark. "There, does that feel better?"

"Yes, much better." Elliott was so attentive that Susan forgot her irritation over another evening meeting.

They cleared off the kitchen table together and had just sat down in the living room when the den telephone rang. In the den, Elliott noticed the open door and rolled his chair over until he could reach it with his foot. Susan was watching, and they had eye contact for a second before the door slammed shut. She cringed at the sound; it felt like a slap across her face. He was in there for only a couple of minutes, but it seemed forever.

"It's just what I expected. There's a problem, and I'm the only one who can handle it. I won't be gone long. Wait up, and we can have a drink before bed." Elliott kissed Susan and left the house before she had a chance to answer.

* * *

Thirty minutes later, Elliott pulled up in front of a seedy looking tavern. The place was empty except for three customers leaning on the bar. There were two men in a back booth. Elliott quickly walked back to the booth and sat down with them. The waitress followed him and waited for his order, "scotch and soda."

A rough, muscular man started to talk. "We got to his place at about six-thirty. He must have fought with his old lady. The guy sat in his car in the driveway for an hour before he took off. We followed him to a tavern just down the street. You can see his car from here. What you want us to do?"

The waitress returned and set a drink in front of Elliott. He waited until she walked away before he responded. "Hal, the guy was given money, a lot of money for the merchandise; and we expected delivery two days ago. According to our source in Florida, they handed it over to him last Saturday. We have some nervous investors who are making demands of me. I want you to find out what is going on and locate the shipment. Then teach the guy a lesson. Don't eliminate him, but leave a permanent reminder to anyone else who may get the same idea."

The second man in the booth, a heavy-set man with tattoos on his neck, pulled a switchblade from his pocket. He flipped it open and ran his finger gleefully along the edge. "Don't worry; we'll teach him a real good lesson."

Elliott spoke to the muscular man. "Hal, keep your friend in line. Remember the main object is to get information. If we don't get it today, leave him with something to think about. And remember, I want him to be able to talk later. Get the message?"

Hal grinned at Elliott and nodded. "Yeah, I get the message." He stood up and punched the other man on the arm. "Come on, Weirdo, let's get to work."

The waitress came back to the booth. Elliott smiled pleasantly at the woman. "They'll be back in a little while; in the meantime, I'll have another scotch and soda."

Elliott nursed his drink as he impatiently drummed his fingers on the table and glanced toward the entrance. About a half hour later, the men returned and slipped into the back booth. The owner of the switchblade pulled it out, pushed the button, and grinned as a bloodied blade protruded. Elliott looked annoyed. "You didn't get the information?"

"No, but don't worry. He'll be seeing things your way." The man reached into his side pocket and tossed something out. Blood splattered on Elliott's tie as an eyeball rolled across the table.

"Jesus Christ, get that thing out of here! What if someone sees it? Wipe up the blood and get rid of it!"

Hal punched his buddy in the arm. "Why the hell did you pick up that bloody mess? You and your fucking souvenirs!"

The man reached across the table. "What should I do with it?"

Hal punched his arm again. "Put it back in your pocket, stupid!"

Elliott took out a wad of bills. "Here, this is for tonight. Keep watching him and his wife. He hid that merchandise somewhere, and I want it found. I'm going to leave now; you two stay here for a while. I don't want anyone seeing us leave together."

* * *

Elliott shouted as he opened the front door. "I'm home, Honey. Let's have that nightcap."

He kicked off his shoes and got comfortable on the couch while Susan made the drinks. As she leaned over and set them on the coffee table, Susan suddenly stopped and stared at Elliott's tie. "Hey, there's blood on your tie!"

Elliott looked surprised but quickly recovered. "Oh, the bartender broke a glass and cut his finger. If I realized that he sprayed my tie, I would have insisted on a free drink."

She loosened the tie. "Here, let me run some cold water on it before the stain sets." He smiled at her. "You're sweet."

* * *

Diane motioned for Susan to come to the counter as soon as she walked in the door Thursday morning. "What's up?"

"I don't know; Tina Collins has called three times already. She sounds upset. Here's her number."

"Thanks. I bet something went wrong at Brighton. I'll call right away."

She took the message to her office. Just as she reached for the phone, the intercom buzzed. "Susan, it's Tina again, on line 302."

"I just got in Tina. How did things go?"

Tina started to cry. "I just feel terrible, Mrs. Mason. Somebody cut out Bill's eye!"

Susan was stunned and didn't respond.

"Mrs. Mason, are you there?"

"Yes, Tina, I'm here. What happened?"

"We waited at Brighton until after five o'clock. The doctor said Bill wasn't a danger to anyone and gave him some medicine and told me to bring him back to the clinic."

"All the way home, Bill kept telling me I was the daughter of Satan and that my time had come." Tina started to sob. "Mrs. Mason, I was afraid of him; so I told him he had to sleep in the car. But after a while, he left and went out drinking. The police called me and said to come to Riley Hospital. They found Bill in an alley behind a tavern. The bartender said two men came in and bought Bill a few drinks. Then they went outside with him.

He must've put up a fight when they tried to rob him, so they cut out his eye. None of this would have happened if they had kept him at Brighton."

"Tina, I can't believe Bill was not admitted to Brighton."

Tina sobbed. "That's not all. He must have taken all his medication because between the alcohol and the drugs, Bill almost died! The emergency room doctor said there's a good chance Bill will have permanent brain damage."

"Tina, what hospital is Bill at now?"

"Riley General. They're going to keep him there until he's stabilized and then transfer him to Brighton. It's all my fault; I should have let him stay in the house."

"Tina, you did the right thing. Bill might have hurt you."

"Can I come in today? I need to talk to somebody."

"Of course, Tina. Have you had any sleep?"

"No, I've been up all night."

"You must be exhausted. Why don't you sleep for a few hours and come this afternoon? My three o'clock appointment canceled."

"Okay," said Tina. I'm so tired that I can't stand up. I'm going to take a nap and come in later."

Susan put the phone down and sat for several minutes letting everything sink in. Then she went and knocked on the door of Dr. Spelling's office, remembering his lecture on her first day. Well, she reassured herself, he wanted to be the first to know about any problems.

"Yes?"

"It's Susan, Dr. Spelling. I need to talk to you. It's important."

"Sure, come on in."

As usual, his desk was overflowing with medical journals and computer printouts; and Susan had to search for an empty chair. It was cool with the air-conditioning on, but Susan's hands felt clammy. Less than two weeks on the job and the first patient she tried to hospitalize ended up losing his eye; and he possibly has brain damage.

"Susan, you look upset. Is anything wrong?"

"Yes, I saw a man named William Collins on intake yesterday. He was psychotic, and I felt he needed hospitalization. And I tried to get him into St. Stephen's, but there were no grant beds."

"Did you try Brighton?"

"Yes, I called and sent my evaluation to the hospital with his wife. I checked back at 4:30, but they still hadn't seen him. I never dreamed that they wouldn't admit him. He was paranoid, had delusions of grandeur, and was threatening his wife."

Dr. Spelling responded, "I take it he didn't get admitted?"

"Right, they sent Bill home with medication and told his wife to bring him here to see a doctor. She was too frightened to let him sleep in the house, so she told him to sleep in the car. Instead, he went out drinking where some creeps tried to roll him. When Bill resisted, they cut his eye out."

"No! Where is he now?"

He's at Riley General. He may have permanent brain damage from the medication and alcohol. The doctor at Riley plans to transfer Bill to Brighton when he stabilizes."

"I'll call the Chief of Staff at Brighton today. We can't encourage her, but I hope Mrs. Collins sues the bastard who refused admission. Susan, I know you feel bad about this; but it sounds like you did all you could."

Susan stood up, too upset to remain sitting. "If only there had been a bed available at St. Stephen's."

Dr. Spelling's voice tightened. "I wish we never had to deal with Brighton. Every couple of years there's an investigation; but as soon as the publicity dies down, they start doing the same damn things all over again! Susan, right now you'd better concentrate on Mrs. Collins. I'm sure she has a lot of guilt over this."

"Yes, she's upset. I have an appointment to see her this afternoon."

"Good. In the meantime, write up a complete report of the incident so I can launch a formal complaint."

Susan walked toward the door. "I'll get started on it right away."

She spent the next hour writing the report. It was 11:30 before she remembered her lunch date with Mark.

* * *

For the second time that day Susan's hands felt clammy. Her anxiety only increased as she got closer to the restaurant. For a moment she sat in the parking lot and contemplated turning the car around to leave, but she didn't.

Mark was already inside. "Hello there. You're just in time; the hostess is getting a table for us."

Susan followed the hostess as she walked through the dining room which was built to resemble an English pub. She wished now that she hadn't agreed to meet in such a cozy and intimate setting. And why wear that blue dress today, knowing it was Mark's favorite?

Mark gave the waitress their order and then leaned over the small table. Susan felt his eyes sweep over her, noticing how good she looked, but not commenting. "All right, now tell me about the new job."

Susan smiled weakly. "It doesn't seem new anymore, so much has happened this week. But if you want to listen, I can certainly use a friendly ear."

Mark winced when Susan told him about Bill Collins. "Susan, it sounds horrible; but sometimes people who should get admitted slip through. You forgot about the pressure we're under to tightly screen intakes when the beds are full, and the staff is worn out."

"I remember. But Bill was psychotic, Mark, and threatening to destroy his wife. I guess one's perspective changes when you're on the outside looking in."

"Are you telling me that you joined the other camp?"

"No, it's just that at the hospital the main concern was getting patients out; and some of the staff thought of the family as the enemy. Out in the community, you've got the whole family to be concerned about."

Mark put his hand up. "Susan, I don't want to change the subject, but we don't have much time; and I wanted to tell you that Karen has left Linton. She got a transfer to another state facility."

"That's great, but I'd be a lot happier if she had resigned."

"Now let's get off the shop talk. For instance, how are your parents doing?"

"Great! They're leaving for an extended European cruise in a couple of days."

"Sounds terrific. I'd settle for a long weekend. How is the rest your life going?"

Her smile faded. "By the rest of my life, you mean my marriage?"

Mark raised his eyebrows. "Do I detect some hostility in your voice? If I hit a nerve, I apologize."

Susan's eyes started to tear. "You have hit a nerve. I don't know if it's me or if I married a paranoid. Honestly, Mark, he is so secretive about his work, you'd swear he was a priest guarding confessional secrets."

"I don't know if Elliott is paranoid, Susan. That's a rather strong term. But you, of all people, should understand about confidentiality. Lawyers have the same ethical code."

"I don't know, Mark. I keep telling myself that; but for some reason, that excuse doesn't satisfy me. It's not just one thing; it's a whole lot of feelings. I don't know, maybe it's indigestion and not my intuition."

"Susan, you are under a lot of strain with the new job. I hate to say I told you so; but it seems to me that we already had the conversation about a new husband, a new job, and all the additional stress in your life."

"I hope you're right. Otherwise, my husband will not turn out to be the man I married which is a little embarrassing for someone in my field. Wouldn't you agree?"

Mark chuckled. "I don't have a word to say. After all, look at me, letting you slip away wasn't the smartest thing, especially for someone in my field."

Instead of feeling comforted about his words, Susan felt resentment. "It's easy for you to say that now. After all, I'm safely married."

Mark's expression turned to hurt. "You're right, Susan, talking about a commitment I should have made nine months ago is inappropriate. Maybe we should stick to shop talk."

The mood now was strained with conversation limited to comments about the food and weather. Susan wanted to lash out at Mark, thinking if only he had committed, she wouldn't be in a marriage that was becoming more difficult by the day. Instead, she forcefully smashed a lump of potato with her fork.

The waitress poured another coffee and left the check. Mark caught Susan's eyes and gave her a faint smile. "It's been a rather awkward lunch."

"Yes," said Susan. "We generate a lot of tension."

Mark put his hand over Susan's, but she slowly pulled away. Mark acted as if he didn't notice and sat back in his chair. "Susan, I'm not saying this to hurt you, but I think that it might be better if we didn't see each other." He paused and took a breath. "I thought that maybe time had healed some of the hurt, but we both have too many bruised feelings to continue a close friendship."

Susan had a sudden panic. Mark had always been there, in the background, but still there. Despite her anger, she was afraid to lose him entirely. "Do you think that's necessary?"

"Susan, think about what happens when we see each other. Then you tell me if you think it's necessary?"

Susan paused for a moment and then gave the only answer she could. "You're right. We have to stop seeing each other."

"There's something else, Susan. You sounded scared when you talked about Elliott. Maybe you're over-reacting; but if there is any trouble, will you promise that you'll call me? Irrespective of decisions made today, I'll always be there if you need me."

"It's getting late, and I have to get back to the clinic." Susan avoided his eyes, smiled, picked up her purse, and left for the ladies room. Thank God, it was empty. She locked herself in one of the tiny stalls, and tears she had been holding back poured out of her in muffled sobs. Why was she reacting this way? What was going on? She was newly married to one man and crying because another was walking out of her life . . . for the second time. All of a sudden, the toilet in the next stall flushed.

"Miss, are you all right in there?"

Susan leaned back against the metal door, filled with embarrassment. Whoever was sitting next door had heard all her sobs. "Yes, I'm okay." She waited for the sound of water running and finally a door closing, and then came out of the cubicle.

Back at the center, Susan dashed to the washroom again. She was splashing cold water on her face when Beth walked in.

"Susan, is something wrong?"

"Oh, no, I'm just washing my face." Susan started to cry again. "I feel like a fool; I can't seem to stop crying. I'll be okay in a minute. I have to be; I see Mrs. Collins in a little while."

"I heard about that; it was terrible. But you shouldn't blame yourself."

"Oh, that is not what I'm crying about; at least it's not the main reason. It's just one of those days. You know, it feels like you're in a swimming pool; and every time you come up for air, someone pushes your head down."

"Yes, I know what you're talking about; I've had a few of those days myself. If you want to talk about it, I'm a good listener."

"Thanks, Beth." She dried her face and put on fresh makeup. Tina was sitting in the waiting room when Susan returned from the washroom. Tina's pale face reflected the emotional strain of the past twenty-four hours. Susan walked over and touched her shoulder, "Tina, let's go into my office."

The next hour, Tina went over the events of the past two weeks.

Susan learned that Bill had been in trouble with the law. Tina was evasive about what kind of legal problems, and Susan didn't feel that this was the time to push for information. When she got up to leave, Tina seemed more relaxed; but Susan knew that the full impact of what had happened hadn't yet hit.

"Tina, do you want to make another appointment? I think it might help to talk."

"Yes, I was hoping I could come back. I don't know what's going to happen with Bill. It's all so frightening."

Susan made the appointment for Monday. By then, Bill would probably be stabilized and transferred to Brighton; and from what Susan had learned about the place, Tina would need to talk.

After charting and clearing off her desk, Susan picked up the phone, dialed, and then crossed her fingers. "Maggie, it's Susan. I was hoping you hadn't left work. Elliott is working late tonight. Would you like to have dinner with me?"

"You bet," Maggie responded. "I'm dying to hear about your new job. Why don't you come over to my place and help me to get rid of my leftovers?"

"Okay," said Susan. "But only if the leftovers are not doggie bags from Linton's cafeteria."

"Don't worry. Those are only for houseguests that have overstayed their welcome. I'll be home by five-thirty. See you then."

"Fine. I'll bring the wine."

CHAPTER 15
BILL AT BRIGHTON

Susan left the office, picked up a bottle of Merlot, and headed for Maggie's apartment. She ran her fingers down the list of names on the wall until she reached Maggie's and pushed the button.

"Susan?"

"Yes, it's me."

"I'll buzz you in."

Susan stopped outside the open door. "Hello, anyone in here?"

"Come on in!" Maggie responded. "Close the door behind you; I'm in the kitchen."

Susan walked into the living room and shook her head at the lived-in look. The couch was the first thing she noticed: comfortable and overstuffed with a wildflower print. Sunday's Tribune was still scattered in various parts of the room. Maggie was fixing a chef salad on the counter in the small galley kitchen. Susan walked in, set down the bottle of wine, and pulled up a stool. "Salad looks delicious. Shall I pour the wine?"

"Sure, Kid. There are glasses in that cabinet over your head."

Maggie pulled another stool over as Susan poured the wine. A few minutes into the meal, Maggie set her fork down. "Well, what's wrong?"

Susan looked up with an amused expression. "You always know, don't you?"

"I do." Maggie laughed. "But you're so easy to read it doesn't take a hell of a lot of talent. If you want to talk about what's bothering you, I'm here; if not, that's okay, too." Maggie lifted her glass of wine, "To friendship."

Susan touched her glass to Maggie's; "Friendship. And you're right, I do need to talk."

"Well, what's the problem: the new job or your new marriage?"

"Both."

"Both! It sounds like you're batting a thousand. Dr. Denning mentioned he was having lunch with you today. One look at the man when he returned, and I knew something was wrong."

Susan's face clouded. "Mark and I hoped we could stay friends, but that doesn't seem to be working. We'll have to forget each other."

"Okay then, we'll save him for later," said Maggie. "So what's the problem at work? You sounded happy when I talked to you last week."

"It's not the job; it's me. The place is terrific, but so far every case I've handled has gone sour. My latest patient had his eye cut out because I couldn't get him hospitalized." Maggie stared at Susan for a few moments. "Do you want to run that past me again? Because either my brain cells are in much worse shape than I thought, or this is a scene from a horror movie."

Susan managed to smile. "I guess I should fill in the blanks."

"That might help." Maggie picked up the bottle of wine. "You grab the glasses; it's more comfortable in the living room. I have a feeling this is going to be a late evening."

An hour and two glasses of wine later, Susan brought up her husband. "I can't talk to Elliott."

Maggie kicked off her shoes and put her feet on the coffee table. She turned to Susan. "Why can't you talk to him?"

"Oh, he can be sweet at times, and I know we're going through a lot of stress. It's hard for two independent people to adjust to marriage."

"That's true, Susan, but you're not answering my question."

Susan's eyes glistened. "I don't know what's going on, Maggie. He's so secretive; he never talks about his work and gets very angry when I ask him anything. He has a terrible temper, and sometimes I'm afraid of him."

Maggie looked alarmed. "Has he hurt you or threatened you?"

Susan shook her head. "No, I don't think he would ever hurt me. It's just that Elliott seems to be on edge; you know, like there's something under the surface. But if he loses his temper, he always apologizes or does something sweet to make up for it. I don't know, Maggie. Sometimes I think he's two different people, but maybe it's just me. After all, everyone needs time to adjust to marriage. I guess I'm just expecting too much, too soon."

Maggie poured another glass of wine. "This loosens my tongue."

"Sure, and when did you ever need help loosening your tongue?"

Maggie chuckled. "Then at least I'll be able to speak my mind tonight and blame the drink tomorrow."

"Uh oh, this doesn't sound good."

"Susan, maybe what you said about expecting too much, too soon is true. But, I have never trusted him. There's something about Elliott I don't like."

Susan's mouth tightened. "And I know what it is! He isn't Mark!"

"All I can say is that I wish you had waited for Mark."

"You never give up, do you? I have to get home."

Maggie pulled herself out of the overstuffed couch. "Look, Susan, please don't go home angry. I can't help how I feel. I care about you, and I worry about you. Do your best to make this marriage work; but for God's sake, don't let pride keep you in something that isn't right. Listen to me sounding like an over-protective mother."

Susan laughed out loud. "That's it, Maggie, you fit the bill perfectly. But I do have to go home. Thanks for dinner and for listening. I'll be talking to you soon."

* * *

It was after 10 o'clock when Susan pulled her car into the driveway. When she opened the door, the first thing she saw was a light under the door of the den. Susan walked over and reached for the doorknob, but quickly pulled her hand back and decided to knock.

Elliott called out, "Susan, I'm on the phone! I'll be right out."

He lowered his voice to a whisper. Susan stood outside the door for a moment, but then walked back to the living room. She turned on a lamp and picked up a magazine from the coffee table, thumbing through it as she waited for him to finish. It wasn't long before Elliott cheerfully opened the door. "Hello there. I was wondering where you were."

"I tried to call late this afternoon, but you had already left. I knew you were having a meeting, so I had dinner with Maggie."

"That was nice; but in the future, I would like to know about these things beforehand. If anything happened, I wouldn't even know where you were."

"Elliott, nothing's going to happen. I did try to call; besides, I don't know where you are most of the time!"

"My business calls for a lot of meetings." Elliott's face darkened. "Why did you need to go to Maggie's apartment? She doesn't even work with you anymore!"

"It had nothing to do with work. I just spent an evening having a pleasant conversation with a friend, something I haven't been able to have with you in some time."

"I don't want you talking about our business with outsiders! I expect loyalty from a wife. I don't know what's happening to you. You act like you don't want to be married." Susan realized things were out-of-control. "Elliott, we're both tired. Let's not blow things out of proportion. I just had dinner with a friend. Things will look different after we get some sleep."

"I have a problem at work; I guess I'm edgy. It has been a long day, and I'm going to bed. Are you coming?"

"You go ahead; I'll be up in a few minutes. I'm thirsty. I want to get a cold drink first."

Susan went into the kitchen and sat at the table wondering what the hell was going on. Elliott was acting stranger by the day. He said something had gone wrong at work. Was that why Elliott was so upset? But since he wouldn't talk about his work, she certainly couldn't help him. Susan got up and turned off the light. As she walked towards the stairs, she passed the closed door to the den. Susan glanced up the stairs and knew that by now Elliott was asleep. She thought about the files in his desk and the recorder on his phone and was tempted to go in and look for some answers. But instead, she shook her head and hurried up the stairs. Susan felt sheepish for even thinking about sneaking into his office. Oh God, she thought as she waited for sleep. Is this what our marriage has become?

* * *

The trainer touched the elephant on his trunk and murmured words of praise as the animal clumsily sank to the ground and rolled over. Randy Sloan and Tom Rivers applauded along with the rest of the onlookers. The crowd slowly thinned as Randy and Tom made their way to an empty bench. Tom cracked a peanut and popped it into his mouth. "Zoos-I love them. They're a great place to work out your problems."

Randy was getting annoyed. "Christ, Tom, you make me watch an elephant doing dog tricks, not to mention that half hour wait for you at the stinking lion house. Come on; it's Friday. Let's get this meeting over. And believe me, our next one will be over coffee."

"How was I to know that you're an animal hater?"

Randy rolled his eyes. "I am not an animal hater, but can we get the show on the road?"

"Okay, okay." Their conversation paused for a moment as they waited for a mother to retrieve a child that had toddled over to their bench. "Our sources on the street say that something went wrong with the shipment due last Saturday. The middleman picked up the drugs in Florida; but somewhere between Florida and here, it disappeared. The guy's name is Bill Collins. He was worked over and had an eye put out. They must have beaten him senseless; he's at Brighton now."

Randy leaned forward, "Brighton State Hospital? That's where they send the vegetables. Do you have anything else?"

"No, just that there's a lot of tension on the street. We know that Elliott Mason is connected, but we still don't have any evidence."

"Well, we may have some soon if Elliott brings me on board."

Randy stood up. "Come on. You like to tour zoos. It's time you visited a people zoo. We're going to see if we can get any information from Bill Collins. But from what you said, it doesn't look promising." An hour later they were sitting in the office of Brighton's chief of social service.

* * *

"Mr. Desmond, I appreciate your position; but you're not aware of what's at stake. We are not interested in bringing charges against Mr. Collins, only in getting information. Actually, after seeing him, I doubt that he even knows his name which is why we need to see his chart. Maybe something was said on the intake that could help us."

Mr. Desmond shook his head. "I'm sorry, Mr. Rivers. Without a court order, there's nothing I can do. I want to help, but my hands are tied."

Tom walked toward the door. "Thanks, I know what you mean. Just one more thing, could you tell me how he got here?"

"Yes, I don't think that would be breaking any rules."

Mr. Desmond flipped open the chart. "Let's see; he's a referral from Tri-Valley Mental Health Center. Oh no, that was last Friday. We admitted Mr. Collins this past Tuesday. He was a transfer from Riley General."

"Are you saying that he was seen here last Friday?"

Mr. Desmond realized that he had said too much. He quickly shut the chart. "I can't say any more. If you will excuse me, I have a meeting to attend."

Randy put out his hand. "Look, we won't be bothering you further. We want to find out what happened to Mr. Collins before he came here. Who referred him from Tri-Valley?"

He grudgingly opened the chart again. "It was a social worker, Susan Mason. And now gentlemen, if you'll excuse me, I do have a meeting. When Tom and Randy left the building, Tom was the first to speak. "Did you hear that? Susan Mason referred him. Is she in on this?"

Randy lit a cigarette. "No, I'd stake my life on it. Collins must live in the area that the clinic serves. She must have seen them at the intake. That means that Bill Collins was off his rocker before he was worked over."

Randy put the car in gear.

Tom asked, "Are you going to make contact with her again?"

"Yes, I think a visit this Monday to Susan's new office would be appropriate, especially since I'll be in the neighborhood. Perhaps we could have a chatty lunch. It's late, Tom; I'll drop you at your car, unless you prefer the zoo."

* * *

Just before noon, Dr. Spelling walked past the open door of Susan's office and waved a hearty goodbye to everyone. He was leaving on his vacation, a ten-day outdoor survival course in Colorado. Susan watched Dr. Spelling as he walked down the hall. "I didn't think he was the type."

Tony laughed. "He isn't. Dr. Spelling comes back exhausted, sunburned, with pulled muscles, and poison ivy rashes. But, he always claims he has gotten back in touch with his soul and, of course, has communed with nature."

Jan added, "Dr. Spelling left Beth in charge while he's away."

Susan stood up. "I don't know about you people, but I'm starving. If we're finished, let's get some lunch."

Back at work, Susan was pulling some charts to review when the intercom buzzed.

"Susan, its Tina Collins on line 304. She wants to know if you can see her this afternoon. I reminded her that she has an appointment on Monday, but she sounds upset."

"Okay, Diane, I'll talk to her."

"Hello, Tina. This is Susan Mason. The secretary said you wanted to come in today."

"Yes, it's important. I have to talk to someone, and you're the only person I can trust."

Susan replied, "I have time now. Do you want to talk on the phone for a while?"

"No, I can't tell you anything on the phone! I have to talk to you in person!"

"All right, I'm just doing paperwork. If you want to come in now, I can see you."

Tina sighed. "Oh, thank you! I'll leave right away."

Susan hung up the phone thinking Tina must have gone to Brighton. If it was only half as bad as Susan heard, she had good reason to be upset.

It wasn't long before the intercom buzzed. "I'll be right out."

Susan was shocked when she saw Tina sitting on the edge of the waiting room chair. She had expected her to look better after a full night's rest. Instead, Tina's face was pale and washed out. There were dark circles under her eyes, and her blonde hair was hanging limp and stringy.

"Tina? Come on in."

Susan closed the office door and sat down. Tina started to cry. She grabbed a tissue, dabbed at her eyes, and then blew her nose.

"I'm sorry, Mrs. Mason. It's just that I'm so upset!"

"I can imagine Brighton must've been a shock to you."

Tina's voice shook. "Yes, but it's… it's something else. I don't know if I should even be telling you!"

"What's going on, Tina?"

Tina looked up suspiciously. "If I tell you something, is it in confidence? I mean, can you tell anyone else?"

Susan reassured her, "Tina, do you remember the form I gave you and Bill the first time you were here? It explained all about that. We keep everything confidential except if you are planning to harm yourself or someone else. But I don't think you've come here to tell me you're going to harm somebody."

"No," Tina hesitated, "what if someone is breaking the law? Do you turn them in?"

"Only if they are a danger to them self or others; I'm a therapist, not a police officer."

Tina took a deep breath. "You're not going to like me anymore when I tell you this."

Susan caught Tina's eyes and smiled. "I may not like what you've done, Tina, but I'll still like you."

"Okay, I have to tell someone." Tina turned her head away from Susan so that they wouldn't make eye contact. "Bill is a drug dealer, mainly cocaine. He takes delivery of the big shipments and then cuts the stuff, but not at home. Bill rents an apartment for that. He gets in touch with the area dealers; they buy the coke from him and mix it with baking soda and bleach to make crack. Then he takes his percentage of the money and turns the rest over to some front group. Bill has contact with only one man, but I think the group puts money up front for the main shipment. It's an investment club; their return, plus interest, comes after Bill makes the sale to the area dealers."

Susan sat back with an expression of disbelief on her face. Tina looked up in alarm. "Honest, Mrs. Mason, I didn't know what Bill was doing. It wasn't until after we married that I found out about this. Then it was too late; I knew too much. I couldn't leave even if I wanted. I was afraid. Besides, I love him!"

Susan stood up, paced around the room, and then returned to her chair. "Tina, why are you telling me about this?"

"Tina started to cry again. "I have to tell someone. I'm so scared; I don't know where to turn! I can't go to the police; this group has connections all over the place. They're all prominent people! Last week, Bill got a big drug delivery. He told me once that he rents apartments by the month so that he can change them every couple of months."

Tina stopped to wipe her eyes. "About a month ago, he took me with him to help because he wasn't feeling well; and he had already made the appointments. That was the first time I ever went with him. I don't even know where the place was; it was dark, and I've never been in that neighborhood. And for all I know, he may have rented a different apartment this month." She lifted her tear stained face. "Yesterday two men came to my house and took me to the hospital to find out from Bill where he hid the drugs."

Susan asked, "Did Bill tell them?"

Tina shook her head. "They couldn't get anything out of him, and Bill didn't even recognize me! I don't think he'll ever be right again. The men said they know that Bill told me where he hid the drugs and that I better come up with the stuff pretty quick. Honest! I don't know where the drugs are, Mrs. Mason; I don't know what I'm going to do!"

Susan sat quietly for a moment. "Tina, I think there's only one thing you can do. You must go to the police."

Tina's eyes opened wide in alarm. "No! You don't know what you're talking about! This isn't a little side-business. There are powerful people involved, and that shipment is worth millions." Tina clenched her hands. "Damn him! Bill's lying there in the hospital and doesn't know or care about a thing, and I'm left here with all this shit!"

Tina jumped up and leaned over Susan's desk. "They'll kill me if I can't find that stuff! You don't understand; they think I'm hiding it! They'll use me as an example to keep everybody else in line." Tears ran down her cheek. "They were the men who cut out Bill's eye!"

Susan stood up again. "Oh my God, Tina, that's all the more reason to get help. You have to go to the police. Or else, my husband is a lawyer; you could talk to him. I'm sure he would help you."

"No, I can't do that!" Tina walked toward the door. "I have to go. Can I come back again? It helps to talk to someone."

"Yes, of course. But please think about what I said. You need more help than I can offer you."

Tina stopped in the waiting room and pulled the blinds apart. "Look, their outside in that blue car. They were following me all day! I have to go. I've got to find it! Or I'm dead!"

Susan put her arm out to stop her, but Tina brushed her aside and rushed out the door. Susan watched as she pulled out of the parking lot. Following right behind her was the blue car that Tina had pointed out. After a while, Susan became aware of Diane standing at the counter staring at her.

"Susan? Is something wrong?"

"No! I mean, yes. I have to talk to Beth. Is she with anyone?"

"Her last appointment left about ten minutes ago; I think she's charting."

Susan could feel her heart pounding as she walked down the

hall to Beth's office.

"Hi, come on in." Beth pointed to a chair. "Sit down; I was relaxing. Is something wrong? You look like you're on your way to a funeral."

"I may be. Beth, this Collins' case is getting unreal. I just saw Tina, and you wouldn't believe the story she told me. Her husband is a dealer, a middleman for what sounds like a drug syndicate!"

Beth put her hands up to her ears. "Susan, do I want to hear this?"

"No, but with Dr. Spelling gone, you don't have any choice. Tina asked me if I was going to turn her in. When I told her 'no', she let everything out. Her life is in danger. It seems Bill received a shipment of drugs and hid it before he became psychotic. The organization is also known as an investment group! Can you believe it? Anyway, they believe that Tina knows where Bill hid the drugs. She was terrified."

"It sounds like she should be."

"According to her, they're the guys that cut out Bill's eye. And those drugs are worth millions. They're not going to let her walk away if they believe she knows the location. Tina said if she can't find them, they'll make an example out of her."

"Why doesn't she go to the police?"

"She's afraid they might be in on it. The group that bankrolled the initial investment is supposed to have some powerful members."

"Susan, maybe she's been around her husband too much. I've

heard of cases where spouses are so compatible they even share delusions."

"Not this time. I just saw Tina's delusion follow her out of the parking lot! Tina pointed out a car and, as soon as she left, it followed right behind. I know this all sounds crazy, but too much of the story fits together. Look, they live in an expensive house; and he doesn't have a regular job. When they came in, she said he was a job broker. We can't go to the police. If she's telling the truth, we may be turning her over to someone with connections to that group."

Beth threw up her hands. "There's not a damn thing we can do. And another thing, I hate to bring this up; but if she's telling the truth and that car was following her, then you may be in trouble too. They know that she came in here to talk to someone!"

Susan hit the arm of the chair. "Dr. Spelling and his damn survival trip! It's the only place where we can't reach him! Beth, what are you going to do?"

"For the moment, nothing; did you chart yet?"

"No, I came right in to talk to you."

"Good. I know I shouldn't say this, but don't chart about anything she told you. Just write that she came in upset about her husband's condition. Susan, if those people are as desperate as she says, they may try to get that record. If there's any hint that you're aware of what's going on, then you'll be in Tina's situation."

Susan reluctantly agreed. "I guess you're right. We'd better protect ourselves. But, I wish there were something we could do for Tina."

"I wish there were too, Susan, but who can you go to for help? No matter what you do, you'll be doing something that could get her into more trouble. Let's hope Tina finds those drugs. But then what? She gets off the hook, but how many other people's lives are ruined with those street drugs! What about your husband? He's a lawyer; maybe he could give her some advice?"

"I tried that. I asked Tina if she wanted his help, but she turned down the offer."

Beth walked around the front of her desk. "Susan, you got my home phone number. Call if anything comes up over the weekend. I'm going to finish up and then get out of here. Right now this place gives me the creeps."

"Don't worry, Beth; it won't take me more than a few minutes to write this progress note. Thanks again for listening." Susan left for her office, anxious to finish Tina's charting and leave for home.

CHAPTER 16

ELLIOTT UNDERCOVER

Susan pierced the yolk of the egg with her fork and watched the thin, yellow liquid pool next to the bacon.

"Having fun?"

"I'm sorry, Elliott. I guess I'm worried about something."

"I've noticed. It's obvious that something's bothering you. Your mind has been elsewhere since Friday evening."

She felt defensive. "Well, I'm not the only one who's letting their work get to them. You've been uptight the last few days."

For a second his face clouded, but then Elliott smiled. "Yes, I guess we both should put work aside for the rest of the weekend." Just then, the phone in the den rang.

He's right, thought Susan; we both have to forget about work. But no matter how hard she tried, she couldn't get Tina off of her mind. She was clearing the table when Elliott returned. "How about another cup of coffee?"

He stared at her with a strange look. "No, I have to go to a meeting. There's a crisis over that problem I mentioned."

She noticed his expression. "Are you all right? You look more than worried!"

"I'm okay. Are you going to stick around here till I get back?"

"Yes, I'm going to call my parents and wish them 'bon voyage' and then read the Sunday paper. I hope you can resolve this problem quickly so that it won't take up your whole day."

Elliott's expression turned grim. "Oh, it will get resolved, one way or another."

Susan talked cheerfully to her mother. She didn't want to have her parents leave on the trip of a lifetime with her on their mind. Susan was digging through the thick Tribune when the phone rang. At first, she ignored the sound, thinking it was another business call for Elliott. But then she realized it was their phone. "Hello." Susan immediately recognized Beth's voice. "Beth, is something wrong?"

"Yes, I'm calling from the office. Someone broke into the Center early this morning. It didn't take long to find what was missing. It was Bill's and Tina's charts."

Susan felt a queer sensation in her stomach. "She was telling the truth."

"Yes, it means that they know Tina was talking to you! Did you chart the way I told you?"

"The only thing I wrote in the chart was how upset she was over her husband's condition. Beth, how did you find out about the break-in?"

"The security guard patrolling the shopping center found the door to the Center jimmied open. They tried to call Dr. Spelling, and his answering service gave them my number."

"What do we do now?"

"We do nothing! The security guard reported the incident to the police. As far as we're concerned, the thief was frightened away before he had a chance to take anything. Remember, we're not supposed to know anything. Besides, why should we miss just two charts when our file cabinets have hundreds of cases?"

"Beth, do you want me to come in?"

"No, let's downplay the whole thing. Just act surprised when you come in tomorrow and learn about the break-in. Susan, the fewer people who know about this drug thing, the better. I'm waiting for a locksmith to fix the door, and then I'm going to go home. I have a date to go shopping this afternoon, and that's just what I'm going to do!"

Susan nervously curled the telephone cord around her finger. "I think you're right. If Tina was telling the truth about everything, then there's no one we can safely go to for help. For the time being, we better agree to keep this to ourselves."

"You'll get no argument from me. Susan, I have to go. The locksmith just drove up. See you tomorrow."

Susan put the phone down and sat for a few minutes trying to put everything out of her mind, but the memory of Tina's frightened face kept coming back to her. Susan wished she could talk to Elliott, but knew that as paranoid as he had been acting lately, that might not be wise. He would probably insist she take early retirement.

* * *

At the airport, Frank and his bodyguard walked down the ramp to where Elliott was waiting. Frank's bodyguard stood a few feet behind, his eyes quickly scanning the waiting area. "Come on. Let's talk over there. It's private." They sat down in front of the window where several planes were stacked up waiting for an empty runway.

"What the hell is going on? Where is my merchandise? You said this Collins guy could be trusted! He takes my stuff and then you have some jerks mess him over so that he doesn't even know his fucking name." Frank turned and faced Elliott. "I sent you to school, set you up in business, paved the way for you, Elliott. And now I find out you're a jackass." He waved his finger under Elliott's nose. "Find the shipment, Elliott, just find the fucking goods!"

Elliott kept his voice calm. "I don't blame you for being angry, Frank. What should have been a perfect set-up went sour. My guys didn't work over Bill's head; he went crazy on his own. I think his wife knows where he put the stuff."

"Then get it!"

"She denies that she knows. I've had her followed, and she's going for therapy at the clinic where my wife works. This morning we broke in and got her chart, and it turned out that Susan is her therapist. Patients tell their therapist everything; it's like going to confession."

Frank didn't look relieved. "Yeah, and priests never tell secrets revealed to them in confession."

Elliott smiled. "Maybe so. But priests don't have spouses, either."

Frank stood up and started walking. "I've got a ticket for the next plane out. I don't want anyone to know I even left Florida. Elliott, a wise man knows when to cut his losses. Give the Collins Babe one more day. If she doesn't come up with the goods, then take her out. Look, have her taken out either way. She knows too much!"

They left the empty loading area and walked down the corridor to another gate. "Strange coincidence, Elliott, your wife being her therapist. Lot of bad luck you've been having lately!" Elliott was silent. Frank quickened his step when he heard the boarding call. As he handed the ticket to the agent, he turned and shouted, "Twenty-four hours, Elliott! Just twenty-four hours!"

Elliott tried to smile reassuringly.

* * *

Susan was towel drying her hair when she heard Elliott shout hello. "I'm upstairs, Elliott. I'll be right down!"

"Susan, are you coming?"

"Yes, in a minute!"

Elliott was in the living room mixing a drink. "What would you like?"

"A tonic and lime, please. How did your meeting go? Did you get the problem resolved?"

"Maybe. We'll know in a day or so." He handed her drink and

leaned close for a kiss. "Hey, you smell good!"

"I've just had a shower. Besides, I'm feeling good. I've decided to take your advice and put work out of my mind. We have a few hours of the weekend left. What would you like to do?"

Elliott paused for a moment and set his drink down on the coffee table. "I think it's time we talked."

Susan was surprised, "What about?"

He sat down next to her and gently held her face in his hands. "I have to tell you something. I know I shouldn't; but if I don't, I'm afraid our marriage will break up." Elliott dropped his hands but continued to look intently into her eyes. "Susan, you must promise me that you'll never tell anybody what I'm going to tell you, or my life will be an extreme danger!"

"Elliott! What are you talking about?"

"You know how you've been complaining about how secretive I am about my work?"

"Yes, and secretive is putting it mildly. But what do you mean that your life will be in extreme danger?"

"Do you remember last week when you joked about me being with the CIA?"

"Sure, and I also remembered how upset you got!"

"Well, I'm not working for the CIA; but I am working as an undercover agent for the FBI."

Susan was stunned. The news was unbelievable, or was it? "What! Why didn't you tell me! Elliott, you should have told me.

Maybe not when we met, but certainly before we were married!"
Elliott took her hand. "I wanted to, Susan. Honestly, I did; but everything happened so fast. I couldn't tell you when we were first dating; and before I knew it, we were married. I guess I was afraid; I didn't know how you would react. Some of the guys told their fiancés or wives, and they walked out on them. I didn't want to lose you."

"I love you, Elliott. I wouldn't have left you. My God, I'm so relieved. You have no idea what I've been thinking! Half the time I thought you were paranoid, and the other half I thought you were doing something illegal. You are a lawyer, aren't you?"

"Yes, of course; and I work for the firm. It's just that I also work as an undercover agent. Susan, the whole fiber of our society is falling apart. I know it sounds corny, but I want to help. Now if it means losing you, then I'll quit. Susan, I guess you're a little shocked."

She gave a faint smile. "That's an understatement. How did you get into this undercover work?"

"I started back in Florida. It used to be that organized crime was fairly identifiable."

"You mean like Frank DiMato…the man you introduced me to, the one at the cocktail party."

Elliott looked away. "Yes, now organized crime is in everything: law, business, medicine, and all the other professions. If you look hard enough at any of them, you'll find a crime. Anyway, to make a long story short, the FBI approached the American Bar Association for someone to work undercover for them. At first, I declined but changed my mind when the evidence of criminal activity involving lawyers began to mount. Instead of just defending their clients, some are joining in the actual crimes. Susan, there's a lot of money in drugs. The temptation is just too great for some to pass up."

"Elliott, this is so incredible! Are you working on a case now?"

"Yes, but I'm frustrated. I haven't been able to get anywhere, and I don't have a thing to go on. I know something big is going on, but this time I don't have a contact." He picked up her hand again. "Susan, I just wanted to tell you what I've been doing so we will stop arguing over my reluctance to share my work with you. Now please don't ask me any more questions. The less you know about what's going on, the less you'll have to worry about."

She shook her head. "Only one more question: how dangerous?"

He looked straight into her eyes. "I could be killed at any time. But you can't think about that, or you may as well stop functioning. I know this is rough on you, but give it some time. You'll get used to it."

"You've got to be kidding. How do you get used to your husband's life constantly being in danger?" Elliott sat down and pulled Susan close to him. "You do love me, don't you?"

"Oh yes! I was so terrified of what was happening. I can't tell you how relieved I am. You gave me the impression that you didn't care about anything but making money. But, you are a very caring person. So much so, you put your life on the line. I'm upset that you didn't tell me about this sooner, but I feel a lot better about us. At least I no longer think I'm married to a paranoid!"

He pulled her up from the couch. "Let's go upstairs and continue this conversation."

Tina suddenly came to Susan's mind. Now she knew that Elliott would be able to help. "Elliott."

He hungrily put his mouth on hers, while he gently pulled her up toward the stairs. "Not now, Susan, not now."

She didn't protest. Making love that night was better than it had been in a long time. Exhausted, but satisfied, Elliott drifted off to sleep. Susan's body was ready for sleep, but her mind raced with images of everything that had happened over the last few days. Again, she saw Tina's frightened face. Susan sat up and looked over at Elliott, deep in sleep. She ran her fingers gently down his back but quickly pulled away when he stirred, thinking she may as well wait until morning. A few more hours wouldn't matter. Relieved that she had finally found someone to help Tina, Susan settled into her pillow and drifted off to sleep.

Susan awakened to the sound of the closet door as Elliott took out his clothes. She glanced at the bedside clock, "Elliott, it's only 5:30. You're up early."

"Sorry, I didn't mean to wake you. I have a case that's going to trial today, and it's the first one on the docket. I need to go in early and review the file." He quickly finished dressing and then leaned down to kiss Susan goodbye. "I won't be home for dinner; its federal business. So don't wait up. I'll be late!"

He ran his fingers down the side of her face. "Hon, don't fall back to sleep or you'll be late for work."

"Don't worry; I won't." Susan suddenly thought about Tina. "Elliott, I need to talk to you. It's important!"

He was at the door. "Sorry, it will have to wait. I can't be late. This judge is a real stickler on punctuality, but I'll try to call you this afternoon."

* * *

As Susan drove to work, she felt optimistic for the first time in weeks. She was concerned about Elliott's involvement in undercover work, but now she understood his secretive behavior. Susan smiled to herself. Elliott had been putting her down for caring and trying to make things better while in his way, he was doing the same thing. Still, being unable to talk with him about Tina was worrying? Well, no matter how late he got home tonight, she would be awake. Maybe he could both protect Tina and use the information in his work.

Diane was standing at the counter when Susan walked in. "Guess what! Someone broke in yesterday, but they didn't take anything. Security must have frightened them away."

Susan feigned surprise. "No kidding! Does Beth know?"

Diane was eager to announce the news. "Yes, the police called her to come in to see if anything was missing. I think they were after the typewriters and copy machine."

"Yes, you're probably right; I've heard they're easy to sell on the street. Please hand me the appointment book. I need to check my schedule."

Diane looked disappointed that the conversation had ended. Susan scanned the list of appointments to find Tina Collins' name. She hoped Tina would agree to get help from Elliott. And since the clinic was burgled, the problem was no longer just Tina's.

She walked down the corridor and saw Beth's open door. "Good morning. Diane told me about the break-in. I was happy to hear nothing was taken."

Beth lifted her eyes in mock surprise. "Sure. Better shut the door."

Susan closed the door behind her and took a seat. "There's something I think we better talk about."

Beth smiled and shook her head. "Has something else come up with the Collins' case?"

"Maybe. Tina Collins has an appointment this afternoon; I'm going to tell her about the break-in. She has a right to know that her chart is gone. And I'm going to try to persuade her to talk with my husband."

Beth looked worried. "Tina should know her chart was taken, and she certainly needs to understand that those people are desperate. Did you tell your husband about her?"

"No, I haven't had the time. Because of Elliott's work, he has contact with a federal agency that might be able to help Tina. I hope she'll agree to talk to him."

Beth looked relieved. "I'm happy that we can finally do something about this mess. Covering this up is going against all my beliefs."

"My feelings, also. We'd both feel guilty if anything happened to her. I'm scheduled to tour Brighton later this afternoon. I'm sure I'll be seeing Bill Collins."

Beth shuddered. "I don't envy you!"

"I'm certainly not looking forward to it. He came to us for treatment and then ends up like that. So, no matter how much you tell yourself it's not your fault, you still feel responsible." Susan leaned back in the chair and searched for words. "I guess that's why I want so desperately to get help for Tina. I don't think I could handle it if something terrible happened to her."

Beth got up and walked toward the door. I've got an appointment in a few minutes." She stopped and put her hand on Susan's arm. "I hope things work out with Tina, but so far she hasn't wanted outside help. She just asked you to listen. Encourage her to agree to seek help, Susan. But don't feel that because of what happened to Bill, you're now responsible for Tina. Remember, these people were dealing drugs long before they walked into our place!"

Susan gave Beth a faint smile. "Thanks, I'll try to keep things in perspective."

"One more thing; I'll be here all afternoon. If you need to talk, I'm available."

Susan looked relieved. "I hope I won't have to bother you, but

I'm glad you offered."

The morning went by quickly; it was 11 o'clock when Susan heard the intercom.

"Susan, there's a Mr. Sloan out here. He says he's a personal friend."

She was off guard. Did Randy know about Elliott's undercover work? She would have to act as if she didn't know anything. Randy was standing in the waiting room looking a little embarrassed when Susan arrived.

"Hello, this is an unexpected pleasure."

He walked up to her and kissed her on the cheek. "I was in the neighborhood and thought I'd see if you were free for lunch."

"Sounds great, as long as it's a quick lunch. I have an appointment at 1:00 o'clock."

No problem. I have to get back to the office, too. How about going to that little place in the strip mall?"

"All right. Let me get my purse."

Susan took a bite of her hamburger while Randy waited for a reply. "Sorry, what was that you asked?"

"I asked if you had any unusual cases. Remember, when you accepted this position you thought you might die of boredom out here."

"No, nothing unusual so far; but I don't think I'll die of boredom out here."

"Have you had to hospitalize anybody yet?"

Susan wondered why he was asking all these questions. Now she was becoming paranoid! She didn't know if Randy was someone that Elliott might be investigating or if he just didn't know of Elliott's undercover work.

"Susan, are you here?"

"Sorry, I'm just not with it today. Yes, I've had to hospitalize someone; but it was just a routine case." She glanced at her watch. Thank God, it was time to leave. "I hate to cut this short, Randy, but I really should be getting back. Next time we'll have a more leisurely lunch."

Randy pulled up to the clinic, and Susan quickly stepped out of the car. "Thanks for stopping by. I'm sorry for the rushed lunch."

A few minutes later Randy was phoning from a service station. "Tom, there something wrong with Susan; I've never seen her so guarded. I want you to check with your friend at Marshall Law and find out if my cover is still intact. Susan's hiding something, but I still don't believe that she is part of Elliott's dealings." Randy returned to his car and sat for a few minutes staring into space. Finally, he shook his head and shifted the transmission into drive.

CHAPTER 17
TINA'S FEARS

Tina was sitting in the waiting room, nervously shifting her weight in the chair.

"Good afternoon, Tina. Come on in."

She got up, followed Susan into the office, and sat with her head turned toward the window.

"Is someone out there? You keep watching the window."

Tina jumped up and walked toward the window. She pulled two slats apart and motioned for Susan to come over. "Look at them; they follow me everywhere I go. At least they know I'm looking for the drugs!"

Susan took a deep breath. "Tina, come and sit down. Would you like a cup coffee?"

"No thanks. I've been living on coffee the past few days. I went to see Bill yesterday." Her eyes welled up with tears. "I can't believe he's the same person. You've only seen him since this started, but he was a real handsome guy. He was smart, too." Tina put her head down. "I know he was doing wrong, but he didn't deserve this! It might sound crazy to you, but I love him. And it's like he's dead now, only not buried."

"It's not crazy, Tina. The man you married is gone. Bill is alive, but he's changed and may never again be the man you remember. That's bound to affect how you feel about him. I'm going to the hospital in a little while; I'll stop in to see him."

"Thanks, but he won't even know you're there." Tina grabbed the arms of the chair. "I've reached the end of my rope. All that's left is for me to run away somewhere. Maybe I can go to Mexico or someplace far off."

"Tina, I want to talk to you about something. First of all, the clinic had a break-in yesterday morning. And when we checked, the only thing missing was Bill's and your charts."

"Jesus! They think I know where it's hidden and that I told you." Tina's eyes opened wide with fright. "Did you tell the police?"

"Only about the jimmied door, not that your charts are missing."

"Thank God!" Tina started to cry. "What difference does it make? If you wrote down what I told you, I'm dead anyway!"

"Don't worry. All I noted was that you were upset about Bill."

Tina looked up at Susan. "You didn't write anything about the drugs? How come?"

"Well, I talked to a psychologist at the clinic. And we both felt that considering what you told us, it would be better for everyone if there weren't anything in writing."

Tina stopped crying and blew her nose. "Thanks. I feel that I can trust someone."

"I'm glad you feel that way, Tina, because there's someone I want you to talk to."

Tina suddenly had a curious look on her face. "Who do you mean?"

"My husband. He has connections with a federal agency, and he might be able to help you."

Tina looked up with interest. "What can he do?"

"To be honest, since I haven't talked to him yet, I don't know what he can do. I only know that the government has a program to protect witnesses, and maybe he can work out a deal for you."

"I don't know, Mrs. Mason. A part of me wants to give it a try, but another part is afraid!"

"Tina, you trust me, don't you?"

"Yes, but you're different. You have to keep quiet about anything I tell you. And, I'm grateful you didn't write about it in the chart. I know you usually do."

"Right, and a lawyer has to obey the same client privilege rules about his clients."

Tina took a deep breath. "Okay. I'll talk to him, but only after I try this last place. Because if I can find the stuff and get it back, they'll leave me alone. I'll call you here tomorrow morning; and if I haven't found it, we'll set up a meeting with your husband."

"Tina, I wish you'd let me set up that meeting today. I don't think you'll be off the hook even if you do find the drugs. Your life could still be in danger."

"Believe me; they only want the drugs. Bill has never cheated them, and if I give it all back, they won't hurt me." Tina was thoughtful for a moment. "I'm going to try it my way first. But in case you're right, and something happens to me, I'm going to give you a telephone number. This number is for the contact person for the group. Bill called this number to make arrangements about how much the drugs would cost and the date of the delivery-that kind of stuff. Nobody knows I have the number. Bill was supposed to memorize it and never write it down. But he was afraid that something might happen to him, so he told me to memorize it, too." She reached over to a pad on Susan's desk and wrote the number down. "Do you have an envelope?"

Susan pulled the desk drawer open and took out an envelope. Tina put the paper in, sealed it, and handed it back to Susan.

"Promise me that you'll get this to your husband, but only if something goes wrong tonight! I'm going back to Bill's old neighborhood; maybe he hid it there." Tina looked intently at her. "I still think that everything will be okay if I find the drugs."

Susan felt uneasy, but she knew she couldn't change Tina's mind. Jesus Christ! This woman is forcing me to sit and wait while she plays Russian roulette with organized crime. "All right. I promise I won't give the number to my husband unless something happens to you. But only on the condition that tomorrow we get help. I know you're frightened for yourself, but those people and their drugs are messing up a lot of other lives, too!"

Tina raised her voice. "Sure, but what about that fucking doctor who wouldn't take Bill into the hospital? What about the lives he's messed up?"

"I haven't forgotten, and we'll talk about what happened at Brighton. For now, let's worry about getting you through the next few days." Susan stood up and noticed how frightened and alone Tina looked. "Are you sure this is the way you want it?"

Tina fought back the tears. "Yes, believe me, it's the best way."

Susan walked around the desk. "Tina, do you need a hug?"

"Oh, you have no idea how much I need a hug!" Susan put her arms around her. "Thanks for listening to me, and especially for not making me feel like a criminal."

Susan watched through the blinds as Tina walked to her car. A few minutes later, she saw two men in a blue Ford follow Tina's red Buick Regal out of the parking lot.

"What's so engrossing in the parking lot?" Diane asked.

"Oh nothing, just thinking, that's all. I got to get going. I have an appointment at Brighton."

* * *

The setting at Brighton was idyllic. Beautiful old oak trees lined the winding paths of spacious grounds carved out of a farm field. Susan passed a quaint, picturesque cemetery that was a final resting place for patient's unclaimed bodies.

The exterior of the main building was quaint with rustic,

ivy-covered stone walls and large, double entry oak doors. Except for the steel mesh on the windows, this place could pass for an old and prestigious university campus. When Susan stepped into the administration building, she noticed signs of recent redecorating with new carpeting and furniture in bright colors which were futile attempts to brighten up the gloomy building. She told the receptionist that she had an appointment with Mr. Desmond. Soon a man in his forties, overweight and balding, was standing in front of her with his hand outstretched. "How do you do, Mrs. Mason? I'm Carl Desmond."

"Hello, I've been looking forward to meeting you!" These buildings must hold a lot of stories."

Mr. Desmond smiled sadly. "Yes, unfortunately, most of them are tragic. Come to my office. I'll give you a little history, and then I'll take you on the grand tour. We have some interesting programs going on in some of these old buildings."

Susan walked with Mr. Desmond from the administration building to the admitting ward where intakes stayed until there was a decision to either put them in the small intensive therapy program or send them along to one of the several human warehouses on the grounds.

"Mr. Desmond, you have a patient of ours who has been here a few days. His name is William Collins. I'd like to talk to him."

"Yes, I've read his chart. Tragic case. By the way, did Mr. Rivers, from the FBI, get in touch with you? It seems our Mr. Collins is popular with those fellows."

"I'm sorry, what are you talking about?"

"Last Friday, Mr. Rivers and another man from the FBI came to the hospital. They were unable to elicit information from Mr. Collins. But you'll understand why when you see him. Mr. Rivers said he would be talking with you further about Mr. Collins' intake interview. He asked who referred Mr. Collins. I hope it was okay to give him your name."

Susan didn't know what to think. Was it someone from the FBI, or the goons that were following Tina?

"Wait here, please. I'll ask the nurse if Mr. Collins is on the ward."

Susan's mind was racing. She wished that Elliott didn't have an evening meeting because she wanted to talk to him as soon as possible. She was overwhelmed. Too many things didn't make sense.

Mr. Desmond finished his conversation with the nurse, looked at Susan, and then nodded toward a man sitting on the bed at the end of the long, narrow room. Susan gently approached him. "Bill. It's Mrs. Mason, the social worker you talked to at Tri-Valley Mental Health Center."

Bill looked up, and Susan gasped as she fought back a wave of nausea. The area around the left eye socket was purple, and yellow pus was running out of the shrunken lid. He had a vacant expression, and she quickly saw that the front of his pants was wet. She looked up and saw that Mr. Desmond had also noticed. He looked uncomfortable; this was not the impression he wanted to make. "I'll ask the nurse to help him change his clothes." He turned to Susan and quietly said, "I'm afraid that Mr. Collins has permanent brain damage. He seems to be getting worse instead of better. That eye socket looks bad. The aides are cleaning it several times a day with an antiseptic wash. But with his poor hygiene, it's impossible to avoid infection."

Susan took one last look at Bill as he sat there in his urine-soaked pants playing with his fingers, totally unaware of her presence. Now she understood why Tina had said it seemed that Bill was dead. He was certainly dead to her. "Mr. Desmond, let's get on with the tour."

"Yes, I want to show you our intensive care ward."

She was happy to see this building's interior brightly painted in primary colors. There were only forty patients on the ward with the young, energetic staff working their hearts out to give these people one last chance. Mr. Desmond had good reason to be proud. But these were only forty patients. Susan couldn't help but wonder about the other thousand or so.

"I'm impressed. You and your staff are doing a terrific job."

He beamed in response to Susan's compliment. "Thank you. Shall we go back to my office now?"

"What about the other programs? I'd like to see where the other patients live while they're here."

Mr. Desmond lifted his eyes from Susan. "I don't think you want to go into those buildings; it's not very pleasant."

She turned and looked into his eyes. "Can you guarantee me that none of the patients referred from our clinic will ever end up in those buildings?"

"No, of course not; it would depend on their condition."

"Then, Mr. Desmond, I really would like to see the rest of the facilities."

He frowned, but gave-in. "All right, but remember these are chronic patients; and many of them have lost their social skills. They'll be grabbing at you, and you'll see a lot more soiling."

Susan realized that he was embarrassed. "I can appreciate that Mr. Desmond; please don't think I'm judging you personally for any shortcomings at this hospital. I know that quality care takes the kind of staff and money that you don't have."

He relaxed a little. "I'm glad you understand. We get a lot of heat from family and community workers, but we don't have the power to change things. So, if you still want the entire tour, let's get on with it."

The condition of the other buildings went from bad to pathetic, as did the patients. Eager for fresh air, Susan reached for the exit door. Before she could grab the handle, the door opened from the other side. She was speechless. Standing in front of her was Karen. Susan glanced back at Mr. Desmond with a shocked expression.

"Susan, I forgot to mention that one of your former colleagues, Karen Morgan, is working here. She used to work in social services at Linton. Do you remember her?"

She glared at Karen. "Yes, of course."

Karen lowered her eyes and stepped aside as Susan hurried through the door. Mr. Desmond, sensing the tension, silently walked next to Susan. "I didn't think that she had the right attitude for the intensive care ward."

Susan smiled to herself. "I think you made a wise decision."

After seeing the last building, they once again walked silently down the beautiful tree-lined path. Mr. Desmond spoke first. "This is how it hits most people: it's depressing. Sometimes this job makes me feel like Sisyphus, condemned to roll a huge stone uphill only to have it roll right back down again. The beds are never empty. When one patient leaves, there's another two waiting." By now they had completed the tour and were back in front of the administration building

"Thank you for taking the time to show me around. Please don't take this personally, but I hope that we won't be sending you many patients."

He smiled. "My sentiments also; it'll give us more time to spend with the patients we already have."

If it's all right with you, Mr. Desmond, I'd like to call my office before I leave."

Mr. Desmond left Susan in his office to make her call. "Diane, this is Susan. I'm about ready to leave Brighton. Since it's almost 4 o'clock, I think I'll go on home. Do I have any messages?"

"Just one. Your husband called at two o'clock and asked me to tell you that he was leaving the office on a business matter and not to wait up for him since he was going to be late. That's all."

Susan wondered if he was doing business for the firm or the government. She felt anxious; maybe it was better if she didn't know. This undercover work was more difficult to handle than she first thought. "Thanks, Diane. See you tomorrow."

Driving home, Susan put Brighton out of her mind and began to think about Tina. Now that Elliott might be able to help her, she hoped that Tina wouldn't find the drugs tonight. If Tina were successful, she would have no reason to cooperate with Elliott.

* * *

After a tiring day like this, Susan decided it was an evening that called for a light salad while relaxing in front of the television. And how much she needed to relax! With a salad and drink in hand, she sat down on the couch and watched her favorite news station. Susan had just finished eating when the local news came on. A breaking news announcement grabbed her full attention.

"Around 3:00 o'clock this afternoon, the police discovered the body of a woman in the trunk of a car in Brendan Woods after a routine check of an abandoned car. The coroner's office reports the woman to be Caucasian and in her late twenties. She was in the trunk of a late model car with her hands tied behind her back, a bullet hole in her head, apparently executed gangland style."

Susan leaned forward and watched intently as the murder scene flashed on the screen. She suddenly recognized Tina's red Buick

Regal. "Oh, My God!"

The newscaster continued speaking in a monotone. "As of now, we do not have the official identity of the slain woman; but we expect the police to release the name shortly."

Then a commercial came on. Susan sat mesmerized, unable to move or think. Once again, the picture of Tina's car appeared.

"We now have an identification of the woman found shot to death a few hours ago. Her name is Tina Collins, and she is married to William Collins, a man who is known to be involved in drug trafficking. Willian Collins is currently at Brighton State Hospital. At this time, there is no known motive for the murder; but it appears to be drug-related."

Susan sat numbly on the couch, trying to comprehend what she had watched and heard. The scene of Tina leaving the clinic at noon flashed in front of her, along with the picture of the two men in a blue car following her. Susan realized that she was probably the last person to see Tina alive, except of course for whoever murdered her!

She paced the floor, going from the living room to the kitchen, watching the clock, trying to use her mind to force the hands to move faster. It was a little after six. She knew that Elliott would not be home before eleven. With her anxiety building, Susan needed to talk to somebody now! Suddenly she remembered the telephone number that Tina had given her that morning. Susan rushed to where she had thrown her purse. Her hands were shaking as she opened it, and rummaged until she came upon the envelope. Susan's bewilderment changed to anger, and she ripped open the envelope. The numbers written in black ink on white paper jumped out at her. There was something familiar about the telephone number, but it took a few seconds to register.

It was the same exchange as their home phone. That meant that the contact person lived in this area! A chill ran down her spine as she realized that Tina's murderer could be within walking distance of her own home. Maybe she had been followed. Was someone watching outside the house right now? If they killed Tina, what would they do to her?

Her mouth felt like cotton. Still holding the piece of paper, Susan went to the kitchen for a drink of water. Then she returned to the living room and sat down staring at the phone. Her fear cautioned her to wait for Elliott. But instead, she found herself rationalizing why she should call. She owed it to Tina. By the time Elliott came home, it would be too late to call. And by tomorrow, the phone might be disconnected.

Susan's hands were clammy as she set the paper on the table and dialed the number. She had no sooner finished dialing when the phone in the den ring. Startled, she dropped the phone back on the receiver and put her hand up to her chest waiting for her heart to stop racing. After a few seconds, Susan picked up the phone and tried a second time. Again, the phone rang in the den. This time she noticed that the ringing she heard on the phone and the ringing she heard coming from the den were in unison. Suddenly, the click of an answering machine interrupted the ringing.

"This is Elliott Mason. I'm out of my office. Please leave a message at the sound of the tone, and I'll get back to you as soon as possible."

Susan stood frozen to the spot, breathing deeply into the phone. The next thing she heard was the recorder tone, and with a puzzled look on her face, she placed the phone back on the receiver. Her mind flashed back to the day that she had cleaned Elliott's office. She remembered seeing the empty slot on the phone where the number usually appeared. Susan picked up the phone and again dialed the number. Once more the phone in the den rang. "This is Elliott Mason."

She shook her head. What was going on? Elliott said he didn't have any leads to this case, but Tina said Bill had been calling this number. Susan's face paled as she slowly walked to the den. She stood in front of the door, staring down at the handle, reasoning that if she didn't go in, there would never be any trust. The suspicion of his involvement would always be with her.

The room was dim. Susan decided to put the office lights on rather than pull the drapes open. She did not want to be seen from the outside as she sneaked around Elliott's office. First, she looked around the top of the desk; but there were only a calendar, some pens, and blank notepads. Then Susan sat down in his chair, and one by one tried to open the desk drawers. All were locked!

She leaned back in the chair feeling defeated, not knowing what to do next.

CHAPTER 18
THE FILES

Susan raced up the stairs, ran into the bedroom, and pulled open the top dresser drawer. There they were, in the back left-hand side, a ring of keys! Elliott kept duplicate keys to his car, office, and house on this ring. Once he had locked his keys in the car, and she had taken the keys to him. She held her breath as she went through the keys looking for a small desk key. Bingo! There it was! Now she hoped it was to the desk in the den. Quickly she ran back downstairs, glancing at her watch on the way. Only 6:45, she had plenty of time; he wouldn't be back before 11:00 o'clock.

She sat on the edge of the leather chair and put the keys on the desk pad. Her hands grasped the arms of the chair; beads of perspiration joined the tears already running down her face. Susan had often wondered how someone could have their whole life flash in front of them, but now all of her doubts and fears were so clear. How could she have been so blind? She reached down and picked up the key. There on the inside panel by her knee was the lock. She put the key in and heard a click as the lock released. The bottom drawer was large enough to accommodate legal sized files. There were only a few files in the drawer; she pulled them out and set them on top of the desk.

For the moment, she was tempted to put them back and push all the horrible thoughts out of her mind. But she knew that now it was too late; things had gone too far. Susan reached over and opened the top folder. She gasped! Inside was a light green chart used by Tri-Valley. She then opened the chart, already knowing what she would find-all of the forms and notes from her sessions with Tina. Her hands shaking, Susan put the folder aside and opened the second file. This one contained a legal document with the heading, Investors Limited Trust. Something clicked. Then she remembered. Tina had told her that there was an investment group that put money up front to buy the drugs at the point of entry.

Susan looked down at the folder again. There were loose sheets of paper: one with a column of names was next to a column that appeared to be investments. She ran her finger down the page and immediately recognized names. Two that stood out were Judge Morris and Dr. Rhoades, both men she had met at the cocktail party last month. Susan jumped as she heard the sound of a car coming into the driveway. She stopped for a moment, listening to her heart pound, but didn't hear anything else. Then she got up, pulled aside the drapes and peeked out the window. She was relieved to see that someone had used the driveway to turn their car around.

Susan sat down again, visibly shaken, aware that Elliott could come home at any moment. She would have to hurry! Susan ran her finger down the column of figures and stopped at the total on the bottom. My God, she thought, if that's how much is put up front, what are they getting after the drugs were cut and resold?

With a shaking hand, Susan reached for the third folder and slowly opened it. This one contained another accounting sheet, hand-written in Elliott's small attractive script. Under the column of expenses was written: Bill Collins, contract fee, with the date that Bill's eye was taken out. Susan's eyes widened at the next entry: Tina Collins, contract fee. Contract fee? Here was the cost of Tina's murder neatly written in the debit side of the ledger!

Susan suddenly felt a wave of nausea and bolted from the chair, ran to the bathroom, leaned over the toilet, and vomited. Her whole being violently trying to reject everything she now knew about Elliott. Too weak to get up, she sat on the floor leaning against the door, her hair damp on her forehead. It was 7:30. Susan had been sitting on the bathroom floor for over a half hour. She pulled herself up, washed her face, walked down the stairs, and back to the den. The manila folders lay on the top of the desk. She sat down and put all of the papers back in the files and returned them to the drawer. She then turned the key until she heard the lock click. Looking around the room to make sure nothing was disturbed, she left the den and closed the door behind her.

Susan went upstairs, returned the keys to Elliott's dresser, and then went back to the living room. She picked up her purse and rummaged through it looking for her address book. Susan walked over to the phone and saw the paper with the phone number that Tina had given her. She picked it up, but then set it down. She punched in Beth's phone number.

After four rings, Susan began to panic. What if she wasn't home? She had to talk to her! But after the fifth ring, she heard Beth's friendly, "Hello."

"Beth, its Susan. I need to talk to you!"

"What's wrong? Are you all right?"

"Yes." Susan tried to control herself. "Beth, Tina's been murdered!"

"Oh, God! No! What are you talking about?"

"It was on the news. Tina was shot in the back of her head. It was a gang execution."

"We should have gone to your husband; he might have helped her."

"He helped her all right. He arranged for her murder!"

For a moment there was silence. "Susan, you're upset. Do you want me to come over?"

"No, it's dangerous here! I have to leave. I just wanted to warn you. I'll tell you the whole story tomorrow, but now I have to get out of here."

"Wait!"

Susan put the phone down and ran from the house. When she reached her car, she took a deep breath and checked the street, searching for someone following her. As she backed out of the driveway, she kept glancing at the rear-view mirror. But she couldn't detect anyone behind her.

Ten minutes later she realized that without evidence, no one would believe her story. Why did she leave those files there? She had to go back and get them; they were the indisputable link between the group, Tina, and the drugs. Susan felt a chill up her spine as she turned the car around, but reasoned with herself to stay calm. She was safe. There was nothing in the chart about the drugs; and she had put everything back in the desk just the way it was. Elliott believed that she was ignorant of what he was doing. After all, she had fallen for his undercover story-hook, line, and sinker. He won't arrive home until late tonight; and if I turn around now, I'll be there and gone before he returns. It will just take a few minutes.

As she turned the corner, Susan's headlights reflected off the back of Elliott's parked car. "Damn!" She pulled the car in front of the townhouse and sat for a moment debating whether she should drive away or go back into the house. She knew that Elliott would never let her divorce him. He would kill her first. Those files were her only way out! She decided that after Elliott fell asleep, she would sneak into the den and steal the files. Susan got out of the car and took a deep breath before opening the door. Elliott was sitting on the couch with the drink in his hand and a pleasant smile. "Hello, I was surprised you weren't home. Where were you?"

She gave a weak smile. "Oh, it was such a boring night I went out for a drive."

"Did you visit anyone?"

"No, I didn't feel like socializing. You're home early!"

"Yes, I finished my work sooner than I expected. I've been home for about five minutes. Let me get you a drink."

"No thanks." Susan wanted to avoid spending time with him. "I'm pretty tired; I'm going to take a shower and crawl into bed. It's been a long day."

He was persistent. "Oh, come on! You'll sleep better. Just have one drink with me."

The last thing she wanted was an argument. "All right, just one. Then I'm going to bed."

Elliott went over to the bar to mix the drink. As he was standing there, Susan's eyes swept the room. Abruptly her eyes moved back to the phone as it triggered a memory. The piece of paper! Before she left the house, she had set Tina's note with the phone number on the table while she called Beth. Susan tried to recall every moment. What had she done with it? She couldn't remember picking it up! The table was too far from the couch for Susan to see if the paper was still lying there.

Elliott walked toward her with the drink. "Here, it's a gin and tonic." He grinned at Susan. "I must admit I make a fairly decent one."

Susan's hand was shaking as she took the drink. "Thank you."

He noticed her shaking hands. "Is something wrong? You seem nervous."

"No, nothing's wrong, I'm just tired."

He lifted his drink and motioned for Susan to do the same. "Then drink up. You're right; you do look tired."

She took the drink and quickly finished it. The sooner they got to bed, the sooner she could come back and get that number off the table.

Elliott smiled. "That's better. Now we have a few minutes before you'll be asleep."

Susan laughed. "Well, I think it'll take a little longer than that."

"We'll see." He leaned close to her, his face only inches away from hers. Suddenly he reached into his pocket and pulled out the piece of paper that Susan immediately recognized. "Were you looking for this, Susan?"

Her face went pale. "No, what is it?"

He ignored her response. "There's only one person who could have given you this number: Tina Collins!" His eyes hardened. "That bitch! I should have taken care of her right away." He looked straight at Susan. "We watched her day and night, and guess what? The only one that Tina talked to in all that time was you!"

Susan moved back from Elliott, but he grabbed her arm and pulled her close. "You know everything, don't you?"

"What, Elliott? I don't know what you're talking about!"

His face turned red, and he started to shout. "Don't lie to me!

You're my wife; you're supposed to respect and love me! I should come first, not those fucking patients of yours. You should have come to me when that bitch gave you this number! But what the hell did you do? You called this number, and then you went snooping in my files." He dropped her arm and pushed her back on the couch. "You would have gotten away with it if I hadn't found this paper. But then I checked the folders in my desk, and they were out of order."

He grabbed her again and shook her. "What the hell were you planning to do? Turn me in Susan? I believed I could trust you, but you're just another Goddamn fucking whore out to get me!"

Susan felt herself getting sleepy. She was aware that Elliott was screaming, but everything was drifting away.

"That's right. The drink was drugged, and you will be snowed under for hours!" Elliott jumped up from the couch and paced back and forth, getting angrier and angrier as he yelled at her. "You bitch, you God damn, fucking pig! I should never have married you, you slut!"

He came back to the couch and glared down at her, his breathing heavy, sweat running down his face. Suddenly he grabbed the coffee table and pushed it over, and the empty glasses when flying. He looked at Susan, his face contorted in rage. He reached down and roughly grabbed her breast as Susan winced with pain. Then he straightened up and unzipped his pants.

Susan was aware of Elliott tearing her clothes off as she drifted in and out of consciousness. She felt trapped in her body. Her mind kept giving instructions to get up! Fight! Run! But her body wouldn't obey; nothing would move. She was suspended in a nightmare. Elliott was above her, screaming and slapping her. Then he came down on her time after time. There was pain, wave after wave of pain, as Elliott violently raped her. Eventually, with his rage spent, the drug rendered Susan mercifully unconscious.

* * *

Elliott walked into the den and sat, slowly drumming his fingers on the desk. The bitch, she pretended to love me to trap me into marrying her. Since she's come into my life, it's just been one mess after another. What's going to happen to me? Frank said that she was my responsibility. All these years of sucking up to Frank, and now she's ruined it all! The fucking bastard, he told me to find a wife with class. Now it's my fault that she's a self-righteous law-abiding bitch. Stupid old man! I should've taken over; he's senile. Elliott could hear his heart pounding. Take it easy. He told himself-first things first. I've got to think. I've got to have a plan before I talk to Frank. He thought for several minutes and then picked up the phone. "Frank, its Elliott. We have a serious problem. It's Susan; she knows everything."

"Can she be trusted?"

"No, she got hold of my business number which she could only have gotten from Collins' wife. There's more: she was out when I returned, and she's been through my files."

"Elliott, you've got a big problem here. What the hell are you going to do about it?"

"Anything I have to-to protect us."

"I'm glad to hear that. But if she's connected to Bill Collins and his wife, we can't afford to eliminate her now."

"Frank, I have an idea. Actually, without Susan, I never would have thought of it. I'll call you right back. I need to talk to Judge Morris."

Twenty minutes later, Elliott was backing the car out of the driveway. The first step of his plan wouldn't require much time; and with the sedative he had given her, Susan would sleep for hours.

*　*　*

Susan opened her eyes and saw Elliott sitting on a chair watching her. Her mind was racing, flashing bits and pieces of what had happened last night. Her muscles ached. She felt as if her entire body was beat with a club. Slowly things came together; and for a moment, she wished she were dead.

Elliott glanced down at his watch, and then stood up. "Get up and get dressed." When Susan didn't respond, he grabbed her arm. "I mean now. Move it!"

She wanted to fight, but she didn't have the strength. It took every ounce of energy to swing her legs down and sit up. As she bent over, the room whirled.

His voice shook with emotion. "Look, this is your entire fault. If you had been a good wife and shown a little loyalty, this never would have happened."

"Elliott, we loved each other. How can you treat me this way?"

He turned to her, looking surprised. "Because you asked for it! Now get dressed."

"I have to use the bathroom."

"All right. Leave the door open."

"For God's sake, Elliott, there isn't even a window in there!"

His face darkened. "Dammit! Listen to me. I said leave the damn door open!"

Susan didn't say any more; she stood up and unsteadily made her way to the bathroom. She used the toilet, trying to pretend he wasn't watching her; and then she washed her face and hands. Susan looked in the mirror and saw that her face was swollen and bruised. The scratches on her body attested to last night's attack. Filled with shame and anger, she fought back the tears and resolved she would get even. For now, she tried to think of a way to escape.

Elliott grabbed some clothes from the couch, approached the open door, and threw them at her. "Here, put these on!"

"I don't want you to move out of my sight!" He grabbed her arm. "If you do, you're going to get hurt. Understand?" She nodded, hoping that if she cooperated, he might let his guard down. Elliott pointed to the couch. "Sit there and don't move."

Obediently Susan sat down. "I'm very thirsty; could I please get a drink."

"No, just sit there!" He thought a moment. "I'll get it for you.

Don't get off that couch."

The kitchen was a few yards from the living room. Elliott got a glass but never took his eyes off her. She waited until he opened the refrigerator door, which blocked his view for a couple of seconds, and then ran for the front door. Susan fumbled with the chain and got the door open. She heard Elliott shout, "Dammit! You fucking bitch!" He came running after her, but she rushed out and was halfway down the stairs when she ran into the arms of a sheriff's deputy.

"Thank God! I need help! It's my husband; he's going to kill me!"

The deputy took her by the arm. "Don't worry little lady. We're going to help you," he nodded to the second officer. "Better get the equipment from the car."

Elliott was standing by the door watching as the officer gently took Susan by the arm and whispered, "Let's go inside for a moment and get a few things cleared up."

Filled with fear, Susan glanced back at Elliott. "I don't want to go back in there!"

"Don't worry. It will take only a minute, and then we'll take you where you can get help. You've been through a lot."

Susan went limp and let herself be led back, feeling relieved that it was all over. At least, she was still alive.

Elliott stepped back as they entered the house. "Officer, thank God you got here. I've been trying to keep her from running away."

She stared in disbelief, not realizing what was going on.

"Things have been getting more and more bizarre! Last night my wife was hitting and scratching herself. I thought she was going to kill herself! I called Judge Morris, and he signed papers ordering a psychiatric evaluation."

The officer nodded. "Yes, we have them; we need your signature as a witness."

Susan screamed. "No, he's lying! There's nothing wrong with me. He's involved in a drug ring. They killed Tina Collins! Listen to me! He's trying to get rid of me because I know too much!" The officer took her arm. "That's all right. Calm down. You can tell your story to the doctor."

She pulled her arm away. "Don't touch me! I'm not going anywhere with you! Let me go!" Susan tried to run out the door but was stopped by the other officer who was returning from the car with a straitjacket.

Elliott leaned his head against the wall and started to cry. "Oh God, I can't bear this! I should have seen what was happening; she's been getting too involved with her patients." He looked up at one of the officers. "My wife's under the care of Dr. Rhoades, but she refused to go into the hospital. I didn't want to force her. Oh God, the doctor warned me that it could come to this!"

Susan couldn't believe what she was hearing. "He's lying. I'm not sick! He's the one! He's a sociopath!"

The two deputies took Susan's arms and started to put the straitjacket on her. She fought, but they were experienced and had a shocked Susan in the jacket within minutes.

As Elliott turned away, the officer patted him on the back. Take it easy, buddy. It's not your fault. She'll get help at the hospital. You're doing the best thing for her."

Susan struggled as the officers dragged her to the car. "You can't do this to me! I'll get you, Elliott!"

CHAPTER 19
I'M NOT CRAZY

The deputies sat in the car and ignored Susan, relieved that she had shut up after twenty minutes of shouting. "It's sad. Here's a guy who's got it all, and then his wife flips out. See, even with money you've got no guarantees! He'll have to take care of this one for the rest of his life."

Susan's throat was sore from yelling. And, the more she screamed, the crazier she sounded. To these policemen, she was just another delivery. The car pulled up to a small hospital. Susan remembered Elliott telling the police that she was Dr. Rhoades' patient and realized that this must be his hospital, the one that Mark described so horrifically. Fried brains, that's how he described Rhoades' electro-shock therapy.

One of the policemen opened the back door of the car. "Come on, Honey, let's go. They're waiting for you!"

Susan hissed. "I'm not your Honey!"

The officer pulled her out of the car and waited while an orderly brought out a wheelchair. "Here are her papers, signed by Judge

Morris. She's all yours. This one has got a good story, the best I've heard this month!"

An orderly wheeled her into the waiting area outside the admitting room and motioned to the clerk. "This is Susan Mason, the one that Dr. Rhoades is expecting. I'll stay here with her; you give him a call. He said he wanted to do the intake interview."

Susan sat quietly, looking around the first floor for exits. She was trying to become familiar with the layout of the area so that at the first opportunity she would know where to run.

Coming down the hall toward Susan was a tall, distinguished-looking man she remembered meeting at the cocktail party. She felt a surge of anger and tried to pull her arms free from the jacket. "Get me out of this, you bastard!"

Dr. Rhoades leaned close so that the orderlies standing nearby wouldn't hear. "Shut up! If you're quiet you might get out of the jacket. If not, you'll get an injection of Thorazine. Take your pick." He stood up and said in a louder voice. "Now, now, Susan, let's be a good girl. We're here to help you. You're just confused and upset. We'll have a little talk in my office and then Joe, our orderly, will take you to your room. The site of a tranquilized Carla falling to the ground flashed into Susan's mind. So she closed her mouth and waited to be wheeled to the interview room.

A woman came from behind them and closed the door. Susan turned around and immediately recognized a fellow social worker. She was wearing the uniform: a suit, not too drab, but not sexy. The woman looked young as if this were her first year out of school. She sat down with a pen and notebook, an eager expression on her face, apparently thrilled to have an opportunity to watch the master at work.

Dr. Rhoades turned on the Dictaphone and began speaking. "Patient, Susan Mason, is a twenty nine-year-old, White, married female brought here by the Sheriff's police for a court-ordered psychiatric evaluation. Patient's husband, Elliott Mason, requested a court order when his wife became a danger to herself. She has been acting increasingly bizarre over the past few weeks, accusing her husband, a successful attorney, of being involved in illegal activities. Last night after watching a news program, she accused him of being responsible for a reported murder."

Susan couldn't believe what she was hearing. It wasn't what he was saying; it was the fact that it sounded just like other intakes she had heard. She turned back toward the social worker. "He's lying! This doctor and a group of other men have hired my husband to represent them in a drug scheme. It's an investment club; they put up money to buy drugs. He paid to have that woman killed!" Dr. Rhoades let Susan go on as he sat with a sad expression on his face.

The social worker looked past Susan, motioned to Dr. Rhoades, and rolled her eyes toward the ceiling. My God, all I'm doing is verifying his diagnosis! She slumped back in the chair, thinking about the intakes she had sat through, taking for granted that the person brought to the hospital was sick and that their wild stories were delusions. She felt a wave of depression but immediately fought it off. I'm alive; at least they haven't killed me. If they were going to kill me, they would've done it already. The orderly took off the straitjacket in the intake room, and for a second Susan thought about making a run for it. But after looking down the long corridor with staff milling around, and the beefy orderly behind her, she vetoed the idea. She put her head down and closed her eyes, appearing defeated, but concentrating her energies into one thought, one image, one word: survival!

Dr. Rhoades stood up. "Take her upstairs, Joe." He handed Joe the chart. "Here are her orders. Make sure the supervisor reads them immediately."

Joe wheeled a quiet Susan out of the room. She felt weak, between the pills Elliott had given her last night and his vicious attack, her energy was completely drained. The orderly took the elevator up to the second floor. Susan paid attention, trying to mentally map every office and hallway between the entrance and the ward. The elevator door opened; and Susan felt a sense of déjà vu as Joe took out a ring of keys and fumbled with them, looking for the one that would open the ward door.

A blonde, fortyish, attractive woman was standing on the other side of the door, obviously expecting them. "Hello, Susan. I'm Miss Kelly, the ward nurse. We're happy to have you here." She pointed to a young girl who looked like a college student standing next to her. "This is Marsha, one of our aides; she will help you get settled.

Dr. Rhoades ordered a private room for you. I'll be in to see you in a little while to go over the routines and rules of the ward. If you have any questions then, I'll be happy to answer them."

The nurse smiled at Susan, took the chart from Joe, and walked back to the nurses' station. Marsha reached down and helped Susan from the wheelchair. She was glad now that she hadn't attempted to run; her legs were so wobbly that she had difficulty standing alone.

Marsha nodded toward the orderly. "Better let me use the chair to take her to her room. I'll return it to the intake room as soon as we get her into bed."

Susan winced. Already she was a nonperson-just another body on the ward, one of the filled beds. Of course, this wasn't true, as she quickly learned. The first thing she noticed on the way to her room was that all of the rooms were semi-private. They resembled economy motel rooms with twin beds, two small dressers, and a desk. Marsha wheeled Susan into her room; and Susan saw that it contained only one bed, a chair, a dresser, and a desk. Marsha motioned to Susan. "I'll take your clothes. There are a gown and robe in the dresser. The bathroom has a sink and a toilet; the showers are across the hall. I'll take you there when you're ready. The doctor will be up in about an hour to give you a physical."

Susan was exhausted. She felt dirty and knew that she sounded like she belonged here. And with the dried blood crusted on her scratches and her stinking body, she physically fit the part as well. "Yes, thank you, I'd appreciate some help." Susan kept telling herself to be polite, be friendly, and get them on her side. Maybe then someone on the staff would believe her. "I don't have a toothbrush or toothpaste."

"Don't worry; I brought some from the nurse's station."

It took every ounce of Susan's strength to take a shower, and several times Marsha had to steady her. As she put on the hospital gown, she could not recall seeing any other patients in gowns. To her knowledge, all psychiatric wards had patients wear street clothes. Maybe she had to wear this for her physical? When Marsha took Susan back to the room, Nurse Kelly was waiting for them.

"Marsha, since you're the aide assigned to Susan, I think you'd better stay and listen to the restrictions Dr. Rhoades has ordered."

The Nurse flipped the chart open. "Susan, I want you to understand that these restrictions are for your own good. As you show improvement, we will lift the restrictions. We believe in being honest with our patients and involving them in their treatment plan right from their admission day. First of all, because of your suicide attempt last night . . ."

Susan interrupted, "What suicide attempt? I never did anything to hurt myself! My husband knocked me out with drugs and raped me, but..." They looked at her as if she were reciting a delusion. Susan stopped speaking at this point. She had better listen.

"You will be kept in your room unless an aide is with you. Dr. Rhoades feels that you may attempt to run away at the first opportunity. So you will be treated as a suicidal patient who is also a potential runaway, and you will be permitted to dress only in a hospital gown."

Nurse Kelly closed the chart and looked at Susan. "You believe that your husband is involved in serious criminal activities, Susan. So, I'm not going to attempt to persuade you to give up your beliefs, but we cannot let you ruin your husband's good reputation. Since you let us know that you intend to contact the authorities with this delusion, we have no choice but to take away your phone privileges. There is no phone in your room and under no circumstances are you to use any other phone on the ward. If you are caught trying to make a call, the doctor has written orders that you will be put in restraints immediately. Do you understand?"

Susan cried out! "Don't you understand? They are working together; this doctor is one of the biggest investors." Nurse Kelly's lips tightened. "Don't try to change the subject. Do you understand the rules?"

Susan nodded her head as she thought that bastard had made sure all his bases had been covered. Just then Dr. Rhoades came into the room. "Well, Nurse Kelly, how is our new patient doing?"

Nurse Kelly motioned toward Susan with an annoyed expression. "I think she's agitated, doctor. Maybe she needs a tranquilizer!"

Susan's heart raced at the thought of getting snowed under again. "No, I'll be good!"

Dr. Rhoades smiled. "Well, I'm glad to hear that. Still, we may order something to help you relax. Our staff internist is busy with a sick patient right now, so I will give you your physical."

Susan went through the examination without a murmur, afraid that more protests from her would only give the psychiatrist an excuse to tranquilize her. When Dr. Rhoades finished, he walked toward the door and turned to her with a sickeningly sweet smile on his face. "Your husband will be here this afternoon; he's very concerned about you."

Susan glared at him. "You two can't pull off this farce forever!"

He shook his head and, with a look of pity on his face, gently closed the door, leaving her alone. She got up from the bed and walked over to the window. The room was on the second floor. The window had the usual steel mesh, not attractive, but it provided protection for jumpers. For a moment Susan thought about yelling down to the passersby, but who would pay attention to a mad woman screaming from the window of a psychiatric hospital? No, Susan reasoned, the only way out of here was to get to a phone and call Mark. She lay down on the bed. He'll never even attempt to find me. The tears were rolling down Susan's face as the door opened. This time Marsha was bringing her tray. It must be lunch, or was it dinner? She was already losing track of time. She raised herself from the bed. "Can't I eat with the other patients?"

Marsha apologized, "No, I'm sorry. Dr. Rhodes has ordered meals in your room for the next few days." Marsha looked sadly at Susan. "Just cooperate, and then he'll loosen these restrictions."

"Oh, Marsha, you're so naïve. You don't have any idea of what is going on." Susan looked at the tray of roast beef and mashed potatoes and noticed that it was cold; and the dark brown gravy had specks of white grease. Susan was tempted to tell Marsha to take it back but decided that she had to keep up her strength if she were to have any hope of escaping.

Susan made a sandwich of the beef and set the tray on the desk. She lay back on the bed with her arms behind her head; and as she stared at the ceiling, Susan wondered what they were going to do to her. The court order could keep her in the hospital as an involuntary patient for up to three days. After that, she either had to be released, sign voluntary treatment papers, or be committed. If they went for a commitment, then she would be allowed a lawyer to represent her at the hearing. Even Elliott couldn't manage to cover all those bases! No, there had to be another reason why she was here. Maybe they were waiting for some time to pass. Right now, Susan could be linked to Tina Collins. If she were killed so close to Tina's murder, it would bring an investigation that the group could ill afford. Susan got up and tried the door; it was open! That meant Dr. Rhoades was following the state rule against locking a patient's room. It seems that the staff was not a part of this; they were only doing their job and taking care of a crazy lady. Susan felt a little better. Dr. Rhoades had much to lose if she escaped; but to the rest of the staff, she was only another patient. She watched the activity on the ward through the cracked door. With everyone wearing street clothes, it took her a while to separate staff from the patients. She stood looking out the door for about a half-hour until she saw Marsha coming toward the room; she quickly darted back to bed.

Marsha walked in with a cheery smile. "If you had enough, I'll take back your tray."

"Thank you, Marsha. Could you take me for a walk out in the day room?"

Marsha turned away. "I'm sorry, Dr. Rhoades left orders that you can't leave your room until he approves." Susan felt a surge of anger. "But the nurse said I could leave my room as long as I have a staff member with me!"

"I'm sorry, the doctor changed his mind. He said you had a poor attitude."

Marsha left the room. Susan felt another wave of depression; only this time she didn't fight it but curled up on the bed and closed her eyes.

* * *

Mark sat behind his desk at Linton State Hospital. He kept an eye on the phone. He should call Susan. Mark reached for the phone only to pull his hand back. They had agreed not to stay in touch. He shrugged his shoulders and halfheartedly picked up a report as he left the office. In the corridor, he saw Jenna walking toward the intake room.

"Hello, Jenna, how are things going on the ward?"

"Okay, but it's starting to get crowded up there. I'll be happy when the hiring freeze is over so you can fill Susan's position. By the way, have you talked to her lately?"

Mark continued walking down the hall. He called over his shoulder, "I'll see what I can do about getting that position cleared. Talk to you later, Jenna."

* * *

The door opened, and Susan awoke to see Marsha in the doorway. Right behind her was Elliott and Dr. Rhoades. Instantly everything came rushing back: the Sheriff's deputies bringing her here, the intake interview, and being placed in the locked ward. She must have fallen asleep. Susan pulled herself to the far side of the bed and turned away, her only means of escape.

Elliott smiled in Susan's direction. "Sweetheart, how are you? I've come to visit you. Please turn around and talk to me, Honey." When he received no response, Elliott turned and looked at Dr. Rhoades and Marsha with an aggrieved expression.

Dr. Rhoades motioned to Marsha. "Why don't we leave them alone? If Mr. Mason sits quietly with Susan for a while, maybe she'll realize that her husband hasn't abandoned her." Marsha nodded in agreement, and they both left the room.

Elliott pulled up a chair and sat by the bedside. After a couple of minutes, Susan turned and glared at him. "Just what are you and your buddy planning to do to me?"

The sickening smile never left his face. "Why, Honey, you're mentally ill. You need help! The doctor and I are just taking care of you."

"Dammit, Elliott! There's no one in the room but you and me, so lay off the theatrics. What plans are you and Dr. Frankenstein cooking up? You can't keep me here forever!"

"I don't intend to. Eventually, our insurance will run out and the only alternative left will be to ship you to Brighton." He feigned a sad expression. "No one will blame me. What else can I do for a wife who needs lifetime care except to put her in an institution? After all, I have a life to live too!"

Susan couldn't believe what she was hearing. "I hate to ruin your plan, but they don't admit you to Brighton unless your brain is like a tossed salad. Vegetables, Elliott, that's all they take at that place."

He grinned at her. "Yeah, I know. It's a terrible thing, mental illness. Some people get better; but then, unfortunately, some people get worse. You've given me a good education. I remember how much sympathy you had for the patient's family. Thank goodness, Dr. Rhoades shares your understanding. It will bring me comfort as I sadly watch you fall deeper and deeper into depression, and there's nothing I can do to help." Elliott patted her hand. "It's terrible to have to see a loved one go through this, but I'm receiving nothing but sympathy. For instance, that psychologist, Beth, at the clinic was very understanding when I told her how you blamed yourself for the Collinses' misfortunes. I explained that I had to send you to your mother's for rest. She agreed that you had been, shall we say, rather emotional lately."

Susan pulled back in disgust. "You're sick, Elliott!

Elliott's eyes flashed with anger. "Shut up, bitch. You're the one on the psycho ward."

She turned away, but he grabbed her shoulders and pulled her closer, lifting her off the bed till she was only inches from his face.

"Remember those commitment hearings you used to attend? All that concern for the scum that shouldn't even be taking up oxygen!" He sneered down at her. "Well, soon you'll be that patient sounding so pathetic that the only humane thing to do is to commit you." Elliott chuckled to himself as he pushed Susan back down on the bed. He was enjoying this, the feeling of total control. All the positive feelings that he had for Susan were gone; now the only feeling he had was anger. She was getting just what she deserved for standing in his way. "What a mess, you're so disgusting. How could I have ever thought you were a classy broad?"

At first, Susan was stunned; and then she was terrified. What if they pulled it off? She'd be a certified nut case; and with Judge Morris in on it, Elliott could probably get a commitment hearing just by showing up in court. "You'll never get away with it! Those hearings are open to the public. Someone will be smart enough to check out my story. If nothing else, it will plant a seed of doubt."

Elliott set back in the chair, deep in thought. "You've got a point." He smiled at her. "Thank you for finding the flaw in my plan; I wouldn't want anything to go wrong."

What had she done? That might have been her best chance, and now she had blown it! Who knows what they would do now?

Elliott laughed. "What's wrong? Getting depressed? Hey, this is perfect." He leaned back and started to chant. "Butterfly net, butterfly net, what do we have here? The Huntress is caught. Let's all give it cheer!"

Susan jumped off the bed, pushed him aside, and ran screaming to the door, "Let me out of here! Dammit, let me out!" She ran halfway down the hall before being tackled by a male aide. Soon there were four people on top of her. She was kicking and screaming, but they each grabbed a limb while Nurse Kelly pulled up Susan's gown and quickly stuck the needle in her hip. The last thing Susan remembered was Elliott standing over her saying, "I don't know what happened. One minute she was talking calmly, and then she jumped up and started clawing at me! I couldn't stop her. She ran out of the room."

* * *

It was dark. Susan opened her eyes and saw a line of light shining under the door. Her mouth was dry. Her muscles were tight, and everything ached. Slowly it came back: where she was, Elliott's taunts, and her reaction. They must have given her an injection; she felt groggy. What time was it? No, what day was it? Had she been here for hours or days? Was that the first injection or the only one she remembered?

Susan tried to move her hands, but she couldn't because they were tied down. She attempted to raise her legs, but Susan couldn't move them either. Oh God, she was in restraints! She couldn't turn her neck! "Help, help, someone, help me!" Susan screamed over and over until her throat was raw. Finally, the door opened.

She saw an unfamiliar woman standing in the light from the hallway. The woman turned on the ceiling light. Susan quickly closed her eyes from the painful glare.

"Hush in here. Stop that screaming! You're going to wake up the whole in the ward!"

"Please, help me. It's my neck; I can't move it!"

The woman came closer to the bed. She was big and maternal looking. "I'm Mrs. Cook, the night nurse. Let me see." She put her hand on Susan's neck. "Yes, it feels like you have dystonia. Don't get scared; it's a common side effect. There's a standing order for something to help with the discomfort. If you are quiet, I'll get something to relax those muscles."

Susan remembered all the times she had seen patients having the same drug reaction. Now she was lying here with her head cocked over to the side, looking as bizarre as some of her former patients. Elliott was right. She did get caught in her butterfly net! Under the sheet, Susan's body felt warm and moist.

After a few minutes, the nurse came back. "I am going to give you an injection of Cogentin. It should take effect in a couple of minutes." The nurse pulled off the sheet. "You've had an accident; the bed is wet."

Tears welled up in Susan's eyes. She had wet the bed! She felt a surge of shame that she hadn't experienced since she wet her pants the first day of kindergarten. Once again, she felt that Elliott and Dr. Rhoades might be able to pull off their plan. She'd fit right in at Brighton with Bill Collins in his urine soaked pants.

"I'll give you the shot and then get someone to help change the sheets and clean you up." She took an alcohol pad, cleaned a small area on Susan's hip, and gave her an injection. "I'll be back; you let this take effect."

Nurse Cook returned, and this time she had an aide with her. The nurse leaned over Susan and asked. "If I take you out of the restraints to clean you up, will you behave yourself? Otherwise, I will put you right back in; and you'll have to stay in this mess!"

Susan meekly answered in the affirmative, all the fight drained out of her. The two women loosened the straps and helped her from the bed, carrying on a lighthearted conversation as Susan tried desperately to hold on to the little ego she had left. Slowly they walked across the hall to the shower room, each woman holding one of Susan's arms. She felt the muscles in her neck relaxing and knew the shot was working. Right now the only thing she could think of was getting a shower and a clean gown. Suddenly she smiled and turned to the nurse. "They haven't got me yet! I'm not like those people at Brighton; I don't want to lie in that mess. My shame is a good sign!"

The nurse looked at the aide and shrugged her shoulders. "Anything you say, dear."

Back in the room, Susan sat on the chair as the nurse and the aide changed her bed. She turned her head and looked away, trying to dissociate from the urine soaked sheets they pulled from the bed.

Mrs. Cook turned to Susan. "All right, back to bed now. We won't put the restraints on. But if you start any trouble, I'll call security; and you'll go right back into them. Understand?"

Susan nodded her head and did not attempt to argue her case. Who would listen? Who would care? Compliance seemed the only way to cope, at least for tonight. She was tired, and the clean bed looked inviting. She lay down and quietly rolled over, pulling the sheet up over her head, trying to block everything out. But sleep was fitful, and the night was long. Susan kept waking up in a cold sweat with nightmares that turned out to be her reality.

CHAPTER 20
RESTRAINTS AGAIN

Susan had just fallen into a deep sleep when the ward noises awakened her. Her tongue had a furry coating. God must be punishing her for all the times she hadn't listen to patient's complaints about the side effects of the drugs. Susan got out of bed, went into the bathroom, and looked at herself in a polished stainless steel mirror, another safety feature found in a typical psych ward. She looked terrible. Her face was bloated, and there were dark circles under her eyes, all effects of stress, drugs, and sleep. How had she ever gotten to this point? Why hadn't she seen what had been going on sooner? What had made her close her eyes to Elliott's behavior? All the symptoms of a sociopath, that's what she denied. Suddenly she heard the door to her room open.

"Good morning. I brought you some breakfast." Susan walked out of the bathroom and saw Marsha standing with the tray.

"Thank you. Sorry, I usually tip for room service; but you people took my bag."

Marsha put the tray on the desk and then sat down while Susan ate. "I'm sorry that you had to be in restraints. It's an unpleasant experience."

"Tell me about it!"

"If you want to talk about anything, I'm here."

Susan turned to her. "Marsha? Do I look like someone who belongs here?" She suddenly remembered the reflection she had just seen. "Never mind; forget I said that. Why don't you tell me what my schedule is for today? Do I get to join in any activities, or do I sit in this room all day?"

"I'm sorry. While you're under observation, you're don't have a regular treatment plan. The doctor feels you have to stabilize first. The best thing you can do is cooperate. Then before you know, you'll be going on day trips; and if things go well, maybe even a home visit with your husband."

A disgusted look came over Susan's face. "I can hardly wait. Marsha, did it ever occur to you that I might be telling the truth? That my husband and Dr. Rhoades are involved in a drug scheme? And that I might be as sane as you?"

Marsha stood up. "Susan, I'm sorry, I can't discuss that with you. Dr. Rhoades left strict orders that we are not to reinforce that kind of thinking."

Susan replied, "I'm sorry, you can't do this. I'm sorry, you can't say that. I'm sorry, you can't think those thoughts. What the hell can I do?"

Nurse Kelly was standing at the door observing, "Very good,

Marsha. I'm glad to see you're following doctor's orders. Now I would like to talk to Susan." Marsha took the tray and left the room. "I'm hoping we don't have a repeat of yesterday's conduct. Your husband is worried about you. You gave him quite a scare. If you can behave yourself, I'll let Marsha take you for a walk on the ward this morning. We're not trying to punish you, Susan, but we can't allow you to disturb the other patients."

Finally, thought Susan, a chance to find a way out of here. "I understand. I promise, no more scenes. Please let me out of this room for a while. I'm going stir crazy!"

Nurse Kelly started to leave the room but turned back. "One more thing. I don't want to hear you telling the staff that ridiculous story about Dr. Rhoades. He's the kindest man I've ever met!" Nurse's Kelly's face flushed with anger. "I may not be able to shake your delusion, but I insist that you keep it to yourself! Do you understand that?"

Susan nodded, wondering why Nurse Kelly was so upset. Dr. Rhoades must have pulled a con on these people. But that was their problem. Right now she was excited about getting out of her room. Any small piece of hope became important.

She found that one of the annoying things about being here was losing a sense of time. There was no clock in her room; and her watch, along with her other possessions, was removed at intake. Susan sat down on the edge of the bed and went through a mental exercise to help her keep track of the day and the date. She repeated it several times until she felt that she knew what day it was. I can't let them win. I must do everything possible to keep my sanity. Just then Marsha came back into the room.

"I can take you for a walk around the ward, but Nurse Kelly told me to warn you to not even think about going near a phone."

"Don't worry; I want to get out of this room. I'll behave."

Marsha smiled. "Okay, then let's go. We can sit in the day room and play cards."

Susan remembered last time she had played cards. It was the day Carla was admitted to the ward. Was it only a month ago? "Thanks, Marsha, but I think I'll pass on the card game. I'm not up to all that concentration."

As they walk down the hall, Susan looked into the other rooms to see if they were occupied. Maybe she could sneak out of her room tonight and use the phone in an empty room. The day room was furnished better, but similar to the one at Linton. Susan looked at the nurses' station and saw several lists taped on the window. One was a suicide precaution list, and Susan's name was at the top. The next one was "runaway watch," and again Susan made the top of the list. The third list was a schedule for EST. Susan shuttered as she remembered what Mark had told her about Dr. Rhoades and his electro-shock therapy. She anxiously ran her eyes down the list; at least her name wasn't there! Marsha interrupted her observations. "If I have time after lunch, I'll come and get you again." Susan got up and followed Marsha without a whimper.

* * *

Back in her room, Susan lay down on the bed and let her mind wander. The EST list made her think of Mark. She sadly wondered if he was thinking of her. He probably didn't even know that she was missing. Susan thought about how she had pressured Mark about marriage. If only she had given him more time. She thought about the feelings they had for each other: the kindness, the respect, the values, and most of all the love they shared. Susan soon drifted off to sleep, the usual occupation of depressed people.

There was a knock at her door. "Susan, your lunch is here." Marsha pushed the door open with one hand as she balanced the tray in the other. "You won't be the only one who will be happy when you can eat in the dining room. I hope Dr. Rhoades takes you off restrictions soon."

Susan smiled, determined to be cheerful. Nothing was going to keep her from getting out of her room this afternoon.

Marsha looked apprehensive, remembering yesterday. "You have a visitor. Now please don't get upset. I don't think you want to go back into restraints!"

Susan's hands started to tremble. "Who is it?"

"It's your husband."

"I don't want to see him!" Susan got up and started to pace the floor. "Do I have to see him?" Marsha was hesitant. "I think so. Usually, patients have the right to turn down visitors; but Dr. Rhoades has a special interest in your case. He said your husband was worried and to make sure he had a visit with you. Maybe you could see your husband for a few minutes, just to let him know you're okay?"

Susan gave in, afraid to appear unreasonable. "All right. I'll see him, but only if someone is in the room with me. I don't want to be left alone with him!"

"Then why don't we take a walk out to the dayroom? That way you won't be alone with your husband, and you'll get out of your room." Susan panicked. She didn't want Elliott to notice that she was allowed to leave her room; he might tell Rhoades it was too risky.

"Marsha, if it's all right with you, I'd rather see him here. I don't want to be left alone with him, but I think he would want privacy. And then could I please take a walk after he leaves? That would help break up the day."

"Okay, I'll go get him." As Marsha turned to leave, Elliott stepped into the room. "Hello, Dear. Are you feeling better? I took the afternoon off to spend some time with you."

Susan smiled, ready to play Elliott's game. "I'm fine, thank you. How are you?"

He turned to Marsha. "You can leave now."

"No!" Susan moved in front of the door. "Marsha, don't go! Elliott, I want her to stay. Are you afraid to have her here?" Susan could see the muscles in his jaw tighten. He wasn't in control.

"No. I'm not afraid, Susan. It's just that I want to be alone with you. I'm sure Marsha doesn't mind leaving us for a while."

"Please, Elliott, I feel very anxious and want her to be here."

His hands grasped the edge of the desk until his knuckles were white. Marsha noticed. "Is something wrong, Mr. Mason?"

"No. Nothing's wrong." He took a deep breath and smiled at her. "I guess this business has upset me more than I thought. Maybe it would be better if I came back tomorrow." He turned to Susan and stared at her with narrowed eyes. "I'm sure my wife will feel more like talking to me tomorrow." When he left, Susan could hear his steps angrily pounding down the hall.

Marsha didn't say a word, but Susan could tell that she was puzzled by what had happened. It was just what Susan wanted, a seed of doubt! "Are you ready to take me out for my airing?"

Marsha smiled. "Sure, you handled the visit with your husband very well. Maybe tomorrow, you'll be able to talk to him for a while. If you keep this up, you'll be out of here in no time."

Susan left the room with her spirits lifting, but it didn't take long for them to come crashing down. In the dayroom, a notice was taped up on the nurses' station window. "Susan Mason, commitment hearing-conference room, Thursday, 9:30 A.M."

Marsha saw the fear in Susan's eyes and followed her stare. She quickly read the notice and looked back at Susan with surprise. "I'm sorry; I thought you knew about this. Let's go sit down and talk."

Susan was stunned. She had forgotten that occasionally with the judge's agreement, a hearing could take place in the hospital. What a fool she had been! She was the one who gave Elliott the idea. Susan knew that once she was committed, they'd have a free hand to keep her here as long as they wanted and to drug her with anything they wanted. It would be in her treatment plan. She followed Marsha to the far end of the empty dayroom. They sat quietly for a few minutes.

Marsha finally turned to Susan. "Look, why are you putting yourself through all this? Why don't you sign voluntary papers? Then you'll probably be released in a few days. It would be a lot easier than going through a court hearing."

Susan tried to reason with Marsha. "You don't understand. Marsha, they didn't offer me a chance to sign in voluntarily because they want me committed."

Marsha patted her hand. "That's not true, Susan. Your husband and Dr. Rhoades only want you to get help."

"All right. Then why don't you go up to the nurse's station and asked them for a set of voluntary papers?" Susan tried again. "You've been assigned to work with me; surely they would want you to try and get me to agree to a voluntary admission."

"If I get the papers, then you'll sign them?"

"Marsha, if you get the papers, I will be happy to sign them. I don't want to be committed; it's a hassle for everyone. But I'll bet one phone call they won't give you the papers."

Marsha laughed. "Come on, you know better than that! You're restricted. Remember, no phone calls!"

"Listen to me, please! I have no intention of calling the police or any agency like that. I only want to call a friend. It's important that he knows I'm here. He's a psychiatrist on staff at the hospital where I once worked. You can dial the number and talk to him. Nobody knows that I'm in the hospital. Don't you think that's a bit more than the usual restriction?"

Marsha was becoming disturbed. "I don't know. They are watching you more closely than any other patient, but maybe they have a reason. I've been working here for only six months; I don't know everything."

Susan realized that she was upsetting Marsha. "Okay, let's take one step at a time. How about trying to get those papers? I really would like to sign."

Marsha looked pleased. "Well, that I can do. And I know you're wrong about not being able to get them. You sit here while I go to the nurse's station." She gave Susan a stern look. "And I can see you from there, so don't try anything!"

After a few minutes, Marsha walked back to Susan...empty-handed. "You're right!" Marsha looked puzzled. "I don't know why, but Dr. Rhoades left orders that you are not to sign voluntary papers." Susan felt her spirits lifting again; she was slowly gaining an ally. Granted Marsha was just a kid, but at least someone on the inside was beginning to question what was going on. Now, all she had to do was convince Marsha to help her make that call.

"Marsha, I know that some of the things I've said have sounded pretty crazy. But considering this episode with the voluntary papers, don't you have a little doubt?" Susan waited a moment, letting her words sink in. "All I'm asking for is one phone call. I only want to let my friend know where I am. Does that sound so unreasonable?"

Marsha sat back and thought a moment. Then she slowly stood up. "I shouldn't be doing this. You know I could get fired. Come on, let's go. There's an empty room across the hall from yours. You can make the call, but then it's back to your room. And whatever you do, don't tell anyone I let you use the phone!"

Susan felt her heart racing. Soon it would be over; in a few hours she'd be safe. With most of the patients attending activity therapy, the corridor was empty; and every room they passed was unoccupied. When they got to Susan's door, Marsha paused for a second; but then she led Susan into the vacant room across the hall. She picked up the phone and handed it to Susan. "Remember, just one short call to your friend, no one else!"

"Don't worry. That's the only call I need to make." Susan dialed the number while Marsha looked on. Suddenly the room was filled with people; and the phone was yanked from her hand. She looked into the angry face of Nurse Kelly flanked by two male aides.

"Marsha, go and wait in my office. I'll talk to you after we put Susan in restraints. Susan knows that she is not allowed telephone calls." Marsha looked sheepish and quickly left the room, as Nurse Kelly turned to the aides. "Get her back to her room."

While the aides held her down, Nurse Kelly went for restraints and a tranquilizer.

The more Susan fought, the tighter they held her. It didn't take long before the nurse was back. They rolled Susan over on her hip. Nurse Kelly jabbed her with the needle, and she felt a sharp pain. Everything started to spin. Within seconds she was unconscious. And it took only a few minutes for the aides to put Susan's limp body into restraints.

* * *

It had been a busy day at the Public Defender's office, and it was late afternoon before Randy saw the schedule of the next day's commitment hearings dropped on his desk. He was engaged in a heated discussion with another public defender. The man picked up the list and scanned the names. "Hey, take a look at the name on the bottom. You'll never believe this! I've heard that a lot of people who go into the mental health field choose it because they need help themselves. I guess this proves it."

Randy took the paper, and his eyes scanned to the bottom-Susan Mason! A commitment hearing at the hospital that Dr. Rhoades operated! What the hell was going on? "I have a call to make. Talk to you later." As soon as his coworker was out of earshot, Randy reached over and picked up the phone. It rang several times before someone answered.

"Tom Rivers."

"Tom, its Randy Sloan. We've got to talk, now! Susan Mason is in Rhoades' Hospital, and she's scheduled for a commitment hearing tomorrow. We've got to get her out of there."

"Take it easy, Randy. We need to talk. Meet me at the entrance to the zoo in a half-hour."

"Shit, not the fucking zoo."

"Yes, it's close and safe."

"Okay, whatever. See you in a half hour."

Randy was waiting at the entrance when Tom arrived, and a few minutes later they were walking down a secluded path.

"She must have found out something; why else would he put her in there? It's a perfect way to keep someone quiet; the Russians do it all the time. We've got to get Susan out of there, Tom. You remember what those patients at Brighton looked like, and half of them are that way because of excessive psychotropic drugs."

They walked until Tom spotted a bench. "Come on; let's sit down for a minute."

Randy impatiently asked, "Well, what are we going to do?"

Tom responded, "Nothing."

Randy exploded, "Nothing! What the hell are you saying? That we stand by and wait for Elliott to kill her?"

Tom remained calm. "No. We're going to stand by until we get the okay to go in and nail Elliott. Randy, you're letting your emotions take over. First of all, if Elliott were going to kill her, she'd be dead by now. And second, she's probably safer in Rhoades' Hospital than she was living with Elliott."

Randy shook his head. "I don't know; I just don't feel comfortable with this."

"Look," Tom said, his face tense, "this is the second time we've had this conversation. Either you're an agent, or you're not. I'm beginning to feel uncomfortable working with you. We're at the end of the road. We know there's a big shipment coming in two weeks and that Elliott arranged for the drug distribution. Should we blow it all and endanger several of our agent's lives because you feel uncomfortable about leaving a woman in a hospital? Where I might add, she is bored, but a hell of a lot safer than you or I."

Randy nodded. "You're right; Rhoades isn't going to do something right underneath the noses of his staff. Two weeks in a private hospital won't kill her. I hope!"

CHAPTER 21
THE HEARING

Once again, Susan slept for hours; and it was dark when she awoke. She felt someone rubbing her body. Susan opened her eyes, confused, and dazed, and saw a strange man standing over her. Her gown was pulled up; the man had one hand between her legs while his other hand fondled her breasts. She let out a scream. The man jumped back and ran from the room, but Susan didn't stop screaming until Mrs. Cook arrived.

"What's going on in here? Stop that screaming!"

Susan cried, "There was a man in here. He was molesting me!"

"Nonsense. You were having a nightmare."

"For God's sake, he had his fingers in my vagina. Look, I'm in restraints; and my gown has been pulled up to my neck!"

Mrs. Cook came over and pulled down Susan's gown. "It must've been Harry; he sneaks out of his room at night. Don't worry; he's harmless."

Susan couldn't believe what she was hearing. To Mrs. Cook, everything was all right since he hadn't hurt her! Susan had been violated; but since she was a non-person, it didn't matter. Oh God, how many times had she not seen or listened? Susan glared at Mrs. Cook, just like any other patient stripped of self-respect, but helpless. "I have to go to the bathroom."

Mrs. Cook put her hand on the leather restraint around Susan's wrist. I'll get some help to take you out of these, but you have to go back into them. The doctor said you have to stay in restraints tonight. If you cooperate, I won't give you another shot."

"All right. But please get me out of these. I have to go! And can you get something for my muscles? They're contracting again."

Nurse Cook nodded her head. "Okay, I'll be back in a few minutes. Keep quiet; I don't want everybody on the ward awake."

The nurse and the aide returned and once again went through the ritual of giving Susan a shot for side effects and taking her to the bathroom. This time when they put her back in restraints, Susan didn't put up a fight. Harry was somewhere down the hall probably waiting for staff to leave so he could come back. She was determined to stay awake; but with the tranquilizers in her bloodstream, it wasn't long before she was sleeping again. It was now only a few hours until her commitment hearing.

* * *

After several hours of tossing and turning, Randy finally got out of bed, walked into the kitchen, and poured a large glass of milk. He had read somewhere that milk contained a natural hypnotic. In his mind, Randy replayed Tom's argument for letting Susan's hearing proceed; and he was still trying to convince himself that it was the right thing to do. Oh well, he reasoned, taking risks and sleepless nights were part of the job. It's just that he always thought that the risks would only be with his own life. Randy finished drinking the milk and hoped it had a hypnotic effect on his conscience. Back in bed again, he glanced at the clock on his bedside table. Two o'clock: it was now only seven and a half hours until Susan's hearing.

* * *

"Wake up; you have to shower and dress."

Susan heard a voice but had a difficult time responding, her drugged mind operated in slow motion. The aide unlocked the restraints. Susan's head began to clear, and slowly everything came back to her. It was the morning of her commitment hearing.

She didn't recognize the expressionless woman standing over her. "Where is Marsha?"

"She's been transferred to another ward. From what I heard, she was lucky not to be fired. The girl pleaded for her job, so they let her stay after she promised to follow doctor's orders in the future."

The woman stared coldly at Susan. "I have a lot more experience than Marsha, so don't even think about trying to manipulate me!"

Susan held up her arms and looked at her aching wrist, bruised and rubbed raw from pulling at the leather cuffs. She glanced up at the aide, a woman about thirty-five, dressed in a white blouse and a pair of navy slacks. She looked like a model for a Marine recruitment ad. Most hospitals had at least one on staff to keeping incorrigible patients in line. Susan swung her legs over the side of the bed and slowly walked to the showers with the drill sergeant right behind her. She stayed under the stream of water for a long time, letting herself cry. Tears mixed with water didn't seem to count.

"Hurry up in there, or you'll miss your breakfast!"

Susan turned off the water, dried herself, and put on her gown. Returning to the room, she noticed that Elliott must've dropped off her clothes, a concession for her sham court appearance. There was a tray of food on the desk. Susan took one look at the cold, greasy scrambled eggs and felt a wave of nausea. She took a couple of bites from the piece of toast and forced the eggs down with large gulps of coffee. For a moment Susan considered refusing to dress but realized that, dressed or not, she would be forced to go to the hearing. If she went in looking crazy, it would only strengthen the case against her. And maybe if she appeared cooperative, someone in the room would listen to her.

She waited alone on the bed, struggling to remember the things that happened in a commitment hearing. Finally, two male orderlies were standing in the doorway. "Let's go, Susan," one ordered. "They're waiting for you in the conference room."

Susan got up and walked down the corridor like a prisoner being walked to death row. The rest of the staff was busy and ignored her as she walked past the nurse's station. An activity had been planned to get the patients off the ward. Susan turned to one of the orderlies. "Commitments make everyone nervous. See, no one will look me in the eye. If my loss of freedom is not acknowledged, then no one has to feel guilty. Ignorance is bliss. I know; I've been there."

The orderly looked away and ignored her comment.

The group assembled in the conference room. Susan was surprised and disappointed to see Judge Morris sitting at the head of the conference table. She knew he wasn't the regular judge who handled commitments and wondered how he had managed to get assigned to this hearing. There was Dr. Rhoades, calmly smoking a pipe; and sitting next to him was a young, collegiate-looking man. On the other side of the table was a court reporter with the machine set up to record everybody's testimony. And then, of course, there was Elliott, her beloved husband. The orderlies seated Susan next to the young man. Judge Morris cleared his throat and said in a loud, forceful voice. "Let this hearing proceed!"

She listened as Judge Morris explained that the usual judge had a scheduling conflict. Then Susan heard the judge say, "For the record, Susan Mason has been offered counsel but has refused to talk with her attorney. Mr. Davidson is present for the hearing."

Susan jumped up and shouted, "No! Correction, sir! I didn't refuse to talk to him! I've never seen him before!"

The orderlies standing behind her grabbed Susan by the shoulders and pushed her down.

Judge Morris looked sternly at Susan. "There will be no further outbursts from you, Mrs. Mason; or I will have you gagged!" Her assigned lawyer, Mr. Davidson, didn't say a word. The hearing continued. Elliott told the judge how his wife has become increasingly depressed over the past several weeks; and her behavior had continued to deteriorate until Susan became delusional and suicidal. He told how she had attacked him at the hospital and how she was ruining his career with her crazy accusations. Then Dr. Rhoades pointed out that Susan was a danger to herself in the community and finished with the recommendation for commitment. Nurse Kelly told of the violent behavior that resulted in Susan frequently requiring restraints which substantiated Dr. Rhoades' findings.

The whole process took only twenty minutes. Susan's lawyer, Mr. Davidson, never questioned anyone; and Susan reasoned that he must be a junior partner in the organization. Judge Morris officiously stated, "Commitment granted!" He signed the prepared papers and motioned for the orderlies to take her from the room.

Susan couldn't move, and her knees felt like rubber. The orderlies took her by the arms and lifted her to her feet. She looked at Elliot who was studying the paper the judge had handed him; he sensed her stare and glanced up with that sickening smile on his face. That did it! Susan felt a wave of nausea; only this time, she lost her breakfast right on the conference table. Everyone jumped up. Elliott shouted, "You threw up on purpose!"

Susan didn't feel any embarrassment. After all, she was no longer responsible for her behavior. Judge Morris gathered his papers and quickly left the room as the orderlies looked at the vomit with disgust. One of them pointed to Susan. "Take her back to her room. I'll get someone from housekeeping to clean up this mess!"

The orderly took Susan's arm and led her out of the conference room. She was dazed and followed him down the corridor with a blank expression. Back in the room, she sat on the side of the bed until Nurse Kelly came in holding out a hospital gown, wanting Susan's clothes in return. She undressed, dropped her clothes onto the floor, put on the gown, and then lay on the bed. Nurse Kelly picked up her clothes and left the room.

Susan knew that ordinarily a patient would never be allowed to spend so much time in bed. She reasoned that the goal of her treatment plan was to have her lose touch with reality as quickly as possible. Even knowing this, she lay on the bed feeling hopeless, cooperating with her captor's plan.

Someone brought a tray, and someone else took it back untouched. Susan didn't move for several hours. She recounted everything that had happened from the day of Randy's party to her day in court this morning. If only she had had something else to do that night, her whole life would now be different. There would be no Elliott, no guilty feelings about Tina, and no memories of Bill Collins vegetating at Brighton. And this, none of this would have happened! She thought of Mark and all their loving times drifted through her head. If she hadn't pushed, she wondered again, would they be together now? Susan sank further and further into depression as she went from name to name and realized that none of them could help her. Even Marsha, who was beginning to question what was going on, was now probably convinced that she was a manipulative psychotic. She had been abandoned!

The hours ticked by, but Susan had lost all sense of time. She had lost all control over her life and was now hoping it would end. Her past would soon be gone, and there were no tomorrows.

Someone knocked on the door, and another tray was brought in and set on the desk. Susan responded by turning her head toward the wall. She didn't speak and didn't feel. The room went from bright to dim, to dark, as she drifted in and out of sleep, repeatedly wakened by the sight of Elliott's smirking face. Finally, the image floated away, giving her a few hours of peace.

The sun came up, and the room was bright again. It was just another day, another shower, another breakfast, another morning of Susan lying in her bed. No one bothered her. She was left to herself. After all, she thought, Dr. Rhoades could afford to be passive and wait for her to hit rock bottom. It wouldn't take long; she had already given up any hope of escape.

The door opened, and she waited for someone to leave the lunch tray. But instead, she heard Dr. Rhoades' voice. "Hello, Susan. I stopped in to inform you of the course of treatment we will be pursuing over the next few weeks."

Susan ignored him.

"That's all right, Susan. You never have to talk again as far as

I'm concerned; just listen. I wouldn't want you to think that we would do anything to you without your knowledge."

Nurse Kelly was standing next to the doctor and Susan pretended not to notice as she saw Dr. Rhoades' hand reach behind Nurse Kelly and fondle her buttock. No wonder she followed his orders without question; they were screwing around.

The doctor continued, "Mrs. Mason because of the severity of your depression, I am ordering a series of electroshock-therapy. I have discussed this with your husband, and he has agreed to the treatment. You are in no condition to comprehend what is happening to you, so your husband has signed the necessary permission forms."

Susan flew up from the bed and grabbed the doctor's hand and sunk her teeth into it. He jumped up yelling and tried to pull his hand away, but she hung on with all her strength. Nurse Kelly reached over and gave Susan a sharp slap across her face. Susan reeled back from the blow and lost her grip on the hand. Dr. Rhoades held his hand out and looked at the bleeding teeth marks.

"God damn you! You'll be sorry you did that!" He turned to Nurse Kelly. "Come on; I need a tetanus shot."

Dr. Rhoades looked back at Susan on the way out. "This won't change anything! You're going to start those EST series on Monday, and you're going to get one every day until you won't even know who you are or where you are. When we're through giving you these treatments, you'll be an imbecile!"

Susan vowed revenge. Maybe she would lose; but over the last few days, she had forgotten how good it felt to fight. Suddenly, Susan recalled the hearing; and she recalled Elliott's shocked face as she threw-up all over the conference table. And then she thought about Dr. Rhoades' expression as he tried to pull his hand free from her teeth. Susan started to laugh. At first, it was a giggle; but then she let out a loud, raucous laugh. The door opened, and Nurse Kelly with two burly aides came into the room. "What's going on in here?"

"I'm not depressed, Nurse Kelly. That's what's going on. I believe I still have my sense of humor. Maybe it's a little primitive, but what the hell! By the way, is Rhoades a good fuck?" She started laughing as Nurse Kelly glared down at her.

"You're going back into the restraints." Nurse Kelly turned to the aides. "Watch her mouth, she bites!"

Susan didn't fight; she remembered how intolerant the staff became when one of their own was injured. And to these people, Dr. Rhoades was God incarnate. "Enjoy your memories, Susan. We'll see how much you can remember by next week! Shock therapy has temporary memory loss as one of its side effects. But, by the time you finish the series Dr. Rhoades has in store for you, your loss won't be temporary." Nurse Kelly left the room leaving Susan strapped to the bed, no longer laughing.

* * *

Mark was editing a paper for presentation at Sunday's regional meeting of the Department of Mental Health. Satisfied that everything was correct, he walked next door and handed the report to his secretary.

"Its fine, Donna. I'll need a dozen copies. Just leave them in the bin when you're finished. I have a few calls to make before I leave."

"Okay, Doctor. Don't forget to take your plane tickets. That shuttle to Springfield is booked solid."

Mark padded the breast pocket of his suit. "Got them right here; see you Wednesday unless I can think of an excuse to sneak out of there sooner. Productive meetings are a rarity."

Back in his office, Mark took a deep breath and picked up the phone. Since Tuesday morning he had been telling himself that it was better if he and Susan didn't talk, but Mark couldn't push from his mind the feeling that he had picked up in Susan at their last lunch. It went beyond fear. He had felt that emotion before. Usually, it came from his paranoid patients. But Susan wasn't paranoid, so what was he picking up?

"Good afternoon, Tri-Valley Mental Health Center. May I help you?"

"Yes, may I please speak to Susan Mason?"

There was a pause at the other end of the telephone.

"Is this a client?"

"No, this is Dr. Denning, a friend of Susan's. Is she in?"

"Doctor, if you'll hold on for a moment I'll connect you to our acting director, Dr. Jordan.

As Mark waited, he wondered what was happening.

"This is Dr. Beth Jordan, the staff psychologist. You're calling to speak to Susan. So you haven't heard?"

He felt his pulse quicken. "Heard what?"

"Susan has taken a leave of absence. Well, her husband has requested it. He said she was depressed and needed to get away. She'll be staying with her mother in Arizona. A patient here at the clinic was murdered, and Susan had some problems coping with the death. I guess I can tell you it was Tina Collins since what happened was all over the news. Her husband explained that she was already upset over losing a patient before leaving Linton State."

Mark remembered Susan's reaction to Carla's fatal heart attack. "Yes, she had a difficult time accepting a patient's death at Linton. With this happening so soon after, it's no wonder that she's depressed. Do you have her mother's telephone number?"

"No, I'm sorry; her husband felt that it would be better if she were left alone at this time. We're expecting to hear from him sometime next week. Hopefully, Susan should return to work in two weeks. I'll be glad to see her; I have some unanswered questions about the Collins' case."

"Thank you for the information, Dr. Jordan. If it's all right with you, I'll call back next week to find out how Susan is doing."

"Of course, it's all right. Talk to you next week." Mark put the telephone down and leaned back in his chair with a grave frown. Susan had visited her mother in the past, and he knew he had the telephone number somewhere in his apartment. Well, perhaps a couple of weeks away from the mental health scene would help her put things in perspective. A few minutes later, Mark was on his way home to pack; he would be leaving for Springfield tomorrow.

CHAPTER 22
THE CANDY BAR

Susan woke as the morning shift was taking her out of restraints. Blessed sleep, a place where time and troubles no longer exist. But bladders continue to function even in the depressed. Susan dragged herself out of bed, angry that her body's needs prevented her from staying in that safe cocoon of sleep. However, the bathroom is not just a small room to care for one's bodily functions; it is also the ideal place for soul-searching.

She had washed her hands and pulled out a paper towel from the dispenser. The image in the polished steel mirror stared back at her while Susan dried her hands. Who was this person? She saw a woman with matted hair and empty, glassy eyes. Susan turned away disgusted. No, this wasn't her; she was an intelligent, attractive woman, not this crazy lady. Susan let out a loud groan and covered her face. She cried for being so wrapped up in her marriage that she hadn't taken the time to visit her parents, she cried for the babies she would never have, for Mark whom she would never see again. But most of her tears were for herself, for she was losing her very being. She studied the image and tried to find the old Susan. How would Susan, the therapist, react? What would she say?

Why did you marry this man? Okay, so you acted without thinking. It isn't the mistakes in your life that are important; it's what we make of them that count. What have you done to get yourself out of this mess? Susan answered herself. I've gotten myself put in restraints, or I've been in bed depressed. What a fool! Why didn't I just ask Marsha to make the call for me on her own time? Mark would've been breaking down the door. I may as well be brain-dead; that's how I've been acting. I'm sure as hell not going to get out of here strapped to a bed. Dammit, Susan, your mind is your best resource. Use it!

Thirty minutes later an aide brought Susan her breakfast. When the aide returned for the tray, Susan again forced herself to be friendly. She was not going to provoke a scene that resulted in restraints. For the next several hours, Susan went over every bit of information she could think of about this hospital: shift changes, meal times, the medication times, and visiting hours. She had to know every routine inside out. Without a watch, it was difficult; but one thing she was sure of, the timing of shift changes. Most hospitals followed the same shift changes. Susan was sitting at the desk trying to think of some grand escape plan when she heard someone knocking at the door. It opened, and an Asian man poked his head in the room.

"Hello. Are you Mrs. Mason?"

"Yes, I'm Susan Mason. I'd prefer being called Susan."

The man stepped inside the room. "I'm Dr. Wong, the anesthesiologist. Dr. Rhoades has asked me to work with him on Monday when you receive your EST."

But of course, there was no way she could get treatments without an anesthesiologist. She wondered if he was a part of the group, but couldn't recall seeing his name on Elliot's list. She considered telling him what was going on but decided he probably was warned about her manipulative behavior. Instead, she listened.

"Mrs. Mason, I stopped by to see you and explain the procedures so you wouldn't be frightened. First of all, you will not have any pain with the treatment; but then I'm sure Dr. Rhoades has explained that to you."

Susan shook her head no.

Dr. Wong seemed surprised. "No? Well, he'll probably come in to see you later. But I'll tell you what to expect. On Sunday evening the nurse will give you your regular medication. I believe the doctor has you on a tranquilizer. Then on Monday morning, I will be administering a muscle relaxant and a slight general anesthetic during the procedure. The only thing you'll feel is having the needle put into your arm. We use only a small electric current, and the only after-affect will be short-term memory loss for about twenty-four hours. Because you'll be getting a general anesthetic and a muscle relaxant, you cannot have anything to eat or drink after midnight on Sunday. Susan, do you have any questions?"

"Yes, will you be giving me all the series?"

The doctor smiled. "Yes, I'll be giving you all seven treatments; that's one series. Most people only need one series. We've had good results from EST, Susan. If things go well, you should feel much better."

She was sure now that he wasn't a part of the group.

"Dr. Wong, I wonder if you could do me a favor."

"That depends, Susan. What you want?"

"I know this sounds silly, but I have a terrible fear of needles. Could you ask the nurse to give me my tranquilizer in pill form instead of a shot? I'm afraid of needles. If I know I have to get a shot Sunday night, I'll be nervous all day."

"Yes, I can do that. For a moment I thought you might be asking me to make a telephone call for you. The nurse warned me that you would probably try. I'm glad you didn't."

Susan smiled. "Yes. I'm also glad I didn't."

The doctor walked toward the door. "Remember, nothing to eat or drink after midnight!"

"Okay. "But you remember-no shot, just a pill." She wanted to be alert as long as possible.

"All right, I'll do that. See you Monday."

On Sunday morning Susan awoke refreshed, but still, without a plan. She sat at the small desk in the room and tried to think of every possible way to get help. She rejected all her ideas when one flaw after another surfaced. Her only hope was to somehow connect to a telephone, even at the risk of being put back in restraints.

Susan walked to the door, opened it a little and watched for activity in the corridor. It was empty. The patients were having dinner, and the aides were setting up evening medications. Susan knew that she would have only ten minutes before the fast eaters would be back on the ward. That left just enough time to call Mark. She looked down the corridor again and then darted across the hall just as the door to the ward opened and Dr. Rhoades entered. He pointed to Susan and shouted, "Mrs. Mason is out! Get her now!"

The aides rushed down the corridor as Susan ran into an empty room and slammed the door. She reached for the telephone while bracing her body against the door and dialed Mark's number as the aides banged on the door. As her heart was pounding, Susan whispered, "Hurry, dammit! Mark, answer your phone!"

The seconds passed like hours. But before the call transferred to the answering machine, Susan felt her feet slowly slide across the floor as the door was pushed open. Dr. Rhoades grabbed Susan as one of the aides pried her fingers from the phone. "Put her in restraints and lock the door. I've had enough of this! If she escapes from her room again, the whole shift will be suspended without pay! Does everyone understand?"

The aides dragged Susan across the hall and threw her down on the bed. As they strapped her in, she heard one aide whisper, "It's against the mental health code to lock the door when a person is in restraints."

The other curtly answered, "That's Rhoades' problem. He ordered it, and I don't intend to lose my job bucking him. Besides, it won't kill her; and she brought it on herself!"

A few minutes later Nurse Kelly arrived with the syringe in her hand. Susan tried to wiggle from the needle, but Nurse Kelly grabbed a piece of flesh between her thumb and index finger and jabbed the needle into Susan's hip. The last thing she heard was the sound of the key locking the door.

Hours had passed, and the fog in Susan's mind was beginning to lift. A key rattled in the door, and she saw a figure silhouetted against the brightly lit corridor. The woman turned on the flashlight and shone it on Susan's face. Susan turned away from the glare as the woman gasped.

"Susan!"

Susan immediately recognized the voice. "Jenna!"

Jenna stepped closer to the bed. "I don't understand, girl. What the hell are you doing here?"

Just then the door opened, and the charge nurse walked in. "What's keeping you, Jenna? Is something wrong?"

Jenna glanced at Susan and saw the panic in her eyes. "This lady needs a shower; she's foul. I think she messed the bed."

"Okay, but be careful; she's a runner. And if she gets away, it's my job. I'll stay at the station until you finish, but make it quick. And remember, she's scheduled for shock therapy in the morning; so don't give her anything to eat or drink."

Jenna and Susan were silent until the sound of the nurse's footsteps faded. "Okay," Jenna whispered. "What is going on? I know you're not crazy, so how in the hell did you get here?"

"It's a long story; I'll tell you all about it while you help me shower. First of all, get me out of these damn restraints and tell me why you are here!"

Jenna unlocked the restraints and helped Susan out of bed. "I work here as a substitute. They call me in when someone is out sick. Remember, I told you I was moonlighting at a private hospital until an LPN position opened at Linton?"

As Susan showered, she told an astonished Jenna what had happened. "This is incredible, girl. No wonder everybody here believes you're crazy. What do you want me to do?"

"Jenna, call Dr. Denning. You can't go to the police; I don't know who can be trusted. Besides, I was legally committed." Susan's voice filled with panic. "I've got to get out of here before they give me EST." Jenna helped Susan dry off and gave her a clean gown. "Look, Susan, why don't we find some clothes and get you out right now. I'll give you my keys and distract the nurse while you run."

"Look at me, Jenna. I can't even stand without your help, let alone run!"

"Yeah, you've got a point."

"No, you've got to get to Dr. Denning! He'll know how to get me released."

"This is unreal! What if I can't reach Dr. Denning? What if he doesn't believe me? We've got to do something else. You're going for shock in a few hours."

Jenna put her fingers to her lips as the door to the shower room opened. "Jenna, it would be better if you didn't talk to Mrs. Mason. She's caused a lot of problems on the ward with her manipulation, and Dr. Rhoades wants only necessary contact until she's ready to cooperate. Besides, I need you on the floor. Get her back to bed and put on the restraints."

"Yes, ma'am. I was taking her back. I'll be right there."

Jenna apologized as she slipped the restraints around Susan's ankles. "I hate to do this; but if she checked you later and they're not on, it will only cause more trouble. I'll put them on loose. My God girl, your skin is raw. You're quite a fighter!"

"Yeah, and I'll probably have the scars to prove it. Please, get in touch with Mark!"

Jenna leaned close to Susan. "Look, I get a coffee break in a little while, and I'll call him then. Just give me his home number. In about an hour you watch the light under the door. I'll flick it off and on, and then you start yelling that you have to go to the bathroom. That way I'll have an excuse to come back." She patted her arm. "See you later, girl."

Susan heard Jenna walk down the hall. She turned her head toward the door watching the sliver of light, afraid to look away even for a second. Susan waited until the light disappeared and then returned. Her mouth was dry. At first she could only make a feeble cry, but soon a yell was heard throughout the ward.

"I have to go to the bathroom! I can't hold it any longer; I have to go now!"

Jenna was yelling as she unlocked the door. "Calm down in there, right now! You'll wake the dead!"

Susan's heart was pounding. "Did you talk to him?"

Jenna leaned over the bed and Susan knew right away that something was wrong. "I couldn't reach him. I forgot someone mentioned Friday that Dr. Denning was going to a conference in Springfield."

Tears rolled down Susan's cheeks. She had been put in restraints and injected with a tranquilizer for telephoning an empty apartment. "What am I going to do?"

Jenna unlocked the restraints from Susan's wrist and reached into her pocket. "Look, we can't get you out of here tonight; but at least you won't be getting a shock treatment tomorrow."

Susan looked at Jenna's hand. "A candy bar! You're right. Nothing to eat after midnight."

Jenna unwrapped the candy. "Hurry up and eat this. I can't stay here much longer!"

"I'm going to put the wrapper under your pillow. When the nurse comes in the morning and takes you out of restraints, slip your hand under the pillow, get the wrapper, and keep it in your fist. Then take it out and show it to the anesthesiologist. In the meantime, I'll talk to Maggie as soon as I get off work. I'm sure we'll think of something. Keep the faith, girl!"

Back in restraints and with the door closed, Susan was left alone. She heard the key turn in the lock and felt the restraints on her wrist and ankles, but she slept peacefully. She was no longer alone.

* * *

Elliott was jarred awake by the alarm clock. Five minutes later it sounded again. And this time he remembered why he had set the alarm. Today his life would become less complicated. An hour later he was sitting in Dr. Rhoades' office. "I spoke to Frank last night, and he's getting impatient. He thought Susan would be taken care of by now."

Dr. Rhoades slammed a chart onto his desk. "I am doing this as quickly as I can! I told you our staff anesthesiologist underwent emergency surgery last week. It was difficult enough trying to find a replacement for my regular cases, never mind this one. We have to do this by the book; I don't want to be left holding the bag. Besides, your wife is not part of our deal. You approached me with this financial investment, and now look at the mess I'm in!"

Elliott jumped up and grabbed Dr. Rhoades by his collar, pulling him out of his chair.

"You bastard! Why did we come to you in the first place? I'll tell you why! Because, Dr. Rhoades, you're a greedy son of a bitch whose professional emblem is a dollar sign! So, cut the crap about your loss of innocence. Frank DiMato wants this matter tied up quickly. As long as my wife remains an articulate witness, we're just a breath away from prison. And need I remind you that your name is at the top of the list of investors!"

Elliott released Rhoades and watched him slump back into his chair. "Don't worry," Rhoades said. "In an hour she'll be an unreliable witness."

A smirk spread across Elliott's face. "I'd like to be there; I'd like to see her body quiver when you turn on the current."

Rhoades shook his head. "No way. That would cause problems. The staff would be suspicious. It's bad enough that we don't have a doctor we can trust."

Elliott stopped smiling. "You're right; I shouldn't even be here. But give me a call when it's over. Frank expects a progress report."

Dr. Rhoades walked toward the door. "You'd better leave; I'm expecting Dr. Wong any minute."

"Okay, talk to you later."

Elliott walked to the elevator, pushed the button, and waited. Soon the light came on, and he gave a friendly nod to the Asian man who stepped out of the elevator.

* * *

Susan awoke to the sound of Nurse Kelly's chirpy voice. "Good morning, Susan. It's time for your treatment."

Out of restraints, Susan reached under the pillow and wadded the candy wrapper in her palm as she was being wheeled down the hall and into the elevator. On the third floor, an aide was waiting for them and pushed open the surgery door. There was an oxygen tank, paraphernalia for administering an anesthetic, and a cart. Susan quickly fixed her eyes on the cart and its contents. There were two electrodes-one for each temple, a jar of petroleum jelly to attach the electrodes, and the sinister box that would send an electric current into her brain. She remembered Maggie describing how years ago the current caused the patient's bones to fracture from the shock. Since then the procedures had been modified. Now the first treatment only caused a temporary short-term memory loss. But with the number of treatments planned by Dr. Rhoades, Susan knew that she would end up with permanent memory loss. He would take chunks of her life away one session at a time until the only thing left would be an empty shell.

Dr. Wong smiled at Susan. "Good morning, Susan."

Dr. Rhoades turned and smiled, too. "Good morning, Susan."

Nurse Kelly picked up the petroleum jelly and put a thick coin-sized coating on each of Susan's temples. She stuck the electrodes to the jelly and stood back.

Dr. Wong came over to Susan's side and picked up her arm. "Susan, I don't want you to be afraid. Remember, I told you that the only unpleasant part is inserting the needle. So please try to relax; it will be over in just a minute. Are you ready?"

Susan gave him a sheepish grin. "No, there's something I think I should tell you."

Dr. Wong leaned down. "What, Susan, what is it?"

Susan held her hand out. She opened it, and there was the candy wrapper sitting in the middle of her palm. "I'm sorry, Doctor, but I woke up a few hours ago; and I was starving. It wasn't until after I ate the candy bar that I remembered the treatment today. I knew you'd be upset. I wasn't going to say anything, but I thought I'd better tell you."

Dr. Rhoades exploded. "What the hell is going on? That bitch is lying! She didn't have anything to eat; she's been in restraints all night. It's a ploy to get out of having the EST."

Dr. Wong looked up with surprise at Dr. Rhoades. "Doctor, this is a patient!" He turned back to Susan. "You were right in telling me about this. It's dangerous. You see, if you vomited during the procedures, you could choke to death."

"Oh, God, that's horrible! You're not going to continue, are you?"

"No, we'll have to wait until tomorrow. I'm disappointed that this has been a waste of time, but these things happen. Just make sure you don't eat or drink tonight, no matter how hungry you are!"

"She's lying! Don't let her con you, Doctor!" Rhoades' face was red with anger.

Dr. Wong turned to Dr. Rhoades. "I'm not going to take the chance, Dr. Rhoades. Her life is my responsibility once I start administering the anesthetic." Dr. Wong started to walk toward the door.

Dr. Rhoades looked at Nurse Kelly. He motioned to Susan and said, "Put her in restraints!"

Dr. Wong turned to Dr. Rhoades. "Doctor, may I talk to you

for a moment?"

Dr. Rhoades walked over by the door. Dr. Wong lowered his voice, but Susan could still hear him. "Doctor, are you sure you want to put this woman in restraints? I couldn't help but notice the open sores on her wrists. According to the mental health code, restraints are not to be used for punishment. Doctor, this isn't the first time I've had to cancel treatment because someone forgot and ate something. After all, she is here for mental health problems, isn't she?"

Rhoades knew he had gone too far. He shouldn't have expressed anger toward a patient, especially this one, in front of another physician. Dr. Wong was not on the hospital staff and, therefore, would have nothing to lose by turning in a complaint to the local medical board.

Dr. Rhoades sadly shook his head. "I'm sorry, Doctor. I've been past due for a vacation, and this patient has been so manipulative that I've lost my patience." He turned to Susan. "I'm sorry I lost my temper. I'll be back to talk with you later, dear."

The doctors left, and Nurse Kelly wheeled Susan back to her room. So far, things were going according to Jenna's plan. Susan was having breakfast when Dr. Rhoades arrived. He stood in front of her and glared for several seconds. Susan felt goose bumps rise on her skin as she waited.

Finally, Dr. Rhoades spoke. "You weren't very funny this morning. You put my career on the line, and that was a stupid thing to do.

But don't worry, you haven't destroyed our plan. You've only delayed it one day. If you have any more ideas for avoiding treatment, I suggest that you think about the alternative plan we have for you. Your deep depression might become more than you can tolerate. It's such a pity when a young person like you commits suicide. I'm sure my compassionate colleague, Dr. Wong, will grieve when he hears about it. He may even feel guilty about preventing us from putting you in restraints for your protection."

Susan did not respond. Rhoades smiled. "Well, Susan, nothing to say?"

Her hands were trembling, but her voice was steady as she replied. "Get laid, Doctor. I think Nurse Kelly is waiting for you in the linen closet!" Dr. Rhoades' face turned beet red, and he slammed out of the room.

Susan slumped back on the bed and thought about what he had said, realizing that she didn't have much time. Rhoades was right; there were many ways to kill her and make it appear to be suicide. They could make it seem that she had hoarded her medicine and then over-dosed. A patient committing suicide on a psych ward was not unusual. Someone could even kill her and make it look like one of the other patients had killed her. There would be an investigation; but, at most, the hospital would receive a slap on the wrist for negligence. And of course, Elliott, her bereaved next of kin, would never push for an investigation. As she lay brooding, someone knocked at the door. "I'm here to check your room."

The aide searched everywhere looking for contraband. Satisfied, she picked up the breakfast tray and left the room.

* * *

Dr. Rhoades hands shook as he reached for the telephone. He changed his mind and instead opened his desk drawer and took out a bottle of pills. His fingers tightened around the bottle as he thought of the pressures he had handled in the past without the aid of prescription drugs. This time was different; now his life was on the line. Rhoades poured a glass of water from the pitcher on the desk, closed his eyes, and waited for the Librium to take effect. Suddenly the telephone lit up and loudly buzzed, breaking into his moment of silence.

"It's Elliott. I've been waiting for your call. What the hell is going on?"

Dr. Rhoades picked up a pen and nervously doodled on his blotter. "There's been a problem. Your wife managed to get a candy bar last night, and the anesthesiologist wouldn't give her the first shock treatment this morning."

"I can't believe this! How did she get a candy bar? Wasn't she supposed to be in restraints?"

"She was," replied Dr. Rhoades. "A patient must have wandered into her room and given it to her. But don't worry, I've left orders to have her room searched tonight. And we'll heavily sedate her. I promise she'll start the shock treatments tomorrow!"

"It's too late. Frank wasn't happy about this outside doctor getting involved in the treatments or with the fact that it will be two weeks before the regular anesthesiologist can finish up. We're going to have to fix this another way."

"What do you mean?" Dr. Rhoades yelled. "Hell, no! Not me, no way, Elliott!"

"I wasn't thinking of you. You wouldn't have the balls anyway. I've got someone else in mind for the job. I'll call you later this afternoon with the details. But we're expecting your cooperation; that's the least you can do."

"Elliott, are you sure that there is no other way?"

"If you have a better plan, then call Frank. I'm sure he'll be happy to hear from you."

"No, I'll cooperate. But I'm not going to do it!"

"That's right; you guys are only interested in saving lives. I'll talk to you later."

Dr. Rhoades hung up the phone and reached for another Librium.

Susan believed that somehow Jenna and Maggie would come up with some plan to help her escape. By late afternoon, anxiety set in when there was no sign of either Jenna or Maggie. Susan's heart raced as she heard the key unlock the door, but her hopes faded quickly as an aide walked in and set a dinner tray on the desk.

"I suggest you eat. You won't have another meal until noon tomorrow. When we return for the tray, we will search your room. We don't want you to repeat the mistake of eating after midnight."

"I'm still going to have shock tomorrow?"

"Yes, you're the first one scheduled. Don't worry; there's nothing to be scared about."

"Then how about changing places with me?"

The aide ignored Susan's comment. "Now, Mrs. Mason, you don't even realize how bad you've been feeling. Believe me, when this is over, you'll be thanking Dr. Rhoades."

Susan stopped; she didn't want to anger the aide. "Is that nice aid working tonight? She's a Black woman; I think her name is Jenna."

"Jenna isn't a regular; they only call her in when we're short of staff. I don't think she'll be here tonight. So far, no one has called in sick."

The door shut, and the key turned in the lock. Susan sat down at the desk, looked at the tray of chicken and fries, and forced a few mouthfuls. Her mind raced with questions. Where were they? All day, and nothing! Did Jenna get in touch with Mark? It wasn't long before the door opened again. "I'll take your tray back. Hey, you didn't eat much; do you want to finish this?"

Susan shook her head and pushed the tray toward the aide.

"I'll be back to search your room." In a few minutes, two aids returned and checked everywhere for hidden food. They even stripped the sheets from the bed and lifted the mattress. Susan watched with folded arms as they remade the bed.

"Okay, Susan, take off your gown and bend over. We have to do a body cavity search."

She couldn't believe what she had heard. Her face paled as the aide pulled on an examination glove.

"My God, this is ridiculous! You can't be serious?"

"I'm sorry. But either you cooperate with us, or we'll call in male aids to assist us. It's your choice."

Susan slowly untied the gown, let it drop to the floor, bent over the side of the bed, and buried her head in the pillow to stifle her moans of shame and rage.

A voice announced, "You can put your gown back on."

Then she heard the door close, and the key turned in the lock.

Susan lay on the bed for a long time and quietly sobbed. Nothing could have prepared her for this! She was violated! And even if she eventually got out of here, there would be no recourse; it was all part of a legal treatment plan! Finally, Susan stood up and walked into the half-bath. She filled the sink with water and washed as best she could. No point in asking to be taken for a shower tonight; Rhoades probably had a guard outside the door. Back in bed, Susan pulled the sheet over her head and tried to hide from the images racing through her mind. She felt as if she were looking through a kaleidoscope. But instead of pieces of colorful glass, she saw ugly fragments of her life: Carla grasping for breath, Bill with pus running from his purple eye socket, Tina with her brains oozing from the back of her skull, Elliott sneering above her as he tore off her clothes and brutally raped her. And now this cavity search, a final rape of her dignity.

CHAPTER 23
ANOTHER HIT

The door opened, but Susan didn't move. "Just go away and leave me alone."

"The hell I will!"

"Jenna!" Susan sat up. "What happened? Did you find Mark? Is he here?"

Jenna put her finger to her lips. "Quiet girl, someone is going to think you're causing trouble."

Susan waited for Jenna to continue. "I'm sorry, I couldn't find him. Maggie and I both tried. We called all the hotels in Springfield, but we couldn't find him."

Susan grabbed Jenna's arm. "I've got to get out of here!"

"Take it easy; you're going over the edge. Don't worry; we'll get you out."

Susan took a deep breath. "Jenna, I was so afraid you wouldn't be working tonight."

"I almost wasn't. I got one of the regular aides to call in sick, and then I called and asked if they were short staff. That little deal set me back fifty bucks. I expect you to repay me tomorrow."

Susan smiled. "Now that you have a financial interest in my escape, you'll be clicking on all cylinders."

"Right, so let's get busy. Rhoades ordered a shot of Thorazine for you that borders on an overdose. It goes beyond wanting you to get a good night's rest. But I'll get the injection ready, so don't fight it; you'll just be getting a placebo. I've hidden some clothes in the next room; and after you get your shot, I'll sneak in with them. Now I have to leave before someone comes looking for me."

"But, what's the plan?" asked Susan.

Jenna stood up and headed for the door, her finger to her lips. "Later. I'll come back in a couple of hours."

Susan paced the floor; she was too excited to sit down. Soon she heard the key in the lock, and the charge nurse walked in holding a hypodermic needle.

"It's time for your medication."

Susan thought it would look suspicious if she suddenly became passive. "I feel fine; I don't need medication."

"That's for your doctor to decide. Now lie down, and let me give you this injection." Susan stared at her without a word. "Or we can put you in restraints. Either way, you're getting the shot. The decision is yours!"

"All right, you win." She lied on the bed while the nurse pulled up the gown and stuck the needle in Susan's hip.

* * *

Elliott sat at his desk and dialed the number. "Larry, I've got a problem that needs immediate attention. Meet me at Sal's in thirty minutes."

Sal's was a hole-in-the-wall beer and pizza joint. The lights were dim, and the place was almost empty. A tall man with a blonde ponytail walked to the back booth and sat across from Elliott.

"What's up?" asked Larry.

"I've got a job for you, and you'll make a bonus."

"Who'd you want taken care of?"

"My wife!"

"What, did you catch her screwing around?"

"No, it's much worse than that. Susan's poking around in our business and can't be trusted. She has become a liability to the organization. Frank wants her taken care of, and it has to be tonight. Try to make it look like a suicide. If that's not possible, make it appear that a patient killed her. She's at Rhoades' Hospital. He'll be at the front door to let you in and go over the details. I'll drive you there in your car and wait for you to come out. We have some time to kill. Let's order a pizza, but no alcohol. I want you to be clear-headed."

* * *

Dr. Rhoades was waiting at the front door and motioned for the man to follow him to the elevators. When the tall, broad-shouldered man with blonde hair exited from the elevator, Dr. Rhoades slowly walked past him and loudly whispered, "My office is here. The lab jacket, belt, and master key are on the desk."

The man grabbed his shoulder. "Hold on! Where are you going?"

Dr. Rhoades looked annoyed. "Look, I'm not supposed to be involved in this!"

The man poked his finger in Dr. Rhoades' face. "If this is messed up, you'll be involved up to your ass. Now get back in there, and answer my questions. I have to know the layout and the routine."

Dr. Rhoades sighed but meekly followed. How ironic it was that he, a professional physician, was now forced to collaborate with a professional killer.

* * *

After a while, Jenna returned to Susan's room with a bundle under her arm. "Hurry, get into these. We haven't got much time. I thought those patients would never get to bed!"

Jenna quietly said, "It's the best I could do, better than running out of here with a bare butt. Okay, let's get serious. When I leave, I'll forget to lock your door. But stay under the covers just in case someone checks on you. The charge nurse is covering two wards tonight. She just left to give injections in the other ward and should be gone for about an hour. After I leave here, I'll unlock the door to the ward. A couple of minutes later, I'll flick the corridor lights off and on. That means I will be passing meds on the other wing and the coast will be clear. So, wait a couple of minutes and then run for it." Jenna handed Susan a key. "This will open the side door to the hospital. Maggie will be waiting in her car just outside the door. She'll drive you to her apartment."

Susan hugged Jenna. "Thank you; you saved my life!"

"You're not out of here yet. Remember, a few minutes after the lights flicker, you take off!"

Jenna closed the door behind her as Susan went back to bed and covered herself with the sheet. In the silent darkness, Susan mentally followed Jenna back to the nurses' station, counting every step down the empty corridor. And then she imagined Jenna and the other aid setting up the medicine cart. But in reality, the aides were so involved with their work that they didn't notice the door to the ward open and a tall man with a blonde ponytail sneak pass the nurses' station. A moment later, Jenna left the station and quietly unlocked the door to the ward. At the same time, Susan was holding her breath waiting for the all clear signal.

* * *

Mark's luggage was still on the living room floor where he had set it thirty minutes ago. The entire day had been one problem after another. First, there was a disturbing call to Susan's mother. After trying several times without an answer, he remembered the recent lunch when Susan mentioned that her parents were leaving on an extended European tour. Elliott had lied to the psychologist at Tri-State. Why? And where the hell did he put Susan for her so-called "rest"? Everything seemed to be going wrong. When he decided to leave Springfield this afternoon, the hotel took over two hours to get him checked out. And now there was this call from his answering service. Who the hell was Dr. Wong? Well, he'd give him one more chance; and if he still didn't respond, then he'd go to bed since it was already eleven o'clock. He had tried to call Elliott Mason, but maybe it was better that he wasn't home either. A surprise visit to his office tomorrow would have better results than the telephone call tonight. Mark dialed again and silently counted four rings.

"Hello, Dr. Wong speaking."

"Dr. Wong, this is Dr. Mark Denning. My answering service said that you've been trying to reach me."

"Yes. This is rather awkward, but there's something I need to check out. I was called in to administer the anesthetic to one of Dr. Rhoades' patients who was scheduled for shock treatments this morning. The patient ate something, after midnight, so the treatment was postponed. But, Dr. Rhoades' behavior was so unprofessional that I went back to the ward and reviewed the patient's chart."

"Was she a former patient of mine?"

No, she had no previous hospitalizations. Supposedly, she's scheduled for shock treatments because of deep depression; but the woman not only was asymptomatic but has received nothing but major tranquilizers according to her chart. And that's why I'm calling you, to find out if she has a history of depressive episodes that somehow did not get recorded. Otherwise, I'm not participating in her shock treatment tomorrow."

"But, Doctor, why ask me if she isn't a patient of mine?"

"I'm sorry; I'm jumping ahead of myself. It's just that I've never come across a case like this. I read in her social history that she worked at your hospital."

"Oh, God," Mark interrupted. "It's Susan, Susan Mason, isn't it?"

"Yes, then you know her?"

"I most certainly know her. And she has absolutely no history of depression or any other mental illness. Doctor, is she a voluntary patient?"

"Committed. That was another strange thing. Susan's commitment hearing was held in the hospital. This arrangement is rarely done and usually only when an interested party has political clout."

"Her husband is a lawyer, and Dr. Rhoades is one of his clients. Doctor, what kind of shape is she in?"

"She seems pretty good, outside of bruises and some nasty open sores on her wrists and ankles. According to the record, she's been in restraints almost every day since her admission."

Mark groaned. "This is unbelievable!" What made Elliott do this?"

"Dr. Denning, I think I will make a professional call on Dr. Rhoades first thing tomorrow. Would you like to accompany me?"

"Thank you, but I can't wait until tomorrow. I have to do something right now."

"Dr. Denning, I can understand your urgency; but Dr. Rhoades won't be there. All you'll do is give his staff enough time to alert him. And remember, legally he is not out of line. The commitment is according to the law. And her husband was given power of attorney, and he signed for her to have to shock treatments. I put Dr. Rhoades on notice about having her put in restraints unnecessarily. He seemed worried that I might report him. I'm sure Susan's probably asleep now. So, why don't you wait and meet me in front of the hospital in the morning, say around eight?"

"You're probably right. It might be better to wait. Okay, see you tomorrow morning. And, Doctor, thanks for calling. Susan is much more than an employee. Thank you for bringing this to my attention."

Mark reached up and slowly ran his fingers through his hair. He thought about the last time he had seen Susan. What did she know that could cause her husband to take such drastic measures? Mark tried to recall everything she had said. He remembered in one of their earlier conversations that according to Susan, Elliott seemed paranoid. What was it that psychologist at Tri-Valley said, something about Susan getting upset over the murder of the Collins woman? Mark tried to recall what the papers had written; it was something about Tina Collins' husband being a drug dealer. But how did Elliott tie-in? And what about Dr. Rhoades, where did he fit into the picture?

Mark walked over to his desk and rummaged through several drawers before he found what he was looking for-a folder with the home telephone numbers of the public defenders who worked in commitment court. Mark held his breath as the phone rang several times without an answer. Finally, on the sixth ring, someone picked it up. "Hello, Randy Sloan."

"Randy, this is Dr. Mark Denning from Linton State Hospital. We met after you were assigned to commitment court."

"Yes, I remember, Doctor. What can I do for you?"

I'm calling because a mutual friend of ours is in trouble. Since you know the legal aspects of committing someone, I thought I'd give you a call."

"It's Susan, Susan Mason. I just found out that she was committed to a private hospital run by a psychiatrist, Dr. Rhoades. Did you hear anything about it?"

Randy hesitated. "Uh . . . yes, I noticed her name on the commitment list last week."

"You know that Susan is as sane as you or I. And I just received a call from a physician who saw her at the hospital. They have been keeping her in restraints since her admission, and she is scheduled for shock treatment tomorrow. You're a lawyer. Is there anything I can legally do to get her out of there immediately? I don't have time to go into detail; but believe me, she's in grave danger!"

Randy felt sick to his stomach. All his rationalizing that Susan was safe in the hospital now looked pretty shallow. If anything happened to her, it would be on his conscience. "Meet me in the rear of the parking lot at the hospital. I have a black Ford. But first I need to make a few calls. You're right though, Susan is in danger.

I'll explain everything when I see you. But please for her sake as well as yours, don't go in until I talk to you!"

Mark hesitated. Randy knew something, and it didn't have to do with commitment court. How the hell did he fit into all this? Was he or wasn't he a friend of Susan's? Mark shook his head. This whole thing was lunacy! There appeared to be some conspiracy that involved everybody but him! "Randy, I don't know if I should trust you; but it looks like I haven't got much choice. All right. I'll wait for you."

* * *

Jenna watched as the aides slowly pushed the medication cart down the wing. After they were several rooms away, she walked over to the light switch.

Susan kept her eyes focused on the sliver of light that leaked under the door to her room. Abruptly it disappeared and then suddenly spread up under the door again as Jenna flicked the lights off and on.

Suddenly Jenna felt someone's presence; but before she could even turn around, she felt a belt twisting around her neck. She tried to scream, but only gurgling sounds came from her throat. Her arms and legs flailed wildly for several seconds, and then she slowly sank to the floor. The blonde man quickly stepped over Jenna's body and hurried down the hall.

Susan slowly counted to a hundred; it was time to run. Suddenly the door opened, and a man entered the room. Susan lay still, afraid to breathe as a man in a white jacket approached her bed. Something was wrong! Jenna would not have given her the signal if an orderly was heading toward her room. The man hesitated. He was trying to acclimate to the darkness. As he stood there, the man busied himself with something in his hands. She gasped when she recognized that he was holding a belt!

It took only a second for Susan to realize that Elliott wanted her dead, and this man was sent to assist in her "suicide." She hoped that his guard would be down since she was supposed to be heavily sedated. As he raised the belt above her head, she rolled over and jumped out of bed.

The man quickly recovered and stepped back to block the door. Behind Susan was a window covered with steel mesh, to her side was the bathroom, and coming toward her was the hired killer. He inched closer as she leaped on the bed and attempted to jump past him. He lunged forward, tackled her, and both Susan and the man landed on the floor. She felt his powerful arms tighten around her; his hand covered her mouth. The man stood up and dragged her toward the bed. His grip loosened as he attempted to slip the noose over her head.

Susan twisted herself to face him and quickly drew back her knee. With all the force she could muster, aimed for his crotch. The man let out a loud groan as she connected; and as he doubled over with pain, she rushed toward the door.

The corridor was empty. Susan ran past the nurses' station to the ward door. There on the floor under the light switch was Jenna. Susan gasped! Jenna was dead! Susan heard a noise and looked up to see that the man, although hunched over, was quickly walking down the corridor. Susan ran for the exit. When she pushed open the door, she glanced back and saw that the killer had recovered and was running toward her. She headed for the elevator but decided she couldn't wait and opted for the stairway.

Thanks to the fire code, the stairway door was unlocked. As Susan opened the door, an alarm sounded. She bolted down the stairs taking them two at a time. Her heart was pounding with fear. She reached for the door to the ground floor and tried to pull it open. It moved a crack and then stuck. Susan was pushing at the door when she heard loud footsteps above her. "Stop running, Susan, it's all over."

She took off again and quickly reached the door at the bottom of the stairwell. The basement was dim, with only a few overhead lights hung between the utility pipes. Susan ran looking for a hiding place. She bumped into several dressers and bed frames but was oblivious to the pain. A small table crashed to the concrete floor, instantly giving away her location. She heard footsteps getting closer and dove under a desk. Her pursuer was bumping into furniture just a few yards away. And then she saw his shoes, standing right in front of the desk. He paused there for a few seconds as Susan's heart beat so loudly she was sure that the man could hear it.

* * *

Mark pulled along-side the black Ford and stepped outside of his car. A few seconds later, he shouted at Randy. "You knew, you knew all along, and you said nothing? You let her marry that bastard!" He moved closer, and Randy could feel his hot breath as Mark spat out the words. "If anything happens to her, I swear, I'll personally hound you for the rest of your life. I'll never let you forget what you let happen to her!"

Randy nodded his head. "Don't worry; my conscience is already doing a good job." They got into Randy's car and raced to the front entrance. Randy pulled his car next to where Elliott was waiting. Randy motioned for Elliott to step out of the car. When he didn't immediately comply, Randy fired a warning shot. He then handed the gun to Mark as he patted Elliott down. "If he moves, shoot him."

Elliott shouted, "What the hell is going on Randy?"

"Get ready for a drastic life style change." Randy cuffed Elliott to the steering wheel, turned to Mark, and took back his gun. "Let's go!" They ran up to the front entrance where Randy pulled out his badge and ID. They entered the intake room. "This is an emergency; we need to find Susan Mason."

The nurse shook her head, "I'm sorry, I'll have to call Dr. Rhoades for permission."

Randy flashed his identification in her face. "No, Dr. Rhoades is under investigation. And unless you are looking for an accomplice charge, I suggest you cooperate."

She picked up her keys. "Okay, follow me."

They took the elevator up to the second floor; and a few minutes later, the Nurse was unlocking the door to the ward. The first thing they saw was an aide standing over Jenna's body. "I just found her; I don't know what happened."

Mark ran over and went down on his knees and put his fingers to Jenna's neck. "She's got a pulse, but it's weak." He began CPR and shouted to the nurse, "Call an ambulance!"

Randy grabbed the aide and pulled her up from the floor. "Which room is Mrs. Mason in?"

She pointed down the corridor. "The last one on the left."

The nurse took over the CPR, and Mark ran toward Susan's room. Randy had already checked it and met him halfway down the hall. "She's gone. There's been a struggle. Whoever tried to kill Jenna now has Susan." They back tracked and checked the other rooms.

When they returned to the nurses' station, Mark was relieved to see that Jenna was breathing on her own. She put her hands to her neck and attempted to talk. "Someone choked me. Is Susan all right?"

Randy asked. "Did you see who attacked you?"

Jenna shook her head. "No, he came from behind and grabbed me by my neck. Then I blacked out."

Randy started for the door. "Let's go. They may still be in the building." Mark held up his hand. "Wait a second." He turned to the nurse. "Is there any place to hide in this building?"

"Not really. You have to have keys. Hold on, I forgot! Try the basement. We've found patients hiding there. Take the stairway; the alarm just went off." Randy and Mark took off running. They had lost so much time that Mark was afraid to even think about what they might find.

* * *

Susan held her breath for what seemed an eternity; but then the man moved on, apparently looking for her in another area of the basement. She waited until she could no longer hear him and then crawled out from under the desk. She saw a dark area and ran toward another hiding place. There were stacks of boxes piled haphazardly along the wall. As Susan ran, she bumped into one of the stacks; and they came crashing down. She ran down another wing to find another hiding place. She came upon a row of hospital beds and looked for one that was in a dark area and crawled underneath it. Soon the man was walking down the aisle checking under every bed. Suddenly, Susan was grabbed by the arm and pulled out from under the bed. She screamed and kicked with all her might, but she was no match against his strength. He grabbed her by the neck and started to squeeze. Suddenly, he stopped as he heard some noise and saw two men running toward him.

"Federal Agent! Let her go!" Randy shouted.

The man pulled her closer and tightened his grip around Susan's neck. Her eyes filled with terror. He had cut off her air supply, and she felt herself losing consciousness.

Randy took one step closer. "Don't be an ass. The woman upstairs is alive. You didn't kill her. All we can get you on right now is attempted murder. Let her go, man, while there's still a chance to work out a deal. We're not interested in you. We want Mason."

The man slowly let Susan drop to the ground. She heard Randy's handcuffs click as Mark rushed to her side.

She whispered, "Elliott put me here; he hired that man to kill me!"

Mark pulled her close. "I know. You're okay now." He helped Susan to her feet. "Come on, let's get out of here."

Several policemen were in the lobby, where one was engaged in a heated conversation with an older woman. "Lady, you'll just have to wait. One more word out of you, and I'm putting you outside!"

Susan smiled. "Maggie, let the poor man alone."

"It's about time," Maggie loudly said. "I've been waiting here for over an hour! I promised Jenna I'd make sure you're alive. The ambulance took her to the hospital for observation. And boy does she need it! She kept shouting that I better get her fifty dollars. Susan, didn't I warn you about Elliott?"

Randy turned Larry over to one of the officers in the lobby, "Read him his rights, and take him to the station. Also, take Mason. He's outside in a different police car. Put them in different interview rooms under guard. Then send an officer to get Dr. Rhoades. He's probably hiding in his office. Keep all of them separated, and don't book them, or let them make any calls until I get there."

Mark took Susan's arm and walked her toward the main door. "Later, Maggie. Susan will call you in the morning."

Randy put up his hand. "I have to get Susan to a safe place."

Mark shook his head. "Not now. After what she's gone through, I'm taking her to my place. You can talk to her tomorrow."

"Okay, but call me first thing in the morning. I mean it, Mark. It's important."

Maggie sighed as Randy stepped next to her. "Look at them. Aren't they just the perfect couple?"

Randy feigned a look of horror. "Forget it! I never want anything to do with matchmaking!"

Outside the hospital, Susan saw Elliott, his hands cuffed, sitting in the police car. As soon as he saw her, he started shouting. "Bitch, this is the thanks I get for marrying you? You God damn whore! You're dead! Do you hear me!" He shouted, "You're dead! You'll never hide! I'll find you!"

Mark half-carried her to his car.

"You're safe, Susan. It's nothing but talk. He's going to be put away for a long time."

Susan trembled and wished she felt sure of that. "Take me away from here!"

They drove in silence until Mark pulled into a parking spot in front of his building. He got out of the car, walked around to the passenger side, opened the door, and gently took her arm. "Come on, let's go upstairs."

A few minutes later, Mark locked his apartment door behind them. He pulled Susan into his embrace. All the fear and terror of the last week overflowed in the safety of his protective arms. Susan sobbed, wracking sobs. He lifted her and carried her to the bedroom. They lay together, Mark holding Susan in his arms until her sobs subsided, and she finally fell asleep. He looked down at her and vowed he would always keep her safe.

THE END

Dear Reader, now that you've finished this book, I really do hope that you enjoyed it. As the author, I have one small request. Readers rely on reviews to decide if this is a book they want to read. So, please, if you can take a few minutes to go to the site where you purchased this book and review it, I would be extremely grateful. Also, if you are on Goodreads or any other reading community, I would appreciate a review there, too. Every review is important. Thank you, ever so much.

ACKNOWLEDGEMENTS

There are a number of people to thank who have aided me on this journey from manuscript to published novel.

Special thanks to:
Roger Race, for his invaluable computer help that started me on this quest. Carole Korzilius, for her helpful editing and her gracious constructive criticism; Therese Kirklys, for catching errors and our numerous late-night literary discussions. Dr. Beverley Pritchard-Anderson for her skill and patience in this exhaustive editing journey. Arlene Ascencio, for her patient reading of my manuscript, her encouragement and invaluable feedback.

My cousin, Carol DeLorenzo, for her input and for listening to my endless, "which sounds" better discussions;"

To David Ter-Avanesyan for his exceptional creativity in designing the book covers.

The late Bonnie Miller, my first reader, and cheerleader.

I also want to thank my volunteer readers and reviewers: Lyn Jesperson, Rhissa Pontrelli, Simone Jacobs, Rosemary DeAngelo, and Carole Dale

Last, but not least, an extra special thanks to my daughter Melissa Halinski, for being a good sport; listening to me drone on about the trials and tribulations of publishing a novel.

ABOUT THE AUTHOR

JUDITH DRISCOLL was born and lived many years in exciting Chicago until the winters finally called her to Arizona. She obtained: a B.A. in communications, an M.A. in psychology, an M.A. in school psychology and worked toward a clinical PsyD. Judith has worked as a therapist in a psychiatric hospital, a mental health center, and as a school psychologist. In grammar school, Judith devoured Nancy Drew Mysteries. However, as a sophomore in high school, the novel Crime and Punishment pushed her in a direction that led to a career in psychology as well as a subsequent career as a crime novelist.

She is now working on the second book in this series of psychological thrillers. Judith considers herself extremely fortunate to have never had a dull day at work. She currently lives in Arizona with Darcy, the wonder dog. who has trained Judith to: obediently cook her chicken and rice because of her delicate digestive system, take her out to the back yard several times a day for a run about, protect her from the coyotes, and give her lots of belly rubs and cuddles.